THE FINAL VICTIM

A Novel

Robert N. McLaughlin

Cloud9 Publishing

Philadelphia, PA

THE

FINAL

VICTIM

ROBERT N. McLAUGHLIN

The Final Victim

Copies of this book may be purchased through online retailers and independent bookstores or by contacting the author directly.

Front and Back Cover Design – Helene McKelvey McLaughlin

Library of Congress Cataloging-in-Publication Data has been applied for

Robert N. McLaughlin

ISBN 978-1-7328468-3-8 (Paperback)

ISBN 978-1-7328468-4-5 (e-book)

Cloud9 Publishing Company, Philadelphia, PA

This book is dedicated to my children – Robert, Laura, and Stephen and my grandchildren - Kevin, Rosemarie, Robby, Anna, Sarah, Vinny, Jude, Lorelei, Veronica, and Sean.

Persevere and remain true to yourself and to others.

You can have your cake and eat it too.

Karma, a person's actions in previous lives, believed to decide his or her fate in future existences.

Sanskrit meaning action, fate. *Definition from Oxford Dictionary of Current English.*

***

"Be not deceived; God is not mocked: for whatsoever a man soweth, that shall he also reap."

Christian New Testament, Epistle to the Galatians

***

What goes around, comes around. *West Philly proverb*

Table of Contents

Chapter 1: Romania 1

Chapter 2: Fear..9

Chapter 3: Home 15

Chapter 4: Le Cafe 23

Chapter 5: Seeking Help 31

Chapter 6: Enroute 39

Chapter 7: Carl..43

Chapter 8: FBI...51

Chapter 9: Newark 57

Chapter 10: DOJ 65

Chapter 11: Sophia..75

Chapter 12: Turnpike 85

Chapter 13: Boiling Pot 89

Chapter 14: Valley Forge 103

Chapter 15: Jack..115

Chapter 16: Carl Joseph Lewis 121

Chapter 17: Ground Zero 127

Chapter 18: Unraveling..133

Chapter 19: Watched..139

Chapter 20: Reassigned..145

Chapter 21: Checkmate 153

Chapter 22: Intruder:..159

Chapter 23: Caught 165

Chapter 24: Pizza Man...173

Chapter 25: West Philly 179

Chapter 26: Doug and Jack 185

Chapter 27: Unexpected Help 195

Chapter 28: Boathouse Row 199

Chapter 29: Ambush 205
Chapter 30: Rescue 215
Chapter 31: Headlines..219
Chapter 32: The Prize 223
Chapter 33: Treason...229
Chapter 34: Final Victim 237
Epilogue 245

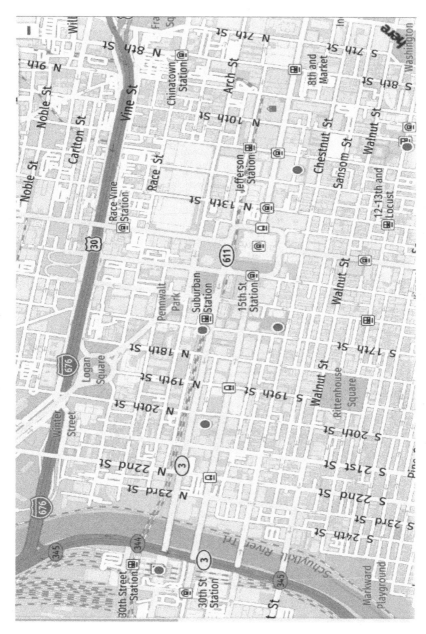

Center City Philadelphia, 30th St. to City Hall

Chapter 1: Romania

Sophia stepped gently onto the veranda overlooking the sandy beach and bright blue waters of the Black Sea. She clutched her coffee mug in one hand and gently swept her other hand through her long and luxurious blonde hair. "Tomorrow comes so quickly. "She said sadly as she turned and looked at her friend and pen pal since high school.

"Yes." Marina replied softly as scenes of the past seven days paraded joyfully across her party-exhausted brain. She recalled it was only a month earlier when she received a text message invitation to join Sophia for an all-expenses paid vacation in Europe. The text was a surprise. Not because Sophia lived in Russia and Marina lived in the United States but it was totally unexpected because there had been a long gap in their communication - almost five years elapsed since their high school graduations from schools on opposite sides of the Atlantic Ocean. After all, life keeps everyone busy.

"No." was Marina's instant reply to her friend's invitation but Sophia insisted. "I have a career that pays me well and includes many perks, expense accounts, airline tickets and hotel rooms." "Just come!" was Sophia's final plea.

The opportunity to see Sophia and to enjoy the sights and scenes in a seaside resort in any European country was flawed by less than perfect timing. The perfect part was that Marina was on a one semester sabbatical from college and in between training fitness jobs. She was working less than twenty hours a week as a barista at a café in center city Philadelphia mixing coffees, lattes, and a wide variety of beverages so she reasoned they could do without her for a week or so. Granted, she needed every part of the income but she couldn't afford to miss this offer to see any part of Europe for the first time. It was also a chance to escape the craziness engulfing America with its coronavirus fears and the growing tensions of the upcoming presidential election in November. The less than perfect part was traveling anywhere during the coronavirus pandemic that had engulfed the whole world since February. Sophia was adamant in her dismissal of Marina's concerns about the virus telling her Romania was open to visitors, her business class ticket would give her safe distance on the flight, and the resort areas in Romania were much safer in the past months with stricter safety measures. The clincher was Sophia's assurance that younger adults were less susceptible to the virus and, if infected, she would incur minor symptoms and fully recover after a short illness. Many in their age range had no symptoms at all. The temptation was great, Marina caved and excitedly agreed. She received a round-trip business class ticket the next day.

So with a single piece of luggage packed full of casual and evening dress clothes and a travel bag on her arm, she flew to Romania. Once she was seated on the plane in her spacious seat equipped with her own viewing monitor with access to a wide range of entertainment options, she laughed at her good fortune: this was the best decision she had made in her young life. Here she was, clutching the flight's menu card, transformed into her favorite storybook character, Eloise, excitedly reading all the scheduled meals she would be served during the six hour flight to Bucharest. She was certain this was going to be the most enjoyable vacation she ever had. And she was correct: the two friends spent the first two days catching up with one another's lives over the past five years, then the parties and nightlife began and never stopped, except for emergency rests taken for beauty sleep and energy refills. Marina felt as if she was in the middle of Dorothy's whirling Kansas tornado, hanging on to a door handle as she was blown from one party to another, from one troupe of attractive people to the next one. There was hardly time to stop and breathe, she was enthralled by Sophia's acquired sophistication and glamorous appearance. Her friend's natural innocence and engaging personality shone through as always but she had grown into a vivacious woman enormously confident in her surroundings and aware of the effect she had on men, all men who happened within her individual circle of light. None of this surprised Marina more than seeing her exotic high school pen pal's unlimited access to clothes, jewelry, cars, and money. There was no end to all of those luxuries and to her readiness to party.

Their friendship began when they met as high school exchange students with Marina first visiting Sophia and her family in Moscow; in return, Sophia spent a few weeks the following summer in Philadelphia. Though oceans apart and separated by languages they were both challenged to learn, the teenage girls had identical interests in the same teen girl obsessions: fashion, makeup, music, parties, and of course, boys. Well, not exactly boys. Boys who had just morphed into young men. The long-distance between them allowed them to share their personal experiences and secrets deeply with each other without having teenage competition and petty interruptions damage their friendship. Their friendship continued beyond high school as pen pals, twitter buddies, readily using the latest social medium to remain bonded to one another. Their funniest on-going joke was how they viewed their famous hometowns: Sophia saw Philadelphia as New York City's little cousin, Marina saw Moscow as the world's grumpy neighbor. That is where their differences ended. The week flew past at rocket speed. Yes, Marina sadly agreed: the vacation and the time with her friend was ending too soon.

Putting on a happy face, *schastlivoye litso* as Sophia would say, Sophia seated herself directly across from Marina; she slowly sipped her expensive coffee, then lifted her smiling face, and cheerfully announced, "Tonight we will have a night to surpass all others. Today we rest on the beach or in the pool. Maybe we shop? But tonight we light up Mamaia. It could go on into the daylight," she teasingly warned Marina.

Half-heartedly, Marina protested, "But I have an early morning flight tomorrow. I haven't packed my things. How can I be out late and be ready to arrive at the airport on time?"

"It is *prostoy*, simple." was Sophia's quick reply. In fact, simple was her most-often used word when she faced an obstacle. Thinking for a moment, she continued. "I will share a tip I learned from my many girlfriends who move quickly from city to city with ease. It leaves a girl with one less bag to carry or fret about."

"What kind of tip?" Marina asked her eternally upbeat pen pal.

"You pack now. Just throw everything you don't need tonight into your luggage bag. I will have someone place your bag in a locker at the airport departing terminal. I give you the locker key, then you get the luggage in the morning when you arrive at the airport. All you need tonight is your travel bag. It's simple." Taking a short breath, Sophia ran her hand through her hair again. "Now let's plan where we go tonight." Marina smiled at Sophia's last remark, there was no 'let's plan' intended, Sophia made every decision by herself.

It was that simple. Every hour she spent in this seaside town in the past week was planned and generously paid for by her free-spending, enor- mously popular and glamorous pen pal. The nightlife in this seaside city and Sophia were perfect matches. They both stopped only after the sun rose, and not always then. Not even the threat continuously posed by the invisible virus slowed the festive crowds of mostly young adults who filled the restaurants, bars, and private clubs. Surprisingly, most places were standing room only, there didn't seem to be a work week in between the weekends. Nearly all the people wore masks to get into buildings but they were removed once the door closed behind them. This was Sophia's world and her flock of fellow night-clubbers arrived early and celebrated long into the morning hours. Where they came from and where they went to after the parties was hardly mentioned. No one talked about work. And they always came back. "Maybe," Marina inquired once to Sophia, "this is some kind of Romanian life-long spring break."

"No" laughed Sophia. "It is the life of young people having fun, enjoying their youthfulness before it is gone too soon."

The final night was a grand send-off just as Sophia promised it would be. Marina took Sophia's advice and agreed to have her largest piece of lug- gage delivered to the airport before they set out for their first stop of the evening. It was fortunate she did so because although the two pen pals were inseparable all week, they lost one another tonight. The 'going home party' as Sophia christened the celebration was completing its third hour with a likelihood of continuing for several more hours. The rollicking evening was full of expensive food delicacies, creative cocktails, and an abundance of party drugs for those who favored them. The loud hammering beat of international dancing tunes and unbridled dancing was reaching its crescendo when Sophia received an urgent phone call. She excused herself from the Bacchic festivities, promising to rejoin the party as soon as she could. She was disappointed to have to leave at this moment but it would be a short absence and it couldn't be avoided. Fortunately, with the party in full steam amid the numerous handsome men and glamorous women, she knew she would be hardly missed; she was certain Marina would be safe among Sophia's friends until she returned.

"Wait here for me." She told Marina as she placed her cell phone into her evening purse, then with a joyful smile, she assured her. "I won't be long. We will end the night with a toast to our friendship and to your new friends."

Sophia quickly turned and hurried away from the table displaying the verve and confidence Marina first saw in Sophia when she was a teenager; Marina was reminded how impressed she was with Sophia at their first meeting. Now she saw she hadn't changed at all, if anything she is still the same precocious teenager who has matured into a radiant beauty, independent and assertive, a lively spirit living an engaging life. Marina couldn't help wonder to herself. Can I ever be like her?

More than an hour had passed and Sophia had not returned. With daybreak slowly approaching but the party winding down, Marina couldn't wait any longer. She was concerned for her friend and decided it was best to go to their apartment, hoping to find her there. Marina expressed her thanks to her new friends, promising to somehow come back to Romania soon. So after bidding farewells and sharing a round of hugs and kisses, and fending off more than one alpha male's tempting invitation to stay just a little longer, she broke away and left the still noisy room. She had discovered in Romania that the world of conquests and romance is not so different in any country. One week was enough for now. It was time to go home

When she stepped outside onto the neon-lit curb, she tipped the doorman then waited only a few minitues before her Uber ride appeared. She handed the driver a paper with the address Sophia had written for her in case she was lost in the city. It came in handy after all. She sat back exhausted. The party ended earlier than expected primarily due to Sophia's absence but that was just as well for Marina. In a few hours, she had to be at the airport terminal to board her return flight to Philly.

Nearing her destination, Marina instructed the driver to stop and leave her off a few blocks away from the apartment. She gathered her purse, stepped out of the car, and paid the fare. She wanted one last view of the seaside to remember. She paused to take in the view of the lamplight on the corner glowing brightly on the promenade that ran parallel to the luxury apartment complex; she marveled how the evenings in this picturesque city never appeared dark or foreboding. They were always quite the opposite. All seven days and nights were cheery and wonderfully gay, indoors and outdoors, day and night. She couldn't remember a week full of so much fun and festivities. Sophia had taught her so much in a week about moving quickly in an ever-faster world of glitz and glamour. She moved silently across the wide avenue to the sea side to take one long last view of the dazzling dark blue spectra of Central Europe's Black Sea. She strolled wistfully along the promenade under the sheltering sky then shook herself loose from her quiet reverie. She enjoyed this short time away from her ordinary life, being freed to see a world normally beyond her reach. But now she had little time to relive the past nights. She had to return to the apartment, change into a traveling outfit, pack her evening clothes and shoes into her light-weight shoulder bag, secure her plane ticket, freshen her makeup, and hurry to the airport. Time always seems to pass swiftly when you have so little time to spare. Wait! Oh no! She suddenly realized she never purchased souvenir postcards of Romania's many vistas and

Mamaia's beaches. This was her intention when she was on the street but she was always hanging onto Sophia's coattails and now she has no time to buy them. Hopefully, she can find them in one of the airport shops.

She took one parting glance at the sea. She would miss this city and Sophia. She turned and crossed back over the avenue to the sidewalk, increasing her pace as she resumed her return to the apartment. As she approached the front of the centuries-old but carefully maintained apartment building, she recalled that Sophia told her there was no need for keys because everyone is safe in Mamaia. But Marina didn't like unlocked doors. She always locked every door at home in Philadelphia. Anyway, she was hopeful Sophia would be waiting for her and she was disappointed when she saw Sophia wasn't sitting there. She fully expected Sophia would be dressed and ready to take her to the airport which would allow her to get ready. That's OK, Marina said to herself, I'm here now. Maybe I can bargain with her for a few extra minutes to freshen up my makeup.

Stepping onto the marble steps, she opened the main door, entered the foyer and walked to Sophia's apartment, then opened the unlocked door. She relaxed immediately when she entered the apartment and saw Sophia's handbag on the chair nearest the front door. She called out softly, "Hello, Sophia." There was no reply so she continued walking into the kitchen area. "Just give me a little time to freshen up," she called out again to Sophia, "I'll be ready to go to the airport in a few minutes." Still not getting a response she walked into Sophia's bedroom. It was empty. Calling out a third time but still hearing no response from Sophia, she checked the bathroom, the last room in the apartment. Suddenly Marina felt strangely uneasy and a shiver ran over her body. Her breathing stopped as she listened for any sound; she felt as if the air in the room had thickened. She suddenly turned around and ran back into the living room frantically looking around to find additional signs of Sophia. She forced her mind and body to stop its spiraling fall into a blind panic, she needed to think clearly: maybe her friend just ran out on a quick errand. Her heart rate and metabolism slowed to a near stop but it didn't last more than a minute.

7

That's when she saw Sophia's shoes lying haphazardly in the hallway leading to the second bedroom. Bright royal blue casual leather flats. Very attractive stylish shoes. She remembered seeing Sophia change from her heels to these flats midway through the evening as the dancing increased. Marina had commented on the shoes this afternoon before she and Sophia left the apartment on separate errands after promising to meet later for dinner followed by a party of all parties. Everything Sophia owned looked expensive and unique, and memorable. Now it was disconcerting. Her shoes, her handbag, but no sign of her. Regaining her normal breathing pace she lifted the handbag from the chair to see if Sophia's cell phone was in there though she didn't fully know what to think if she found the phone was in there or not. She opened it anyway. The phone was not there. A chill touched the back of her neck and filled the room.

A few miles away, a dark rental car raced west on the highway from Mamaia towards Bucharest. A somber-faced man in dark sunglasses sat comfortably behind the wheel. He was listening to classical music through his phone. He had a good day, a successful day: he earned his exorbitant salary and he made his powerful client happy. Soon he could relax on his flight home. In a matter of only hours, he planned to keep his dinner date later that evening at an exclusive restaurant. First he had to deliver the rented car and the body inside its trunk to a pre-arranged location. Within hours of that exchange, his Swiss business account would be generously credited for the services he rendered. "Prostoy." He said out loud. Pleased with himself, he pushed a pink cell phone and a flowery-decorated appointment book deeply into the passenger seat and concentrated on the road ahead while he was being serenaded by the soft but melancholy strains of Rachmaninoff's Preludes.

Chapter 2: Fear

Marina finished checking every inch of the apartment and as she did so, she became more concerned and more frightened. There was no note, no text message on her phone, nothing from Sophia that would give her any comfort against the worrisome thoughts that were filling her increasingly panicking mind. She wasn't certain what to do next. Who should she call? During this entire week, she met many people but only at nightclubs and though they were friendly and polite, most seemed to be as new to Sophia as they were to Marina: a wide collection of party people who frequented the clubs for social fun. In the daylight hours during this whirlwind week, there were two female friends who visited, slept, then shopped and dined, but they left days ago. Marina knew some first names but little else. It was Sophia who led them to and from the apartment to sleep, eat, refresh, dress, and go out to the pool, the beach, and always to more clubs. It didn't matter all week to Marina if she was introduced to anyone formally or if she remembered anyone's name, phone number or address. She was with Sophia to party and enjoy herself. Now she wished so much that she had made at least one acquaintance. She was alone and worried about Sophia. And for some reason, she was frightened for herself.

Her fear had to be overcome because she had to get to the airport. She needed to get her luggage out of the storage locker. At least the locker was in the same terminal as her departure gate. "Oh! The locker key!" she gasped out loud. She walked over to the living room coffee table. There it was lying next to her airline boarding pass folder with her boarding pass and ticket receipt. Sophia had placed the key exactly where she told Marina it would be. "It will be with your tickets so you don't forget it." Marina chuckled, thinking how she almost forgot both of them. Sophia was not only glamourous, she was smart and she thought of everything. Moving from room to room, she cleared her mind in order to identify what else belonged to her, gathering it all up: her personal toiletries, makeup items, brush, comb, and the works. Staying awake through the night made it impossible to expect miracles from her makeup, so she settled for a basic cover of lipstick and eye shadow, throwing everything else into the makeup pouch. She placed her goofy foldup cloth sun bonnet over her hair, opened the apartment door, closed it behind her and trotted down the stairs to the lobby. She'd text Sophia when she got to the terminal. "Airport." She told the doorman. "The Tarom Airlines terminal." She was willing to accept anything that would deliver her quickly to the first leg of her journey home.

The activity at the airport was light, likely related to the early hour of departure. Her luggage cooperated and waited in the locker for her to turn the key and free it briefly before she deposited it at the luggage check-in area, then she stood in another line to check in for the flight and watched as her seat number was scribbled on the top of her boarding pass. She was getting closer to home. Upstairs in the terminal shopping mall area, she saw travel postcards but she was too worried to take the chance she might be delayed at the register and miss her flight. The photos in her cell phone would have to serve as replacements for postcards of Mamaia.

"Gate 7? Philadelphia?" she asked an airport employee as she walked briskly through the terminal. That was how she found her waiting lounge. It was helpful that numbers and the names of large international cities are easily understood in most European countries. Romania was no different. She arrived at her gate and found a seat near the ticket agent podium just outside the door that led to the ramp on which passengers were loaded and unloaded onto the plane. Now she could calm herself a little while she watched arriving passengers walk off the same plane that would begin her journey home to Philly. It seemed to her it was only a few days since she arrived and now her vacation was ended. During all this stress to get herself from the apartment to the departure gate, she had little time to think of Sophia. Up until a few hours ago, the week had been stress-free: all the laughter, the dancing, and some romance chased the real world into a corner. It was difficult to believe it all happened in one week. Only these last hours marred a perfect vacation. None of this stress would've occurred if

Sophia hadn't disappeared. It wasn't like her. Not this week anyway. Marina opened her cell phone and texted a message.

"Thanks, dear friend for wonderful, memorable fun. Wish I could hug & kiss you goodbye. Getting on the plane soon. Text me ASAP."

For the first time since arriving at the terminal, the voice on the loudspeaker gained Marina's exclusive attention. "Flight 1617 to Bucharest is now ready for boarding. All passengers must be prepared to board". All announcements in airports must be alike, she thought. The voice was always calm, flat, and unfeeling but never accepting of any questions. Just do as I say was its calm message. The voice continued. "Please show your boarding pass to the gate agent prior to entering the ramp to the plane". Instantly, the majority of waiting passengers stirred and readied themselves to approach the gate. In her stressed condition, Marina was frantic upon hearing Bucharest announced as the plane's destination. She was going to Philadelphia. What happened to Philadelphia? There was no mention of Philadelphia and this upset her. Her concern must have been visible on her face. A distinguished looking older gentleman wearing wireless ear phones and sitting diagonally opposite from her caught her attention and he smiled politely at her as he removed his ear phones. She noticed him earlier while she canvassed the people around her, looking for Americans also flying to Philadelphia. There were no Americans she could pick out of the thin crowd. The number of persons going to Philadelphia was less than she expected, she was the only one.

"I see you are somewhat confused young lady." The man said to her as he placed his ear phones into his travel bag. "Maybe you are going elsewhere? Don't worry. Nearly all flights from here land in Bucharest. It is the capital city where they collect additional passengers then fly throughout Europe and the world."

His English was near- perfect with a continental accent. It was comforting to Marina to hear the brief explanation. Blushing with embarrassment, she immediately recalled that she did fly here from Bucharest. "Thank you. I understand now. I forgot I flew here from Bucharest. I only looked at the destination city on the ticket."

"It happens to all of us," the man assured her with the voice of experience. He bowed his head and closed his bag, ready to approach the ticket agent now that the boarding sequence was announced. The brief exchange lessened her anxiety level and she was grateful for his polite confirmation that she was on the correct plane.

Gathering her shoulder bag and relieved to know she was headed home, she joined the other passengers in the queue in front of the gate agent's podium. Thoughts of a short nap before landing in Bucharest ran through her mind. That would be welcome, she was hopeful she would be seated in a row all to herself. Why not? This was a big plane and there were so few passengers in the waiting area. Her thoughts were interrupted by the gate agent who checked her boarding pass, smiled brightly at Marina and placed a gold card in her hand. Startled to be singled out and unsure of the significance of the gold card, Marina hesitated slightly before moving down the boarding ramp. The card had an image of the airline's business logo on the top of the card, below the logo were three lines of royal blue text in English: "Compliments of Tarom Airline," First Class Seating, and on the third line Marina's name. Flabbergasted, Marina returned the agent's smile and graciously accepted the upgrade, knowing instantly that somehow her pen pal was the source of yet another unexpected kindness. It was Sophia's way to show her the vacation was continuing through her flight home. It felt for a moment as if she was standing next to her. In a flash of memory, all of the past week's extravaganzas merged with this final exciting gift to fill her with the child-like joy a princess would experience in a Disney fairy tale, but in a split-second she realized all of it was becoming darkly colored by Sophia's disappearance. In her strongest hope, Marina told herself Sophia would awaken in a few hours from some unintended sleep and reply with a frantic apology. Things happen. It's that simple. That's what Sophia would tell her. Prostoy.

Once she entered the plane, she was escorted to her gifted seat by an airline stewardess who seemed more excited about her good fortune than Marina was. Of course, the stewardess was unaware that Marina was torn between Sophia's generosity and her disappearance. The first class seat could be called a berth because its luxuries included among its many added perks a personal control for expanding the passenger space to maximum sleeping comfort. How she wished all her friends could see her now. Once the plane was airborne a nap was first on her list though she planned to take some phone selfies and several quick clicks of her luxury accommodations. As passengers filed onto the plane, she people-watched those who steadily joined her in this lap of luxury. A young couple boarded after her, then several older couples, a few single men including the polite man with the wireless ear phones, and a women in a fashionable navy blue business suit set off by a string of pearls. The woman's choices were tasteful, authoritative, and feminine. Marina enjoyed watching people. Her mother told her that even as a child she was easily entertained by strangers, sometimes staring for hours at people as they passed by her home, on the beach, anywhere. She was also satisfied with her first impression of the polite man; he was obviously wealthy. That piece of detective work brought a chuckle to herself. Obviously wealthy? Not so fast. After all, she, a barista from Philadelphia, was in first class, too.

After the passengers were seated, counted, the luggage stored in place, and the safety instructions delivered to passengers, the plane moved out onto the runway. Marina opened her purse and removed her boarding pass from the boarding pass envelope to confirm the arrival time on her plane ticket before she positioned herself for the nap she was certain would cure her present anxiety: breakfast can wait until the plane landed in Bucharest. She folded the pass and looked down as she slid the pass back into the envelope. Marina froze in horror. Suddenly, she was immobile, unable to breathe. She opened her mouth wide to suck in air; she was unable to speak or cry out. Her eyes remained glued on tiny spots on the boarding pass holder. Dark spots. What she saw was clear and strikingly ominous. Blood. Tiny spots of blood.

Chapter 3: Home

Minutes passed before Marina regained control of her mind and body. She drew on the yoga exercises in her fitness training program to confront the overwhelming crush of stress and shock. Although seated thousands of feet in the air, she was able to calm her mind and body and recover her senses. Of course, the best way to calm down would be to receive a response from Sophia but there had been no reply to any of the texts or phone calls she sent in the past twenty-four hours. The discovery on the boarding pass folder was extremely disturbing. The blood spots, if they were blood spots, were alarming enough, but Sophia's silence was adding serious fuel to her mounting fears: fears she didn't share with her parents when she texted them after landing in Bucharest at 8 AM. It was 1 AM, seven hours earlier in Philadelphia, when she texted them, telling them everything was fine, that she was moving steadily closer to home. She signed off with a final promise to call them when she arrived in New York City, just before completing her last leg of an arduous journey. She didn't want to have her parents worry, at least not until she was right in front of them. Hopefully, she would have better news.

Her search for answers to Sophia's disappearance consisted of continued texts and cell calls to Sophia's phone between takeoffs and landings. She forwarded these texts to her friend, Marc in Philadelphia, creating a small degree of comfort for her while she was alone so far from home. Outside of her family, Marc, a fellow fitness trainer and friend, was the only person she felt comfortable contacting at this time. It was also true he was becoming more than a friend. In the past month she spent most of her non-working hours with him. She liked him and she was certain the attraction was mutual; she liked that when they were together they laughed a lot. That was always a good sign for her. She knew he would listen and console her, sometimes he would think for her. That's also why their business relationship worked so well. That's how it was in the best relationships: no one was right all the time and listening to two voices and opinions often increases the chances of a higher percentage of being correct. Sometimes she found herself sharing more information and trials with him than with her family. Why? She didn't exactly know why, but it worked for her. It just happens. In his initial reply after she told him of her gruesome discovery on the plane, Marc suggested, "Maybe it's your own blood. Think back. Did you cut or scratch yourself? Is it possible that the spots are from your make-up brushes, containers?"

"No." She assured him. "It's blood. I know it. And it's not mine."

Just speaking with Marc was helpful and her mood was lifted after each text or phone call. They kept her connected to home, and best of all, occupied her mind. She had less time to think worse things. This is how they worked at the fitness center together. They shared strategies and solved problems with each other's clients together, trading off ideas. It helped them both. The phone calls made the layovers in the airport terminals bearable whether it was his voice on her phone or whether it was seeing his words appear on texts. A calmness enveloped her and soothed her. Occasionally, she was lulled to sleep, short naps acquired through peace of mind or exhaustion? Both were welcome sedatives self-administered on such a long flight home. No childhood nightmare she ever experienced was worse than what she endured during the hours between her discovery of the spots on her boarding pass envelope and her imminent arrival into Philly. She was able to get some rest on the final leg home from New York City to Philadelphia only because she was in the good old USA, closer to home, safe and sound. These last two facts allowed her to drift into a welcome deep sleep somewhere over North Jersey. Her last thought as she drifted off to sleep lingered on the possibility that she missed something important in her last view around the apartment. Exhaustion temporally erased that concern. Sleep, nature's most effective cure, enfolded her.

The arrival in Philly felt like a rescue. It was a relief from over-thinking, from her own fears, and from her non-stop worrying for Sophia. Her first steps onto the dark blue carpet in Philadelphia's International Terminal A freed her from the imprisonment of the long journey home. Marc met her outside the baggage claim area after she exited the terminal. He embraced her, placed her luggage in the trunk of his car and drove her to her apartment while she spoke briefly on her phone to her parents. Home at last, Marc convinced her to rest, promising her he would drive her to her parents' home the next morning so she could tell them the events of the final night and Sophia's disappearance. He spent the night on her living room couch, serving as a much-appreciated private security guard after her tense trip home; he promised to drive her to see her parents when she woke in the morning, Tomorrow she would share her concern and confusion with her family, her friends, with anyone who would listen and hopefully they will convince her there are numerous reasons to expect that everything will turn out well, that she shouldn't worry. Tomorrow will bring good news. Tomorrow the two pen pal friends will laugh about this one bad day that will be lost in future years underneath the memories of the rollicking, glamourous party week in Mamaia.

****

Back across the ocean, it was mid-morning and Sergei Gazunov was sitting alone in an ornately decorative and spacious outer office encased in near-total silence. Most visitors to this room, to the entire palace, are both awed and unsettled by its sterile essence of starched opulence, their minds and bodies stiff with heightened tension. Gazunov was not among those disarmed by this room. After all, he had visited this palatial building many times in his career, sat in this very room, sometimes waiting for hours, not moving at all. For him, it had become a comfortable place where he received congratulatory compliments after completing many successful assignments, where he was told how much his service was appreciated and graciously reimbursed. Today, this visit was going to be different than his previous visits for one single detail: today he would report on another completed assignment, one of many he's completed for this man over several decades. However, his excitement was increased tenfold today because this would be his final report on what had been his last assignment. He had beaten the odds and survived the rigors of his profession. It was a rare achievement.

"Gazunov. It is always good to see you." The words came sudden and crisp having the form of politeness though there was no warmth in their delivery. "Please join us." invited the short, stiff-mannered man, who motioned Gazunov to follow him. These last words were spoken in the same manner as the greeting but were expressed more as a command. Gazunov chose to quietly ignore the man's tone of voice and his rigid manner. He knew his own worth exceeded this self-important office-dweller. Gazunov rose confidently from the centuries-old antique chair and smiled to himself thinking this man would tremble if he was ever invited to sit in the chair that Gazunov had just vacated. Little men who serve important men command boldly but fear the shadows around them. Such a man was of no importance to Sergei. The man he was about to speak with was the person whom he primarily wished to please. Gazunov followed the man into the interior office, anxious to tally another complimentary review, some short praise, and likely a generous financial bonus as a parting gift.

"Greetings." was the first word Gazunov said as he entered the lavish room and proceeded to walk towards his boss and good friend.

"Greetings to you, Sergei," added The Man. They exchanged handshakes and a sincere embrace. "Please be seated." The Man offered, as he pointed to one of three parlor chairs a short distance from an extravagant cherry wood antique desk. "Are things good for you? " He asked Sergei.

"I am well, sir." Gazunov's replied as he circled the chair and stood waiting for his host to be seated. "I trust it is the same for you." This was the simple truth from Sergei. Today he would do something that few men in his position have ever done. He will retire to a quiet life reading books by a fireplace far away from late night calls, cryptic messages, and journeys taken on a moment's notice. He will not end his life killed on a street corner or buried in a remote grave, never found, and mostly forgotten, never decorated for his life of service to his country.

The Man, dressed in a perfectly-tailored dark blue business suit, selected one of the chairs across from Gazunov, sat down, then nodded, signaling for Gazunov to sit. "Yes, I am glad things are well for you, Sergei, and for me. We have shared many days of troubles and successes and we deserve these good days." Twisting slightly in his chair, The Man seemed to change voices. "You have always done as I asked. Now …"

"As you ordered, sir." interrupted Gazunov.

"Yes." The Man replied. "That is so, and always as a trusted friend."

"Even more than a friend, sir" was Gazunov's earnest response though even in Gazunov's own ears it sounded like a scripted response drawn from a ritual associated within the circles of a clandestine brotherhood.

"You are my loyal bodyguard, Sergei. That is no secret in this room between you and me. You have protected me when I was in peril. You have silenced harmful voices here and around the globe. That is why you were sent to Romania, on a task no other man could accomplish."

The Man held back more words and gazed intently at Sergei as if acknowledging some unspoken thoughts before he continued. "For all these tasks you have earned a hero's reward, the gift to spend the rest of your days as you please: raise a garden, read books, and drink vodka all day. "And" he laughed, "No interruptions ever again."

"You are gracious, sir." Sergei said, swelling with pride of what the past thirty years represented in his lifetime of service.

The Man waited a polite moment to allow Sergei's appreciation to linger, then turned to business. "Now, tell me about Mamaia."

In Gazunov's experience with his host, this request was not a request for details as much as it was a need for the Man to hear directly from his agents on missions that were of prime importance to The Man and his clients. He wanted Gazunov to tell him how this mission was conducted, to assure him it was fully completed. Finished. Rising a bit in his chair, Gazunov announced in his most confident tone, "It is done, sir. I trust you are informed. There were no complications."

19

Silence ominously filled the room. Gazunov's words hung in the air as if they were not heard. His host's facial expression was blank. Frozen in place, Gazunov waited for his host to speak, not understanding the sudden change in his host's demeanor but suddenly expecting to discover something was seriously wrong.

"No." was the word spoken by his host. The word jolted Gazunov, a single word breaking the cold wall of silence.

"No." repeated The Man, staring hard into Gazunov's eyes, maybe into his soul. "The assignment is not completed."

Startled by not hearing an expected pronouncement of flattery but instead hearing words that chased away the dream of retirement he reveled in only moments ago, Gazunov, lurched forward.

"Not completed?" He asked incredulously. "What do you mean, sir? Not completed. The target is delivered, her diary and phone delivered." Shaking, he reached into his pocket, found a paper, and offered it. "Here's the receipt for everything delivered."

The Man sat back, achieving what he intended to see from his friend. Shock. Dismay. Confusion. Disbelief. All of it. He knew how to motivate men like Sergei. This loyal friend. "All that is true," he calmly replied, "but what I need to see is missing. It was not among her possessions and not on her person. Obtaining that information was the primary reason for your mission."

Rising from his chair, The Man continued to speak. "I was assured by others that what I wanted was in her possession, with her wherever she goes: in Mamaia, everywhere, always with her." Stepping back to his seat, he added, "I am aware now that you were not told what that specific item is. That was of course an unexplained and inexcusable mistake. The person responsible for the mistake has paid for his error.

Now looking defeated and breathing hard, Gazunov offered his regret and acknowledged his failure. It didn't matter if he did all he was told to do and if something was left unsaid to him. The Man was not pleased; the mission was not completed. "I am sorry I failed you. What can I do?" was his weak reply.

"No, Sergei. It is not your failure." assured The Man, "but you are the only one I trust to get this task completed and soon. It is very important to me and many others. These others are very rich men, not as powerful as me, but powerful enough to be listened to." Pausing, then adding with an insincere smile, "We all take orders from someone, do we not Sergei?"

Walking over to his priceless fifteenth century desk, The Man pressed a small brass button on the side of it and the cheerless man who ushered Gazunov into the room returned holding a manila envelope which he handed to The Man. Opening the envelope, The Man pulled out a blue folder imprinted with a single word, *Omega*. He held up the folder to Sergei and said coldly, "Here's your task. Everything you need to know is in there. You must understand, Sergei, this is a matter of great importance and the soonest delivery of this prize to me is mandatory." He placed the folder back into the envelope, formed a slight smile, and handed it to Sergei, "One last mission, my good friend."

Chapter 4: Le Cafe

Several days passed and there was still no word from Sophia. Numerous phone calls and texts went unanswered. Using the internet to contact managing personnel at the apartment complex in Mamaia was fruitless. Language was a problem. No one could provide any information on Sophia's whereabouts, whether she was still in Mamaia or elsewhere. The only relief Marina had from this worry was her work and her friends especially Marc who was always at her side, leaving her only for his client's fitness training appointments and when Marina worked at Le Café.

Her parents' reaction to her final night in Romania and to Sophia's disappearance was predictable. They were relieved to have their daughter home; she was safe and sound and their concern for Sophia was genuine. Listening to Marina's account and seeing the blood-stains on the boarding pass amplified the realization that their daughter might also have been missing. What to do next? That was the bigger question.

After much discussion, her father urged her to contact the police. "I'll take you downtown to police headquarters and we can ask if there is someone who can take your information and check out Sophia's status. There must be some way to do it officially."

"Dad, I don't have any real information to give them, just her name and where we stayed."

"That's a beginning. All you're asking is for someone to check on her welfare. You have reason to believe she was harmed. Tell them about the boarding pass. Give them a photo. That should spark their interest."

"Maybe." Marina muttered as she looked at her father who she knew was trying to help her and help Sophia. "But, let me think about it. Maybe one more day." Then sitting up and stiffening a bit, she announced. "I'm going to work today at the café." Then added unconvincingly, "It will keep my mind occupied. Maybe, another day will bring good news." Taking her handbag from the coffee table, she stood, embraced her Mom and Dad and moved towards the door. "I'll call you later."

"Promise?" her Mom said. "Call me when you get there and call me when you leave." She added, insisting more than asking.

Already in motion towards the car, Marina turned and beamed a smile. "Yep. I promise. I love you guys."

****

Le Cafe was located a few blocks west of City Hall on the ground floor of a three story building in the midst of retail stores, hotels, and restaurants. The Covid 19 pandemic arrived in Philadelphia in March, slowly at first with numbers of cases rising in bunches by April. In the span of a few weeks all businesses in center city and around Philadelphia were shut down and remained so for the months that followed. Businesses were now slowly recovering as the number of coronavirus cases lessened but everyone was on a daily coronavirus watch. This strain of virus was proving to be resilient and persistent. Many businesses like the fitness center where Marc and Marina had personal clients were mandated by state decree to remain closed for health and community safety purposes because the virus was quickly transmitted from person to person. Restaurants, specifically cafés and take-outs, were given permission to remain open as they were considered essential for the community. Many people in center city relied on in-dining food services such as restaurants, cafes, and fast-food chains. Marina like many people was forced to temporarily shift careers knowing instinctively that this virus might not be going away too quickly. People had to eat, they didn't need to stay fit. Le Café had become a necessary source of income but it soon became a source of new friends and acquaintances. She enjoyed working with her co-workers and with most of her customers. There were obnoxious or nasty people everywhere, fortunately they were major exceptions to the many who flooded in to Le Café.

"Hey! Welcome back." A middle-aged woman called over to Marina as Marina entered the café. Peggy, one of the friendliest co-workers in the café, shared shifts as a barista with Marina. Peggy continued filling a dou-ble-latte special with caramel syrup for a young girl wearing a school blazer "Missed you last week." She told Marina. "Hey, your seaside resort tan's not showing." She added with a hearty laugh. Over at a second barista machine, Nelson, fresh out of high school working his first full time job, looked up when he heard Marina's voice, then he did as he al-ways did whenever he saw her for the first time each day: he began whis-tling the Beatles' tune, *Here Comes the Sun*. It was embarrassing, not for Nelson who was smitten with Marina's good looks and her shoulder length dark hair that he preferred she wear in a ponytail, but it was cer-tainly embarrassing for Marina. His mini-crush was cute. Actually, Marina thought it was extremely sweet. But it always made her blush. She glanced over and smiled at Nelson who couldn't look happier.

This was her second time working in Le Cafe. She liked working here while she was attending classes at a local university in the city. Her fellow baristas and barristos, whatever the proper terminology is, were listed as such on the payroll staff and considered to be one big family similar to how all the boys, girls, men, and women who worked or performed at the Walt Disney properties were referred to as Disney cast members. This too was a happy place. After all, people came to get their morning, afternoon, evening, midnight, and all-day- long coffee rush. They brewed refined and dried coffee beans that magically created smiles from frowns. Something like that. That light interlude ended when a mature male voice barked, "Marina, you're on register 4 through the dinner hours."

"Happy to see you, too," was Marina's playful reply to Fred, the café man-ager. Fred always sounded tough and disagreeable but he was a teddy bear if you did your job well. Less than 'well' wasn't acceptable. You had to do it better than 'well' and Fred decided what constituted doing a job well. That was some of the café family. Then there were the low hourly wages, the occasional tips, and the unlimited cups of coffee that were barely sus-tainable. The customers were the added attraction for Marina. The stream of customers never ceased. There was always someone in the café from the morning rush through the casual mid-morning, and then the lunch crowd, followed by dinner and followed again with evening regulars until closing well past midnight. Coffee in its many forms - plain and exotic, bitter and sweet blends, consumed with or without pastry deserts - provided the fuel that energized thousands of downtown patrons every day even now as everyone is burdened with masks, with hands wrinkled from being soaked with varying mixtures of disinfectant and soap. It was like being entertained by a steady influx of actors in a community repertoire company, like Seinfeld characters in a play about nothing where so much happens. You never knew who would enter the café: who might enter your life, irritate you, enrich your life experience, or just ruin your day. Marina treated them all the same, the regulars as well as the one and done tourist coffee drinkers.

"Gotta have my dark coffee beans." The words interrupted her train of thought and were pleasantly broadcasted across the room as the latest customer entered the café, gaining everyone's attention and bringing Marina down to floor level fast.

"Gotta think today is a bear claw day." The voice continued as its visage stepped to the counter and faced Marina with a mischievous smile. Carl was a regular, her favorite ex-con who also happened to be the first and only private detective she ever met. If all PDs were like Carl, then all the TV series and all the detective genre book series were really fiction. Carl was not smooth, slick, nor, obviously, was he quiet. But he did command attention. Nothing subtle about Carl. He had a foul mouth, too. But not around her, not outside his circle of friends and enemies. He had a reputation that he could out-cuss the devil's own champion without including a single word of good English or repeating the same word twice. It was nothing he was ashamed of. After all, he attributed that skill from his effective communication classes in the penitentiary. None of them were formal college accredited courses. In his public role as a novice PD, he tempered his language to fit his clients, his surroundings; otherwise his natural default was to communicate effectively using earthy words. After all, he was educated enough to know that one man's plain old nuisance might be another person's pain in the ass, but in his expressive description, the same man was a fucking asshole.

"You chose the perfect bakery item, Carl." declared Marina in a soft voice. This was a daily ritual where Carl gave her the honor to select whatever bakery item Marina felt was the best treat for that day. "It makes me feel like you are part of my day, Lady M," he told her the first day the ritual began. Nothing too personal was intended by either party, just funny pitter- patter. 'Sweet' was how Marina described it to Marc and to others. Today Carl threw her a curve, choosing a pastry but leaving the final decision to Lady M. Marina was ready for it.

"How was your va-cay? Don't see any sunburn?" Carl almost sang the words to her.

Marina smiled as she took a bear claw from the display case, put it on a small paper plate and placed it on the counter. "I was up too late every night to wake up early and get to the beach." she countered as she finished pouring his black coffee into a porcelain mug. She totaled the purchases and beamed brightly, "So, no tan but it was great. The week was wild."

Carl placed a twenty on the counter, collected his change, and left a tip. "That's good. Soon as you can, join me at my table and tell me all about it," then laughing, he added one last dig. "You never know. I might want to go to Bulgaria someday."

"Romania! Not Bulgaria!" corrected Marina. It was now a running joke between the two of them since she first told him about her friend's sudden offer. "Hell!" was Carl's first thought. "Romania. Bulgaria, Serbia, Herze-govina. Who even knew where any of these countries were or even if they were countries, or if any of them had beaches?

The crowd began to thin out after 9 AM so Marina took her fifteen minute break and made her way to the booth in the far corner where Carl ate his

daily breakfast and conducted his official business in his unofficial headquarters. No clients were visible so she slid into the booth and sat across
the table from him. She wanted to tell him about Sophia, about how frightened and worried she was. She hadn't told the police or any person in authority yet. She decided to tell Carl. She trusted him. He was a private detective. It's possible he might have been able to tell her what to do next.

Uninterrupted, Marina recounted the details from the separation of the two
friends at the party on the last evening to having received no response
from Sophia right through this morning. Carl listened, hardly saying a
word. When Marina ended her story, she was exhausted and spent. Carl
stared at his hands, looked to the ceiling fan above him, and shrugged. "So
she's gone. No return calls, and no one else you can call." He paused, and
wondered aloud. "Blood stains?"

"Blood stains." Marina confirmed.

"It sure looks bad. I don't know what you can do. That's in another country. Normally, I'd call it in. But there's a few problems. I don't speak Romania and I don't have the police station number in Romania." Taking a
moment to sip coffee from his mug, as if ingesting some elixir of wisdom,
he furrowed his brow. "We call someone who does. That's what we do."

"Who's that?" asked Marina.

"I don't exactly know. Maybe we begin with the police, the FBI? The Romanian embassy?

"OK, maybe I should call the embassy first." Marina chimed in. "They can
check on her."

"Sure. Try that." Carl was pleased he was helpful but embassies, glass
skyscrapers, offices full of lawyers and men and women in uniform were
not in his comfort zone. He'd leave that to Marina. He picked up his cell
phone and notepad and headed for the exit. He looked back over his shoulder, laughed, and said, "Let me know what you find out in Bulgaria."

"Romania!" was all Marina could manage. By now, the line at the counter was lengthening for the mid-morning rush. It was back to work. Now, at least, she has a plan of action. But how does she contact that embassy? To-night she'll ask Marc to help. She agreed it's a beginning and it seems like a smart thing to do.

Chapter 5: Seeking Help

Later that evening Marina told Marc about her conversation with her café friend Carl and how he thought it would be helpful to contact the Romanian embassy. She was relieved when Marc's reaction was prompt and positive. He agreed contacting Romanian authorities seemed to be the quickest way to find her friend, the authorities there can check the hotel and even the hospitals in case there was an accident.

"Yeh, it makes sense to me" He said. "It seems like the correct first step." He walked over to the sink and filled a glass with water and leaned against the counter. "Filing a missing person's report at the local police station here in Philly for a Russian woman who is missing in Romania isn't going to help us much." Hanging his head and running his hand through his sandy brown hair, he added another thought under his breath, "And that's if we even got as far as filling out the paperwork."

It had been three days and there was still no word from Sophia and no clue where to go next. Marc was trying to be helpful but it was exhausting and it seemed hopeless. Hell, she might be back home working or out partying not aware that anyone was worried about her. He knew that was possible except for one glaring fact: there were no responses from Sophia to Marina's many text messages and phone calls. Yes, there could be a reasonable explanation. But what he also knew was that he wouldn't go this far even for a casual friend let alone for someone he hadn't seen in more than five years, but then it was Marina's friend so he was in it for the long haul, secretly hoping the next text message on Marina's phone would be from Sophia and it would end all the mystery and drama.

"Yes". This was the right first step he repeated to himself.

They did a little online research and discovered Romania had a regional office of the Honorary Consulate to Romania in center-city Philadelphia located at 19th and Spruce Street. The number of official Romanian embassy offices in the United States was few. The primary embassy staff was located in Washington, D.C. and there were four General Consulate offices across the United States with one in New York City whose office was responsible for matters concerning Pennsylvania and several other northeastern states. It was decided they would visit the Romanian consulate office on Spruce Street the next morning and tell them why they were concerned and ask for their help in contacting Sophia. Feeling relieved that some positive decision was made, Marina ordered dinner for two from a local restaurant who made deliveries during the viral outbreak. Marc brought along a choice bottle of cabernet as well as a six-pack of beer purchased from one of the city's new IPA breweries. After more than three long days of worry, it was time to share a glass of wine and perhaps a few beers with good food and try to have a fun conversation about the happier part of Marina's vacation in Mamaia.

Not yet fully committed to sharing a bedroom, they enjoyed the food, red wine, beer, comfortable fun and laughter, then he parted with a few kisses, but not enough to light a fuse and prompt an invitation from Marina to spend the night. Marc headed home after the local late news.

Marina, garnering just enough energy to brush her teeth, managed somehow to toss herself onto her queen-size bed. She was spoiled since her teen years with having a large bed to herself. It gave her room to spread herself across the wide expanse and never feel she was hindered by any restrictive boundaries. It was really the only time she felt she was not hemmed in by one thing or another. Tonight none of that mattered. She wouldn't have trouble falling asleep tonight. She was numb to any more thinking of any kind: her brain was locked down for the evening. It could've been the wine.

In the morning, they visited the consulate but the visit wasn't very productive. The office personnel were as pleasant as the people she met in Mamaia but they knew less than she did about how to find Sophia. Though gifted with a variety of Romanian souvenirs – a travel mug, a set of coasters, playing cards, several ball point pens - in the red and white colors of its national flag – they were no substitute for the lack of progress on finding a way to contact Sophia. The single piece of information provided to her was the name and email address of a contact at the Romanian General Consulate in New York City. She was told she would have to make the initial contact herself. All in all, it wasn't a total waste of time, at least she had a Romanian contact in New York City. Additionally, there was an unexpected bonus, a pleasant surprise that helped to give the visit a small measure of success. When they arrived at the office, they waited in the lobby where her keen eye spied a set of *Inside Romania* travel booklets on the reading table. Each booklet had several tear-away travel postcards inside. Placing several of these into her handbag, she now considered her Romanian vacation complete: she had her set of souvenir postcards.

Once outside the consulate, Marina and Marc went their separate ways. Marc hurried off to a fitness training appointment with one of his clients but not before assuring Marina this first meeting was a good thing; She smiled weakly at his attempt to make her feel more positive then headed in the opposite direction towards the café where she was scheduled to work the dinner shift through ten PM. She was relieved to have some time alone to take a short walk downtown with her own thoughts. It was refreshing for her. She needed the fresh air and sunlight and the comfort of the normal comings and goings of pedestrian and automobile traffic that was so familiar to her. Rittenhouse Square was a block from the consulate office so she chose to walk through the park on her way to the café. The square was one of five original open-air locales planned by Philadelphia's founder William Penn to preserve land for its city residents to enjoy as public parks and gardens and general use open air spaces. The park was later bordered by a variegated collection of a few urban mansions, 19th century townhouses, and buildings in Italianate and Art Deco styles of eras past. It was further updated in 1913 when decorative wrought-iron railings, miniature pools, and classical fountains were added to mimic the French gardens so popular in Paris at the turn of the twentieth century. Today several high-rise residential condominiums and exclusive hotels overlook the park and provide a picturesque background. Upscale restaurants and cafes line the one block long southern side of the park. The square has always been Marina's favorite city park because it offered a sanctuary from the chaos of city life all around it. Sequestered a few blocks from City Hall and the accompanying hustle and bustle of endless traffic on the wide multi-lane expanse of Broad Street, the park provided its residents and weary office workers with an oasis wherein they could relax under leafy trees. The rectangular fountain and the season-weathered sculptures and statues lining the pathways crisscrossing the park provided a respite from the monotony of the tall buildings that populated most of downtown.

The park's proximity to Broad Street was important as well. Broad Street threaded through Philadelphia like an asphalt-paved river snaking its way simultaneously north to the suburbs and south to the city's waterfront on the Delaware River. It was the Delaware River that put Philadelphia and Pennsylvania on the map 400 years ago. Geography wasn't a subject Marina cared about but she knew Philly put her closer to the rest of the world. That's why she was so excited by the offer to go to Romania. She studied her city's history and geography in school and remembered enough to know the river flowed south separating Philadelphia and Pennsylvania on the west side from Camden and New Jersey on the east side, then continued further south past the state of Delaware, into the Delaware and Chesapeake Bay Canal, finally disappearing into the Chesapeake Bay. This is what she liked about Philly. It had communal neighborhoods but it promised a quick access to the world beyond. She hoped to travel to places both far and wide, east and west, and north and south. Romania had been her first journey beyond Philadelphia, beyond home. She couldn't help thinking what a wonderful gift Sophia had given to her. How quickly that excitement, now only a week old, had abruptly turned into fear and confusion. These feelings would end soon. She was certain. Just one text from Sophia would bring all of the previous week's fun and excitement back. Then a harsh car horn startled her back to reality. "Yo! Lady. You gotta get your head...." More horns and the heavy rumbling sounds of a city bus and a trash truck drowned the annoyed driver's final words as Marina stepped back onto the curb. One red light later she walked into the café, smiling and greeting her customers and co-workers as though she didn't have a worry in the world. Coffee seemed to be the cure for everything, even if she was just serving it up to others.

Her shift went smoothly. She kept her mind occupied though she couldn't help checking her phone for messages all day. She called Marc an hour before leaving work and told him she was too tired for company, that she would take a meal home with her from the café. He understood her request to be alone for the evening. "Sure." He agreed. "Just call me when you get in the apartment? OK?" That was a standard request by Marc whenever they parted or whenever she was going out with friends. Marina thought it was sweet and considerate. At first, she worried it was too possessive but in time she liked his concern. It was sincere. He cared about her.

It was nearly 10:30 PM when she entered her apartment and her cell phone rang: she recognized the caller ID.

"Hi! Mom. Yes. I got your message. I'm fine. I'm just getting home from work." Listening as she placed the tin-foil tray of food on her kitchen table, she shook her head. "No. Not much help but we did get a number to call in New York City". She listened to her Mom's questions and answered them in a litany of short clipped responses: "Uh Huh. Yep. Tomorrow. "Her mother continued speaking as Marina placed her keys on a hook fastened to the wall. When her Mom finished speaking, she ended the call as she always did. "OK. I love you, too. Goodnight, Mom."

The café meal was good: a fresh garden salad with chicken slices, a balsamic dressing added flavor, a small roll, no butter, was complimented by a glass of white wine. She carried the dinner into the living room intending to watch some mindless program like The Masked Singer. She found nothing interesting as she browsed through the television programming. It was useless, she felt restless; she couldn't stop thinking about Sophia. No matter what she thought or how she tried to soothe her mind, she was worried. She was having second thoughts about being alone; it wasn't such a good idea after all. A second glass of wine softened her for the Sandman as her

Mom used to call the inevitable bringer of sleep. She moved into the bedroom, propped herself up with pillows against the headboard and set the television on low volume. The wine worked: she missed the late news broadcast. Thirty minutes later her auto-timer shutoff the television. All was quiet. She drifted away into the silent peacefulness between midnight and daybreak.

Hours passed before a slight noise interrupted her slumber and stirred her awake. Opening her eyes, she shifted her body to her left and stared at the alarm clock on the side table closest to her headboard. It was 3:37AM. It wasn't unusual for her to wake in the early hours of the morning but this time she felt uneasy. There was no definitive source for the sound she heard or thought she heard. Nevertheless, she was awake. She laid still, held her breath, and listened. There was nothing. Waiting a few minutes longer, she decided to use the bathroom, she didn't want to have a nature call wake her again before daybreak. The bedside nightlight shone just enough to guide her to the short hallway and into the bathroom where the door was always left open at night. She didn't like closed doors, always imagining there were things hiding behind them. It was likely the result of having too many ghost stories and spooky fairy tales read to her in her childhood. Ghost stories were entertaining and gripping stories when other people were around or with the lights on but not when you lived by yourself. She was convinced closed doors and dark rooms were even scarier and creepier when you were an adult.

Gaining some comfort from no longer hearing any sounds except her own breathing, she finished in the bathroom and walked down the hallway into the bedroom. She froze instantly; even her heart seemed to stop when she noticed the bedroom was pitch black. Stepping a half-step closer, she saw the night light was missing. "What?" was her barely audible response before she could act any further; she barely heard her own muffled scream as a gloved hand was placed firmly over her mouth and a forceful grip encircled her waist.

"Do not scream. Don't make not a sound." A voice commanded in her ear.

Instinctively, Marina's training kicked in. Literally. Surprising herself and her attacker with her own skills, she was able to maneuver her freedom by loosening his grip around her waist; then tangling her legs into his, she shifted her body weight and watched him tumble to the floor. She fell also but she rolled swiftly into the hallway. It was her only way out.

The attacker rose off the floor on one knee and pulled out a gun. "Too late for you and for Sophia." were the only words the figure in the darkness spoke before two loud shots were fired at her.

"No! No!" with arms flaying and legs kicking, Marina tensed her body for the force of the bullets just as a loud alarm filled the room. The bullets impact never hit their target. Marina was in her bed not in the hallway. She would live. It was a dream. A nightmare. "Holy shit!" she exclaimed.

Gasping for air, on the edge of hysteria and hoping to confirm she was still alive, she shifted her eyes swiftly to the still ringing alarm clock. It was 6:30 AM. Her normal setting. She reached her trembling hand across the table and turned the alarm off. She looked back at the nightlight. It was in its outlet, still lit. It was a dream, a nightmare. "Thank God." She whispered. But now she knew she needed help, for her own sanity but also because she no longer felt safe and she didn't know why she would dream anyone would want to kill her…and Sophia.

Chapter 6: Enroute

"Any checked luggage. Mr. Kohler" asked the young woman at the Austrian airlines check-in counter in Vienna as she took the round-trip ticket to Newark, New Jersey from the tall, scholarly looking man.

"No checked luggage. One carry- on and a brief-case." replied the traveler. Sergei hadn't even looked at the e-ticket before handing it to the ticket agent. He received his information in a text: flight number, destination, and seat number, always business class. That's how all his travel arrangements were handled. What was the old American TV show? Yes, *Have Gun, Will Travel*. That was him.

Sergei's final destination wasn't Newark. He would never step out of the terminal. Once he exits the plane, he will wait at a pre-designated gate for a text message and he will be given further information regarding his transportation to Philadelphia.

He had been in the United States several times before but never in the same place twice and never under the same name. Every occasion was for business only with limited tasks assigned and little reason to linger after completing his work. He never acquired a taste for American culture, its music, its open friendliness, its abundance: certainly not its unending noise and its freedoms. It is true that being free to enjoy life and its luxuries is a welcome alternative to the way he spent the majority of his life but he didn't agree that both were possible or necessary for everyone. His childhood and the years between then and now proved to him that life was not fair, it was never fair. You were lucky, or clever, or gifted, or smart, maybe one, all, or none of those things. He liked to think he had been all of the things on the front end of that list. He believed you made your own luck and there was always the chance it could turn bad. Very fast. You had to adapt, be valuable, be productive and own a skill of some distinction. Most importantly, you had to avoid making mistakes, and if a mistake was made, you had to correct it immediately, hopefully before it was discovered. This flight to the United States was the result of a mistake. It wasn't his doing, just a lack of communication from a courier to him. The courier was not going to make any more mistakes; he already paid for that mistake in full, now Sergei was going to fix the resultant problem for his client and his client's important friends.

"Find the girl and the prize." were the instructions he was given in the fewest words possible, plain and simple, just what he would expect to hear from his friend. It was the standard fare from his client, spoken in his client's cold, matter-of–fact, business-as-usual pattern of speech. "Find out what she knows." The Man continued. "Then remove her and anyone she shared it with. Bring the prize to me." Yes, The Man could laugh and share stories easily and put others at ease but his business was always dealt with in this same bland, terse manner. No verbosity. No frills.

The word prize always made Sergei smile. It was strange how The Man used 'prize' as a code word for whatever thing of value or importance was at the center of an assignment. The 'prize' was the important deliverable to be retrieved like Hercules' golden apples or Jason's Golden Fleece, or the head of Medusa. It was rare when the prize was described in any detail. Often, a separate courier would be sent afterwards to retrieve whatever 'it' was. But 'it' was of no concern to Sergei. He followed orders and never failed. This is the reason he was more determined than ever to succeed now. What was to be his final assignment had been tainted with somebody else's failure. Though not his doing, he was being given an opportunity to undo its blemish on his personal legacy. He would patch this blemish and leave his record of accomplishments perfectly intact. He expected it of himself and he knew his client expected no less from him.

The Man did have intermediaries who he used to communicate with Sergei, these persons gave him information and directed his movements. These individuals, men and women, were always as few or as many persons as was considered necessary to complete the task. There was never a lack of money or support of any kind for any of these assignments. The only requirement was to be successful, then forget it ever happened.

40

The task in Romania had been personally difficult for him, not because he wasn't up to the task. He was. Technically, it was, as he liked to say, simple. However, it was also a unique challenge for him. He normally walked away after completing every assignment like most people would leave their office at the end of a working day: he never looked back and he was always pleased with himself. This should've been the case in Romania but it wasn't. He did as he was told but he wasn't told everything. Now, because a courier forgot or neglected to pass on to him one additional request, he had to revisit the assignment and complete it, but now he had to go to America, into the lion's den. He recalled how it began for him.

Having completed recent assignments in England, on the continent, and in the Middle East, he was enjoying a pause between tasks at his rural home that was far enough from the city to make it inconvenient for anyone from the city to visit him. That is how he relaxed and replenished himself for his work. The previous six months were a mix of contradictions for him and for the world. The closing months of the 2019 were quiet and the incoming year looked to be more of the same, but by the end of January a crisis was on the horizon. February and March fostered in a Greek chorus of coronavirus alerts and warnings. All normal human activity throughout the world was halted as the new virus spread death and mayhem across the globe, initially in Asia and Europe, then it devastated the United States. Countries were soon shuttered, services limited, and infections and death counts rose quickly and steadily.

Sergei stayed home. He had practiced social distancing all his life. His wife, now deceased, and his two daughters often commented that he was never missed in his community as he was never home and if he was home he never went anywhere. The months following the coronavirus' initial outbreak saw increasing infections and soon cities, towns, and villages had very few people on the streets, and then only persons out for necessities. In the spring, nature blossomed wholesomely, seeming to thrive greener and brighter than ever, possibly because there were less people, fewer cars, and a limited number of factories pumping carbon dioxide and other pollutants into the air. Once the early days of summer arrived and the deadly statistics reversed, he knew he could expect a call. He was right. He received the call in late October.

"Mr. Gasanov, your connection is open. Your party is ready to speak to you." The voice on the other end said. "Please wait for a voice, then acknowledge your presence on the call."

There was a noticable beep on the connection, then a voice spoke. The connection was faultless, it sounded as though the speaker was standing in the room with him. "Only you can save us"' was how the phone conversation began. "Otherwise, I would not burden you."

Sergei recognized the familiar voice and he knew it was his time to go back to work. Pleasantries were formally exchanged and were followed right away by a short but concise outline of the urgent problem that needed his attention.

"I understand, sir" Sergei responded several times during the one-sided conversation. He knew that his duty was to listen and to hear clearly what is being said. It wouldn't be repeated. He didn't know then how much this call would test his allegiance, make him question his own humanity, and worse of all, he never thought he would inflict such an unforgivable scar on his soul. Now, one week later, it was done. He did as he was told to do, just as he is going to do now. He would move forward and not look back. The passage of time had always brought him a self-justifying comfort.

He boarded the plane to America for the seven hour flight. Now he could rest his eyes and his mind in one of the few places where he ever felt at ease and safe - in an aluminum cocoon thirty thousand feet in the air, far above the clouds, in between continents. Here he was not wary of the strangers around him who didn't know him or care why he was traveling thousands of miles to Philadelphia to find and kill a young woman he's never met nor ever seen.

Chapter 7: Carl

Breakfast at her kitchen table wasn't an option this morning. Marc was the only person Marina called when she gained her composure after the nightmare. She told him about the dream and how real it seemed. He wanted to go to her right away but she insisted he stay at his apartment. She didn't want to be sitting alone just waiting for him to come over. She needed to get out of the apartment, to go somewhere she felt less jittery.

"I'll be fine." She insisted. "It'll take me only a few minutes to shower. Just stay there, please."

"OK. I'll wait but I have my phone and car keys in my hands." He felt useless standing there doing nothing. He wanted to jump in his car, race to be with her, to protect her. She sounded calm enough after she explained the dream and she assured him she was overcoming the initial terror of it.

"All right." He agreed but he wasn't happy about agreeing to stay put. "I'll wait here but keep your phone on. Keep it near you. Put it on speaker and keep talking to me." He knew he was rambling nervously, still he felt useful this way. "Stay on the phone even while you are in the shower so I know you're safe. I'll be listening. Then leave it on speaker even while you're driving in the car, OK." Then he repeated himself, "Until you're here. OK."

"OK." Was her weak reply. Leaving the phone on and pressing the speaker button actually did make her feel safer; she instantly began to feel calm.

Marc was outside his apartment before she even got in the shower. He sat in his car, anxious and tense, holding his cell phone, with his car keys in his ignition, just in case he needed to go to her. He had recited to himself what he would do. He would call 911 first, then race to her in his car.

She showered and dressed in record fashion and arrived outside Marc's place within twenty minutes though it seemed to him as though he had sat in front of his building for an hour. Marina shutoff her engine and didn't move for a minute or so, then put her hands up to cover her face and cried uncontrollably even before Marc could open her car door. He helped her out of the car, put his arms around her and held her tightly.

"You're safe now." He told her. "I have a few coffee pods and some day-old Danish. How's that sound? I didn't want to leave here for anything until you got here."

"That's fine. Thank you." Marina responded through her tears. Her eyes and low voice betrayed how tired she was from the past week of sleeplessness and now from this terrible nightmare. "I …" she tried to speak but broke down, crying fitfully in his arms.

Once upstairs, Marina drank a half-cup of coffee and shared a Danish while Mac downed his normal dosage of two cups of Sumatra dark blend coffee. The Keurig machine and coffee K-pods made everyone's kitchen a mini-café. Not much was said. In a short time, Marina agreed to lie down in Marc's bedroom at the backend of the apartment. It was quieter there. He waited until she was lying down and her eyes were closed before he moved back to the front room of the apartment. He made a few calls and sent several texts to his clients to reschedule his appointments for the day. Several hours passed before Marina woke and shuffled slowly into the living room. He stood up as she entered. "You look better. How do you feel? Were you able to sleep at all?"

"Yes. I was sound asleep. I feel better, much better." Sitting down on a small sofa, she pulled her knees towards her chest and wrapped her arms around her legs. "I'm sorry for getting you up so early and breaking your day apart."

"Don't be. I'm glad you called me." Then he added an obvious fact. "I'm a lot closer than your parents."

"I didn't want to scare them. But to be honest, I thought of you right away." She realized that this call for help took them a step closer in their relationship. If she wasn't so tired, she would've blushed, or more likely, she would've never said that at all. Oh, well, she thought to herself, time will tell but she was glad he was here.

Marc looked at her, nodded, and walked over to the coffee pod rack. "Caffeine or decaf? Same brew as this morning?"

"Yes. Decaf. The same as earlier." She was feeling calmer now. "It was good. Helped me sleep."

Marc placed the decaffeinated K-cup coffee pod into the Keurig then abruptly changed the subject. "Let's talk about what you're going to do. Do you still want to call the consulate in New York City? But maybe you need to do even more than that."

"More? Like what more?" Marina was wide-eyed at that suggestion.

"Well, you can go to the local police, maybe the FBI? I don't know. You have to go somewhere, to someone, to get you some real help. You need to find a person who is interested. Somebody who wants to help."

"Uh Huh." Marina agreed but she wanted it to end today with one call to the consulate. "But if the consulate finds Sophia and she calls and tells us she's OK, then we're done. Right?"

"Yes, that's right." Marc responded brightly. Of course, he would be very happy for Marina if that happened but he added what he thought was more likely. "I just don't think they will find her so fast and I don't think you want to wake up in the middle of a nightmare every night until they locate her. It can't hurt to seek some professional help to find her."

"Professional help? Who's that?"

"The police. The FBI."

Really. Who do we tell? Marc, I don't know any police, certainly not any FBI agents. Do you?"

45

"No." He sat still, arms at his side, thinking. Then he raised his hands into the air. "Carl! What about your café friend, Carl? He might know who to call, what to say. He's got to know some policemen, maybe a captain, maybe he has a contact in the FBI."

"Do you think he can help?"

"He says he's a private detective, right? He knows the city police, probably knows some Feds, too." Pausing for a moment, he asks Marina. "Do you know how to contact him?"

"No. I only see him at the café. We talk a lot and share stories over coffee. He never gave me his phone number, no information, I don't even know his last name. He never asked for mine. There was no reason to ask."

"We got a reason now." was Marc's curt reply. "Let's go find him… after we call the consulate."

An hour later they were sitting in Marc's apartment. The telephone call to the Romanian consulate in New York City didn't last very long. The official they were directed to speak to was polite but generally dismissive of the need for urgency. Yes, he would forward their concern and Sophia's name to the appropriate authorities in Bucharest but it would take several days or longer before they could expect a response. Marina's frustration was increasing. It was clear the higher level diplomatic channels were too formal and too slow to be any more helpful than their counterparts in their Philadelphia consulate.

As soon as Marina ended the call, Marc rose from the kitchen chair, lifted his house keys off the magnetic hook on the side of his refrigerator and announced in a strong voice, "Let's go! Let's find Carl." Then before Marina could reply, he took her by the hand and led her out of his apartment door.

Just as Marina had predicted, Carl showed up at the café after the morning rush, like clockwork. He later explained to Marina why he was always so punctual. It wasn't something he was taught while growing up as a kid. As a matter of fact, he was always late. But he didn't suddenly develop a new-found respect for time, not his time nor anyone else's time. He learned to be punctual during his five years in prison. When you're locked up, he told her, everyone and everything thing is on the clock. You learn the importance of being on-time: both the fruits of being punctual, and the cost of being late. In prison all time was measured: seconds, minutes, and hours all counted. Time was a central part of the overall discipline in a prison. He didn't mind so much at first. It was just a routine. When he was first placed in a cell, he wasn't frightened. He was alert like a big cat. But as time passed, he became dulled by the slow passage of time. He became institutionally depressed by the monotonous routine. He was soon horrified to realize he was now one of those persons in movies he'd seen as a kid, the guy who was locked in prison, or stranded on a desert island who chalked, scrapped, or carved each passing day in blocks of six vertical strokes on a stone wall or on a tree, then added one diagonal stroke across the first six marks, signifying a week had passed, and continued doing that same thing until he could walk out and leave that record of personal confinement behind him forever.

That was the hardest part of prison he said to Marina, "Each day had the same number of seconds, minutes, and hours as every day outside the Walls but they ticked off so slowly, so monotonously that time felt like a mini-sized version of water torture where you were strapped on your back, eyes open, not able to move your head or your body one way or another while water dripped onto your forehead and there was nothing you could do about it."

This was when he began to respect time as an ally, as a partner in his daily plans. Don't be late was his new mantra. Don't be late. Don't be late. Unless of course, sometimes there was a good reason for being late.

Marina and Marc were sitting at a table for four just inside the front door of the café; that made it easy for them to spot him. She saw Carl instantly when he entered. Even wearing a Covid 19 mask couldn't hide the fact that he was smiling at her. His smiling eyes were the give-away clue of the big smile under his mask.

"Hey, whaddya doing on this side of the counter?" was his greeting to her. "Did you lose your job or did your secretly rich father finally buy the place and turn it over to you." He laughed. At the same time he noticed the tall young guy seated next to her. It wasn't anyone he knew or ever saw before. Carl's education as an undergraduate of Prison U taught him to see more around him than most people; he figuratively grew eyes in the back of his head and developed a keen sense of observation and caution. He was now earning his master's degree on the streets of Philly.

"Will you join us?" Marina's asked. "I need your advice."

"My advice?" he wondered as he sat in a chair on the opposite side of a table for four. "Well," he said half-laughing, "try the double café latte with cinnamon, add a warm crumb bun with butter. You'll be set for the day."

Now Marc and Marina were laughing. Marc liked this guy's smooth vibe and his sense of humor and instantly understood why Marina talked so much about him. He was glad he met Marina before she met Carl.

"No, Carl, I don't want advice about picking a coffee" Marina answered. "It's something entirely different. It's about a friend of mine." She interrupted her train of thought when she realized she hadn't introduced Marc. "Oh, wait. Carl, I'd like you to meet my friend Marc. He and I work as fitness trainers. He's helping me find a friend."

Marc nodded to Carl and raised his hand slightly as part of his new normal for acknowledging introductions in this present pandemic world. Carl did the same. Even fist bumps were becoming suspect.

"What kind of advice?" Carl was sought out often by friends and acquaintances and he tried to avoid being a free adviser, a not-for-profit investigator. But he always listened.

Marc could see that this could become a lengthy discussion so he interjected. "Let me get you a beverage while Marina fills you in on some details. What'll you have?"

"Great." Carl could see he was at least going to get an immediate payment for his nugget of advice, whatever advice it was he offered. "I'll have the double café latte with cinnamon, and a warm crumb bun with butter." They all laughed.

Less than a half an hour passed: three coffees, a few more crumb buns were consumed, and the whole story of the several days since Sophia's disappearance was shared with Carl. The manner in which Carl listened to Marina's recounting of events, and at times calmly interrupted with occasional questions or requested clarifications on details, presented another side of Carl, a more inquisitive and serious business part of his personality. Now he was ready to address her first question. What should she do next?

Sitting back in the chair, he placed his lean but muscular arms on the table. "Going to the local police, even downtown to headquarters only four blocks away from here isn't going to help you find your friend," he paused. "They have no interest, no jurisdiction, and no contacts with Romania in Philly, or in NYC, and certainly no direct contacts in Romania."

Marina shifted her eyes to Marc, now feeling more despondent while listening to Carl's words. This wasn't going anywhere either, she said to herself. Marc turned his eyes from her and back to Carl who started speaking again.

"You need to try talking to the FBI. They understand these things. They have experience and methods that cut out standard protocol in times of urgency." Reaching into his pocket, Carl pulled out a pen and a small note pad that he turned over to the back cover and opened it to the last fresh blank page, and began writing.

"Here is a fella who might be able to help. I know he'll listen. I'll text him now and introduce your name to him in the text." Handing her the small paper, he added, "His name is Doug Frister. He's young but he's a smart and experienced agent. He's respected in the police community. He hears things, listens, shares. If any agent will help at all, it will be Agent Frister."

"Thanks so much." Marina said. "I'll call him right away." Instinctively, she reached over to touch his hand, to show how thankful she was, then stopped, remembering the virus protocol. "This is some hope for now."

Rising from his chair, Carl readjusted his mask, nodded at both of them and prepared to walk out the door. He stopped and said, "Let me know what happens. Good luck." Now looking only at Marina, he added with a visible twinkle in his eyes, "See you tomorrow, and thanks for the coffee and buns." He walked out of the café onto the sidewalk.

Not much had changed though. Sophia was still missing. Now FBI agent Doug Frister was their next best hope.

Chapter 8: FBI

The Department of Justice, or the DOJ, occupies eleven office buildings in the Washington, D.C. area and has offices and employees all across the United State and overseas. Generally American citizens don't know these buildings exist, reasonably assuming there is only one gigantic central Justice Building in Washington, D.C. Most Americans couldn't find any one of these eleven buildings, nine located within blocks of the White House. Deciding which building to visit and who to contact within it with complaints or requests would require some research and a bushel of perseverance. The opposite is true for the men and the women who work in the DOJ. When the time comes when they want to contact you they will have learned everything about you or about someone you know or you met or you associated with at home, work or elsewhere long before they contact you. Until Marina reported to the Romanian consulate that Sophia was missing, no one knew Marina existed. Now someone at the Department of Justice headquarters at 950 Pennsylvania Ave, NW, close to the National Mall, was very interested.

Slightly after the dinner hour in D.C., a balding, slightly anemic, and unfriendly man in his late fifties picked up the 'clean' office phone on his desk and spoke into it loudly with years of authority in his voice, "No. It has to be tomorrow." His voice rose higher as he continued. "Just get me a seat on Amtrak's Acela going into Philadelphia. No, I'll go alone. Text me the ticket information before 9 PM tonight." He moved his finger to end the call, but stopped and voiced a final instruction. "Don't put it on my calendar."

Not waiting for an answer, Jefferson Crandall, Assistant Deputy Attorney General, hung up the phone. He was pissed. There were enough things to do here at headquarters but now he was ordered to travel to Philadelphia on less than a day's notice. Granted it must be important if the top man insisted it required Crandall's personal attention, a precautionary measure requiring his own eyes and ears. Hopefully, it was nothing too serious and he would discover it was not necessary for him to be inconvenienced, nevertheless it was better to be safe than sorry. In the previous two decades, he received very few requests to become involved in regional district business but in the past three years such requests from the top floor had become almost commonplace. The Justice Department had become a personal civil and criminal law office dedicated to a single ever more-demanding client. Nevertheless, when he received a call from his superior he did what he was told to do. If there was concern at that high level, the pressure to push the panic button was growing and he should be concerned too. He knew very little about Omega and he didn't care to know more. He was cleaner that way. Nevertheless, he knew he had to be in Philadelphia tomorrow morning, so he would be there.

****

Shortly after Carl's meeting with Marc and Marina, one-hundred and forty miles north of Washington, D.C. and a few miles outside of Philadelphia, in a quiet tree-lined neighborhood with professionally coiffured lawns and gardens, a young light-haired, baby-faced agent of the Federal Bureau of Investigation, the FBI, was seated at his breakfast nook in the three-story home he and his wife Ellen purchased three years earlier. He was finishing his morning coffee while routinely posting online his daily report on the progress or the lack of progress on one of his district cases. The posts went directly into the active records in the local FBI office located on the sixth floor of the Federal Building at 6th and Arch Street, ten blocks south of City Hall. It was a non-descript entry on a normal day and he had no way of knowing that it would be the last such day he might have in the next few months.

Douglas William Frister graduated from Stanford University, earned a law degree at the University of Notre Dame, served an apprenticeship with the a prestigious law firm in New York City, then surprised everyone but himself when he chose to accept a position in his hometown's District Attorney's office. Doug's father was a retired city detective and a former beat cop. That is what inspired him to choose law enforcement as a career. It's also what contributed to his respect and camaraderie with the men and women at every level of law enforcement including security personnel, patrolmen, firemen, and the many office staff who made protecting others their life work. He benefitted from his previous assignments in New York City's five boroughs. The area and wide scope of investigations and the on-the-street experience satisfied his sometimes immature view of danger. In other words, it was exciting.

His wife also a lawyer and she worked across the river in Camden, the largest city in southern New Jersey. Ellen spent as many nights and weekends working as Doug did. For the time being, children were a future part of their lives as they both were industrious, enjoyed their work, and barely had time to celebrate a monthly dinner out on the town. They did manage to eke out a summer vacation once a year, but it was always made to fit in around their current projects or assignments.

Like any large city, Doug knew Philadelphia had its share of crime, all types of crime, though the numbers didn't compete with the constant overdose of criminal activities in the Big Apple. Overall, he was glad to be located closer to home. It didn't change his responsibilities, workload, or his excessive work habits but he did get home faster at the end of a long day or night. He could sleep a little longer in the morning, letting the birds wake him up, previously he would be well on his way to New York before the birds woke up. The biggest gain for him and Ellen was that the number of nights he spent away from home lessened now that his distance to and from his operations center was reduced by several hours. Some agents adjusted comfortably to being on the road. He wasn't one of them. He had a good reason to be home and Ellen felt the same way.

Buzz. Buzzz. Buzzzz… The cell phone vibrated next to him in a slow dance. Doug's cell phone ring was indicative of who he was, it was bland and sedately efficient just like him. But he did inject a hint of urgency in its ring pattern and that was also a mark of his own personality. The first buzz was followed by a slightly more elongated ring, buzzz, and each additional ring increased in length and volume. Time was important to Doug and he liked to be reminded to never waste it, for himself, or for others. He had been a track athlete in high school and college, he knew how important every piece of a second could be in a race. He transferred that same urgency and awareness to his career, it was an important trait for every member of law enforcement. He glanced at the caller ID on his phone's video screen, then smiled. This could be interesting he thought to himself. It was Carl, a local contact and sometimes unofficial partner who is an occasional and reliable source in and around the city. Doug liked him. Carl was unique and unlike many street sources, extremely informed and reliable.

"Hey, Carl. What's up? How ya doing today?"

"Doing good, my man. Doing good. How about you"? It was Carl's standard prelude to acknowledging and offering a greeting before getting to the reason for his call. He continued. "I gotta ask you to do a friend of mine a favor." He sounded rushed.

"What kind of favor?" Doug was taught to be wary of favors but in his line of work he also accepted the fact that favors were part of making progress or trading for information now or later. Favors can be an extension of help, or a step into hell. He asked the first critical question, what kind of favor, now Carl's answer would determine how far this conversation went.

Carl slowed down his tempo, "My friend visited her girlfriend in Bulgaria." He paused. "No, no." He corrected himself. "It was Romania. Anyway, just before she got on the plane to come home, her friend disappeared. After the plane was airborne, she discovered blood stains on her boarding pass envelope." Carl took a deep breath to let his information register with Doug. He knew hearing something for the first time required the speaker to slow their delivery. "She hasn't heard from her since that day. No return calls. No texts. Nothing."

"What makes you think I can help her?" Doug was puzzled why this missing person in Romania would be something he could be helpful with. "Has she contacted people in Romania? Like the missing girl's parents."

"She did speak with the Romanian consulate offices, first in Philly, and yesterday in New York City." He continued, "But no, not the parents, no friends. She has no personal contact information to start her search."

"Then, why do you think I can help her?"

"Just a hunch. She just wants to know if the girl is missing or if she is just very late answering her texts, emails, and tweets."

There was no voice nor any sound for a few seconds. Just quiet stillness. Dead silence.

"Doug," Carl shifted his tone, addressing the agent with a more personal plea, "I have a feeling if you make a few phone calls, send an email, you might get a quick answer, and maybe even find the girl is sitting home with a dead cell phone battery."

There was still no response from the other end of the call.

With a final effort to convince Doug to commit, he threw out his closing sales pitch. "I'll owe you one."

Chapter 9: Newark

Sergei was awakened from a deep slumber by a slight succession of air bumps caused by air turbulence somewhere over the western side of the Atlantic. The flight was now two hours from the New York metropolitan area, Newark was less than twenty miles south of New York City. The opportunity to rest was a welcome treat for him although it did wipe out the main meal served two hours earlier in the flight, a full dinner-size presentation with a choice of salmon or filet with an accompaniment of vegetables, sliced potatoes in German sauces. That was a disappointment for Sergei. He enjoyed food both as a necessary nourishment but often times more for its presentation, exotic flavors and creative pairings. He wasn't expecting all of that perfection on an overseas flight but he did regret missing the free meal. Fortunately, his bumpy wakeup call occurred just before the serving crew began delivering its late-afternoon snack. The plate of cheeses and meats was partnered with dainty desserts and would give him enough sustenance to keep the food-forager part of his brain at bay until he enjoyed dinner at a full restaurant on terra firma in Newark.

As he pulled his tray down in front of him, the stewardess set a snack plate on it and smiled sweetly and inquired, "I hope your rest was pleasant, sir. Welcome back."

Both surprised and delighted by her brightness, he smiled for what seemed to the first time in days. "It was very relaxing. Thank you." Then, unable to resist inserting a flirtatious tone in his ordinarily bland demeanor, he added. "It's a treat to wake up in the presence of such beautiful company. And just in time for needed nourishment."

The flash of charm achieved its goal. "Sir, would you care for a beverage? A glass of premium wine, perhaps?" asked the stewardess in her most pleasant tone of voice."

"I'd prefer a bottle of pilsner, with a glass. Please." answered Sergei.

The choice to approach Philadelphia through Newark was not Sergei's decision. Nothing about his travel arrangements were ever decided by him. There were professional associates who handled every move he would take and they knew when and where he was going before he did. But they never knew why he was going there and who was sending him. It wasn't their business to know. Besides, it was dangerous for anyone to know too much. Twenty-first century technology made it easy to simultaneously allow someone to know everything at one time but allow others to only know what it was necessary for them alone to know. All communications, marching orders, and reservations were relayed, made, and changed in seconds. Even now with the complications of the pandemic, there were methods available to find an easy and quick way to get around protocols and barriers in order to get to a destination. This assignment to America was a prime example. Sergei's recent string of texts included a text with a plane ticket for him to travel from Vienna to Newark and another text told him to exit the plane, wait inside the terminal at Gate D for more details. He knew why and where he was going but how he got there was decided by others. He felt fortunate though. He preferred Newark over any of the New York City airports, and for this assignment a direct flight into Philadelphia was not a good choice. This plane would land in an hour. The snack and pilsner were perfectly timed.

The final approach was smooth and the slight tilt of the wings and a bumpy wheel-ground contact caused an audible number of gasps at touchdown. Otherwise, Sergei would've voted a perfect ten for the pilot's performance into Newark. The three bells signaled an all clear for passengers to move about the cabin. Yes, thought Sergei. The USA. Home of the Brave. Land of the Free. The combination of those three letters followed by those two phrases always sounded to him like an American Madison Avenue commercial when they were intoned with the voice of superiority that usually accompanied those words. It wasn't that he was repulsed or even envious, no, he just didn't appreciate the fact that most people around the world agreed with that commercial pronouncement. Well, at least they would've agreed before the past four years, before the man presently in the White House became America's leader. Sergei smiled when he re-called the joke a fellow FSB agent told him two years ago.

"Yes, my friend. This man is president by default."

"By default?" Sergei answered "Do you mean because Russia helped him to get elected."

He stared at Sergei, belly-laughed in his face and shouted, "No! No!" he protested. "By default! Because it was 'de fault' of the sixty-four million stupid Americans who voted for him."

So now here he was in the home of the brave, land of the free, and headed to Philadelphia, America's Cradle of Liberty. Such a young country with so many slogans.

The Newark Airport complex included three large terminals A, B, and C. In addition to providing air transportation around the world, each terminal serviced millions of travelers every year with a shopping mall, multiple dining choices and bar lounges, and of course multiple ticket gates and waiting areas. Sergei's Austrian Airlines flight from Vienna arrived at the international hub, terminal C. His next scheduled destination was Gate C-71, fortunately located in the same terminal as his arrival gate. It was a short walk from his arrival gate requiring only his legs and his respectable command of English. Although he wasn't expected to make use of the transportation loop inside the airport, he was briefed on the availability of the air train monorail that traversed the half-moon rail line connecting all three terminals. It was quiet, smooth, modern, open twenty-four hours every day, and free. There were no plans for him to ride the train but it was helpful to know it was available if necessity demanded he use it.

Gate 71 was carefully chosen as there were no waiting passengers, no other persons in the area. Sitting in the middle of a row in the waiting area and facing out to the aisle, he could see anyone who might approach him from either side of the concourse. His briefcase and his travel bag were on the seat next to him, Thirty minutes had passed very slowly while he waited for his contact. He was finishing his American breakfast, his first cup of Starbuck's famous coffee and America's most famous breakfast sandwich, a McDonald's Egg Mc Muffin, with cheese and bacon when his cell phone buzzed. A text message appeared on the cell phone's small screen. It was a phone number and beneath the number, a single word, *CALL*, was typed next to it. Nothing else. He rose from his seat, gathered his empty cup and food wrapper and deposited them in the trash container at the end of the row. Reaching out for his briefcase and travel bag, he walked over to the wide wall of windows far from anyone else and looked out onto the airport runways, then he placed the call. "Hello." was all he said.

The voice on the other end spoke in a slow and clear rhythm, stopping in between sentences, as though waiting for Sergei to ask for clarity or to interject a question. There was no sound from Sergei who listened intently, his face masked in total concentration.

"Proceed to the rental car area. A tall young man dressed in a pair of faded jeans and a dark blue shirt and wearing a Brooklyn Nets baseball hat will be carrying a cardboard sign with the name Mr. Baskem on it. He is your driver. You know what to say and what he will answer. Follow him. He will take you through baggage claim and out into the short term parking area. Get in the back seat of the car. He will drive you down the New Jersey Turnpike towards Philadelphia. He doesn't know any more than that." The voice stalled a few seconds, and added one word. "Understood?"

Barely waiting for Sergei's "Yes." the voice continued in the same slow manner, "Once you are on the turnpike, tell him to stop at the Richard Stockton rest area just before Exit 7A. Send him into the food court for coffee, then call this number I give you now. I will then give you the name and address of your hotel in Philadelphia. When he comes back, tell him to drive you to the Valley Forge Sheraton hotel outside Philadelphia and have him park in the rear corner of the parking lot. Show him what's in the trunk. Then leave the keys in the car. Another car will arrive to take you to your hotel in Philly. Your reservation is under Kohler, Walter Kohler. If you have an emergency, or need any assistance, call the agreed number. Otherwise, neither you nor I will communicate with each other until you have completed your assignment."

Sergei asked the man to repeat the first part of the one-sided conversation. After doing so, the man confirmed Sergei's acceptance with a one word inquiry. "Understood?"

"Yes." The word left Sergei's lips just as the cell call was disconnected on the other end. He never questioned the security measures taken by his associates but he couldn't keep himself from being annoyed at the drama and paranoid machinations involved in every new operation. He missed the days when he was totally responsible for completing every piece of the plan. What was it he was told that an American once said? Maybe it was Ben Franklin? "Too many cooks spoil the broth."

Sergei gathered his briefcase and travel bag and followed the main aisle away from the secure passenger area to find the baggage claim area. Just as he passed the security check-in area, a large blue sign was clearly visible in the near-distance hanging from the ceiling directly over a down-escalator. The sign was emblazoned with Baggage Claim on it in four-foot high black letters and beside it, just as large, incorporating a touch of international signage, was an black arrow pointing downward to a wide open lobby area with multiple baggage conveyors. The conveyors sat dutifully waiting to receive the valuable possessions being unloaded from arriving planes and distribute them to their owners. Before he stepped onto the down escalator, Sergei stepped aside to survey the baggage claim area from his vantage point above the open floor. He was looking for his ride to Philadelphia among the many arriving passengers who were busy racing from one baggage conveyor to the next trying to determine which conveyor would be chosen to unload their flight's baggage. It always appeared to him that every airport baggage area presented travelers across the world with an opportunity to play luggage lottery and win a head start in the race to exit the airport and move-on to their targeted destination, competing to be first to leave everyone else behind them. Sergei surmised that Americans might be more involved in it. Americans always seemed to be in a hurry to get somewhere whether they were coming or going. Winning anything was another American trait that amused him.

Viewing the number of people around him, he was reassured to see most people wearing masks. The world media outlets published daily accounts of United States' citizens' strong resistance to donning masks and defying social distancing directives in public places and at public gatherings. Hell, even their president refused to wear a mask and forced those around him to flout the use of masks. It was hard for him to understand Americans. With more than 290,000 Americans dead from the virus and another 50,000 predicted to die from the virus before Christmas, it was hard to believe there were so many who refused to wear masks. This wasn't the case in the airport. Most were masked, few were unmasked, all were forced into a measure of social distancing, particularly where people were required to form lines for services: ticket lines, fast food counters, and the few restaurants that were open were mandated to reduce the number of patrons and have as little as twenty-five percent of their dining areas open for table service. Still, there were those stubborn people who refused to cooperate, for no good or sensible reason. Freedom? It was insane.

These Americans were a puzzle. Generous, competitive, friendly, boisterous, combative, united, independent. One nation? Yes, Many nationalities? Yes. But a difficult people to control. What was it he was once told, "Their diversity creates a maelstrom of cultures that leads to loud inter-family discussions and friction but the fundamental basis of their brand of democracy allows a compromise that ultimately rests on the common desire for the same human wants." In his mind it wouldn't work everywhere; it wasn't worth the trouble. Just give everyone a job, food, and some entertainment. He knew the strong survive. It's the natural order of things. There are some who would say it is not the natural order to steal from others, to enslave or kill others, and have an abundance while others have nothing, Sergei would simply answer, yes, it is. He sees it every day; he saw it his whole life: an equal share, maybe, an equal voice, never.

He abandoned this thoughtful analysis and returned to his mission when a black baseball cap flitted into view, then out again, lost momentarily in the steady stream of people moving back and forth between baggage conveyors. He stared closely until the jeans, dark shirt, and now the visible Brooklyn Nets patch on the front of the hat completed the description. There in the carrier's right hand was a white cardboard sign with Mr. Baskem spelled out in black block letters. Dodging his way through the river of people between him and the black hat, he approached the young man.

"Good afternoon," Sergei said in a formal business manner. "I am Mr. Baskem."

Chapter 10: DOJ

Traveling anywhere was always an unpleasant part of Crandall's duties at
the Department of Justice. He hated stepping outside his insular confines
at the firm's Washington D.C. headquarters on Pennsylvania Avenue. He
had the same negative feelings about traveling more than thirty years ago
when he left his home in Mississippi for the first time. In the passing
years, he proceeded to take one hesitant step after another, plodding his
way through undergrad and law school, eventually landing a political in-
ternship that he parlayed into a career inside the most powerful law-en-
forcement institution in the United States. Now he lived in a townhouse in
the middle of the political universe, in a world far away from Mississippi.

Seated in the first class car of Amtrak's Silverliner headed north to Philadelphia, he wondered how many of the three-hundred million citizens of
the United States knew the advantage Boston, New York, Philadelphia,
and Washington, D.C. have over the other twelve largest cities in the
United States. He would tell them right away that it isn't the World Series
Championship that each city had captured within the past twelve years because he knew what it was and he was particularly aware of it today. Today the advantage provided him with a welcome alternative to the rigors
of flying through Dulles Airport to Philadelphia International Airport. He
was doing what he routinely did whenever he visited one of the cities on
the northeastern seaboard, he was riding on Amtrak's Northeast Corridor
Regional Passenger Rail Line.

The NEC, as it is commonly referred to, is Amtrak's premier rail-high-
way; an extensive network of rail lines running north and south that con-
nects these four metropolitan cities in the northeastern corner of the
United States. The Acela train that Crandall was on this morning traveled
at an average speed of 80 mph, with peaks at 150 mph. The rail service,
anchored in each of these four cities by massive train stations built by the
original railroad companies, was appreciated by the thousands of daily and

weekly commuters who lived along the corridor and within the ring of cities and the communities surrounding them and commuted between Boston and D.C. Among these thousands of commuters, no one was more thankful than Jefferson Crandall. He didn't like airplanes and he considered the rail line to be his personal limousine up and down the coast. Nevertheless, displaying his in-bred narrow-mindedness, and despite his fondness and obvious preference for the NEC service, he repeatedly and publically voiced his opposition to increased funding for Amtrak's operations. That was primarily due to that fact that his own state of Mississippi had little passenger rail service between its cities and nearly zero to any state beyond its borders. The way Crandall saw it was if Mississippi didn't get any of that money, no one else needed it. He also didn't like visitors coming to Mississippi anyway and he seldom travelled outside of Mississippi except to his necessary residence in D.C., and on occasional semi-job related no-cost-to-him junkets which he never reported to anyone and no one in his department ever questioned. In his self-justifying way of thinking, he paraphrased an old adage, "what's good for the goose is ...the goose's business."

Today, his favorite mode of transportation would deliver him to Philadelphia's Penn Station, also commonly known as 30th Street Station because the station sits alongside the Schuylkill River at the corner of 30th and Market Streets. This building was a favorite of Crandall with its exterior constructed with granite and adorned with architectural Roman and Greek columns at the west and east entrances displaying a balance between classical and modern architectural styles. Inside, the main floor is a vast waiting room populated with high-backed wooden benches set alongside the twelve track locations where departing passengers line up inside roped areas before descending the stairs and escalators to the tracks below. In the center of the hall is a large digital board hanging from the three-story high ceiling. On the board are the schedules and ever-changing messages updating its passengers on train movements and the occasional delays. At the east end of the hall just inside the entrance and visible from every corner of the main floor, a bronze statue is mounted on a twenty-foot marble pedestal depicting the archangel Michael, eyes cast down, lifting the body of a dead soldier out of the flames of war. The archangel's presence prompts admiring glances and thoughtful reflection as it stands silently in the great hall bordered by commercial offices, restaurants, retail shops, and fast-food food courts for travelers with street access from Market Street for the general public.

The Acela express discharged a number of riders in Baltimore and Wilmington but just as many new passengers boarded at each station heading to Philadelphia, New York, and Boston. As the train departed Wilmington, DE, Crandall folded his morning newspaper, pushed back what little was left of his three eggs, a slice of toast, cup of fruit (berries) and opened his cell phone. All this comfort on a sleek Amtrak express train, he thought smugly. No dimming airplane lights or safety instructions. He checked his latest DOJ news links, email, Facebook, Twitter and Instagram pages while he finished off his second cup of de-caffeinated coffee: black, no sugar. He began planning his interview of the young woman who had suddenly become such a major concern. His first question to himself was, why? Exactly why was Marina Carlton, age 25, single female, fitness trainer, barista, active on social media, with no other distinguishing details of interest other than a recent week vacation in Romania, identified as a possible threat to National Security? Why and what kind of threat? He even had subordinate staff members run an analysis on her but no worrisome connections surfaced of any kind. Up to the moment before he was asked, no, commanded to dig deeper, she was virtually invisible. She was registered below zero by his intelligence-gathering professionals.

He was an organized person who liked order and control; he thought of himself as a master planner. That was his skill, his value to the department. Though plans can go awry, resulting from an error, a personal mistake, even an act of God, it was more due to a poor plan. He was always able to resurrect a plan; that's why he was assigned to shadow Omega as an observer. Now he was inserted into it. Nevertheless, here he was freezing his busy calendar and on his way to Philadelphia. He was never congenial or accepting of an interruption to his own calendar and today's out-of-office trip was no exception. The train ride and the quiet out-of-the-ordinary breakfast softened his discomfort. He was hopeful the rest of this day would turn out as well. In less than forty minutes he would arrive at 30th Street Penn Station. It could've been worse, he could be headed to New York City.

The Acela express arrived into Penn Station's underbelly on schedule. Stepping out of the train on the lower level, Crandall rode the escalator up to the main floor and glanced to his left to acknowledge the statue he had grown fond of since his first arrival into Penn Station but he did this primarily to get his bearings. Penn Station's primary entrances and exits were east to the Schuylkill River and west to University City, the south side of the station was lined with several entrance/exit doors, as well as shops and eateries adjacent to Market Street, the main traffic conduit in and out of the city. Because he never knew what track he would arrive on and because the odd and even tracks were on opposite sides of the hall, the escalator could deliver him to either side of the main floor. The statue was at the east end of the station and acted as a reliable north star, telling him immediately which way to go. He could do the coordinates from there. He turned right and walked the length of the station, exiting directly out to 32nd Street facing what local residents would call University City because both the University of Pennsylvania and Drexel University campuses and a number of other colleges and universities were located in that western part of the city. New and old traditional academic and dormitory buildings dotted more than fifteen blocks of West Philadelphia. As his standard practice with Uber service calls, he walked to the cab station area carrying his black briefcase and waited for his Uber car. He knew it would be a sleek, shiny steel gray Acura. Within minutes, the Acura with LK43 at the end of its license plate, pulled up near the cab line. He double-checked his phone for the license plate, saw the Uber decal, and lowered himself into the rear of the car.

The Uber driver looked through his rear view mirror, smiled, and said, "Good morning, Sir." Then wanting to confirm the Uber phone order, he added. "U.S. Customs House, correct?"

"Change of plans." was the stiff, formal reply. "Rittenhouse Square."

"Yes, sir." The driver answered as he pulled out into the traffic that circled the station and turned left onto Market Street heading east towards downtown. In the distance stood City Hall, the large gray, granite architectural centerpiece at the crossroads of the city, where a statue of William Penn in his Quaker attire stood on the top of City Hall in a symbolic vigil to remind its citizens of his hope that his city will endure as a City of Brotherly Love.

Crandall typed in US Customs House on his Uber order but he never planned to go to the local DOJ office first, he always intended to meet with Marina first. Not wanting to be traced to his meeting with Marina nor be distracted from his first order of business, he phoned his office manager last evening and told him to notify the DOJ Philadelphia Regional director that he would be making an informal visit to the Philly office in mid-afternoon to discuss pending department policy changes. There were no policy changes being planned but he wanted to fill-in his calendar and legitimize his presence in Philadelphia. Marina chose Rittenhouse Square for this informal visit. He agreed and asked her to come alone. His pretense for meeting with Marina was to have an informal discussion concerning a call he received from the Romanian Embassy in D.C. although there had been no such call. A public park was as good a place as anywhere. There were coffee shops and plenty of benches where he could conduct what he thought would be a short interview. He was all set. His office manager had his cell phone number if there was any urgent need to contact him. He would accept no calls until he completed his interview with this young woman who had suddenly become the most important individual on the DOJ's unofficial hot list.

Rittenhouse Square turned out to be the ideal meeting place. The morning sun shone brightly on the tree covered square nestled in between the nineteenth century townhouses, chic restaurants and luxury hotels. The warm weather cooperated fully in supporting the outdoor rendezvous, and also rewarded tourists and city dwellers who planned to spend the day outside picnicking, bike riding, or just walking to discover Philadelphia's nearby colonial history. The mid-morning hours produced fewer visitors in the square: two residents walking dogs, a few students grabbing fresh air while participating in a virtual online class for the fall semester, and the routine flow of people on errands navigating to and from their offices. That left unoccupied benches spaced far apart available for her appointment.

Marina was nervous when she received yesterday's phone call from a woman identifying herself as an administrative assistant in the Department of Justice who said she was calling Marina in response to her recent inquiry to the Romanian Consulate. Marina was thankful for the fast response but she was surprised to have it come from the Justice Department office in Washington, D.C. The conversation was one-sided with Marina's participation limited to two one-word answers, both "Yes." At the end of the phone call, Marina sat perfectly still, staring at her cell phone trying to register what just occurred. In that lightning-fast conversation, she agreed to meet with an Assistant Attorney General from the United States Justice Department, a Mr. Jefferson Crandall, the next morning, alone, in the park. The assistant said the meeting would be less than an hour. One of Marina's two Yes words was spoken in response to the assistant when she asked Marina if she preferred to meet in Rittenhouse Park instead of Washington Square. Marina selected the park because it was outside and if necessary there were public places adjacent to the park to retreat to if the weather forced them indoors. She was being careful about the virus and was now accustomed to carrying her mask and practicing social distancing, a small bottle of disinfectant was stashed in her backpack. She was sitting on the waist high wall at the southeast corner entrance of the park at 18th and Walnut Street, facing the one-way traffic coming west on Walnut Street from the direction of City Hall. She was told to watch for a man in a dark suit with a black briefcase. That very short list of descriptive information for Mr. Crandall was barely helpful in finding a lawyer in a city full of lawyers but she would do her best. She chuckled at the thought that the only thing they forgot to ask her to do was to wear a red rose in her hair and rent a poodle to sit on her lap. Well, she reasoned, mid-morning in mid-week in Rittenhouse Square in the middle of a pandemic should thin out the number of people she would have to sift through her personal eye-scanner.

The single exception to the instructions from the DOJ assistant who told her not to tell anyone about the meeting was that she did tell Marc about the call and the meeting. He was both surprised and concerned by the Department of Justice's sudden interest in Marina but he was pleased Marina was going to have someone in authority listen to her. Nevertheless, he strongly disagreed that she go to the meeting alone. If for no other reason, he felt his presence would give her support and keep her calm.

"It's not necessary. I'll be fine. My god, he's from Washington. The Justice Department!"

The discussion continued with voices rising on both sides and finally ending when Marina, exasperated with their disagreement, compromised. He could be nearby. Even now, she could see him across the street leaning against a traffic pole, pretending to read a magazine. He was her safety valve. Marc planned to shadow them to wherever they moved, keeping her in sight at all times. It was settled. The night before they agreed they'd walk together to the park, then separate, Marina would sit where Marc could see her at all times. Cops and Robbers? No, it's bigger than that, he thought. This was the U.S. Department of Justice. This is cloak and dagger stuff. What have we gotten into?

****

There are four main streets that crisscross Philadelphia, moving people from the four corners of the city into center city, all converging at City

Hall, and back out again. Market, Chestnut, and Walnut move traffic east and west; Market is the major thoroughfare, a two-way street running east and west through the city (one way east from 20th Street to City Hall). Chestnut is a one-way street running east from the city's western boundary to the Delaware River; Walnut is a one-way street running west from the river, out to the western boundary of the city. Broad Street runs north and south. The city's geography is defined by the Delaware River in the east, it is the landmark best used for navigating your way around this city of 1.5 million people.

Jefferson Crandall's Uber driver was familiar with center city's street layout and its traffic pattern of alternating one way streets so he drove east on Market Street, turned left onto 20Th Street, right onto the JFK Parkway, then right onto 17th Street and finally right onto Walnut. It was like a mouse maneuvering its way through a maze. Crandall leaned forward from the rear seat when they turned onto Walnut Street. "Drive slowly when we come to the square. I'm meeting some people and I want to see if they are here yet."

Holding a recent photo in his hand and scanning faces as they approached the northeast corner of the park, Crandall recognized Marina sitting on the waist-high wall at the entrance to the square. Perched on the wall with her legs dangling, and holding onto her handbag with a backpack slung over her shoulder, she looked like the college student she was. He was unprepared for how young she looked. Her hair was longer, at shoulder length, and darker than in the photo he was given. He decided the difference could be attributed to the recent closure of barbershops and hair salons for the last five to six months mandated by cities and states to reduce the number of cases and deaths during the height of the coronavirus epidemic. Barbershops and hair salons suffered a similar economic setback two generations ago when the hippie era and the Beatles long-haired invasion struck in the sixties. By leaps and bounds, the coronavirus' economic impact was a huge disaster, it wasn't only young people whose hair was getting longer; it was everyone. In only a few months after the outbreak, men's and women's hair was longer and grayer, and not by choice; facial hair was also back in favor by default. Beards, five 'o clock shadows, three-day stubble were all in abundance. With men working at home, or just not working, grooming took a holiday.

Putting aside the long hair, he was satisfied it was Marina and it was helpful she was punctual. He directed the driver to continue on Walnut Street across 18th Street, passing the corner where Marina sat, and told him to slowly pull alongside the sidewalk that rimmed the north end of the square He was now approximately thirty feet beyond Marina. With the hired Acura in park, he paid the driver his fare and climbed out of the car, adjusted his suit coat and prepared to meet Marina Carlton, the young woman who would never guess she was the center of attention of some very important people on both sides of the Atlantic Ocean.

Chapter 11: Sophia

Not wanting to startle her with his sudden appearance, Crandall entered the park at the 19th street entrance, followed a path to the center of the park, then walked out of the park to the sidewalk alongside 18th Street where he shifted his briefcase to his more visible left hand and casually walked north to Walnut Street where Marina sat waiting. He did all this so Marina could see him approaching her from a short distance. He was certain she was nervous enough without feeling she was being ambushed from behind. Marina caught sight of him walking towards her, matching him perfectly with the sparse description she was given, his dark suit and the black briefcase clutched in his left hand. The single addition to his attire was a black cloth mask. As he slowed his step and made eye contact, she took a deep breath, pulled up her teal-colored mask and braced for his greeting.

"Excuse me young lady." He asked politely. "Are you Ms. Carlton?"

Crandall wanted his words to convey how perceptive and confident he was in the manner in which he identified her so quickly. Of course, Marina had no idea he had a recent photo of her in his briefcase that removed any chance he would be wrong. In addition to knowing what she looked like, he knew her life story. That's how professionals worked best, he thought to himself: take the guessing out of every situation whenever you can. It's nice to have the resources of the Justice Department as his private investigator. Taxpayer contributions at work, he chuckled at the thought.

"Yes, I am." Marina answered with a pleasant but nervous smile.

She noted the perfectly-tailored suit he wore and felt momentarily subservient by the air of self-confidence this man from Washington, D.C. exuded. He looked comfortable with the self-knowledge that he was an important person. Nevertheless, with some apprehension but also with relief, she was glad he was here. Now maybe things will start happening and Sophia will be found. The sleepless nights and the nagging worry for Sophia's welfare will hopefully be gone, left in the past.

Displaying his DOJ credentials, Crandall formally introduced himself and invited Marina to choose a spot for their conversation. She led him back into the park, to a lone bench in a corner at the opposite end of the park where there were no people and very little traffic, vehicular or pedestrian. The one-way street that circled the park was seldom busy. Directly behind them, screened by a cluster of shade trees and separated from the park by a narrow street, stood several late nineteenth century residential townhouses owned by wealthy city residents on the city's social register, unremarkable houses valued at millions of dollars. It was an ideal location for a quiet conversation.

Even before they reached the bench, Marc planted himself comfortably at a table on a restaurant's outdoor patio situated diagonally across from where Marina was about to sit. He and Marina had agreed on that bench the night before. He had a clear view of her with no obstructions. Placing his single spy prop, the city's morning Inquirer, on the table, he watched Marina approach the bench, stop, and then sit on the left side of the bench just as he suggested she do. He told her this would let him see her face as she turned to listen and speak to the man from Washington who would now be seated at the opposite end of the bench with his back to Marc. With that vantage point, he could see her facial reactions and know if he should intervene. He had thought of bringing a pair of binoculars he owned from his earlier years of camping but they were too large, too obvious. The much smaller opera glasses he purchased a year ago at a performance of Aida at the Academy of Music were ideal for this amateur bit of surveillance but they were at his parent's home, too far for him to go on such short notice. No. He was in a good spot. He would order a coffee, his final spy prop, and observe and wait. He watched as they both removed their masks once they were somewhat distanced from one another.

"Well, Ms. Carlton." Crandall began. "I was given some information from the Romanian Embassy office in Washington but only that you were concerned for your friend. I understand you contacted their Philadelphia and New York consulates."

"Yes, that's right. I was afraid she was harmed so I tried for several days to reach my friend by phone calls and texts but I didn't receive any replies. I didn't know what else to do. Another friend suggested I call the Romanian offices. I did. They were easy to find on the internet."

He was impressed. Her response was just as precise as the single page summary a member of the department's research team had prepared for him to read on the train, that summary was now sitting in a thin red file folder in the briefcase lying beside him. While she paused for a breath, he interrupted her with a clarification meant to emphasize there was no urgent or personal reason for his interest in her inquiry.

"Normally, Ms. Carlton, the Justice Department wouldn't interest itself in requests for information between private citizens and acquaintances in other countries but your request indicates you suspect something ominous and it came to my attention as I was preparing to come to Philadelphia for a scheduled business meeting today in our regional office. My curiosity as a career investigator led me here today."

With that declaration of personal distancing from the subject at hand, the Assistant Attorney General seemed to relax; he slid further back onto the stiff wooden slats on the bench, put his professional investigator face on and proceeded. "Please tell me what happened to your friend in Romania?"

Knowing this interview was her first opportunity to share her fears for Sophia with a government official, she spent a few hours last evening practicing what she would say and how she would present her story. She was determined to speak in a clear and controlled manner. Proving to herself that practice does not always make perfect, the opposite performance occured as a rush of words poured out of her mouth as if she expected at any moment a hidden timer would release a loud gong announcing to her and to anyone listening that her allotted story time had ended. Fortunately the advice she often gave to her fitness training clients came quickly to mind. Pause. Breathe. Focus. Proceed.

In that moment, a warm breeze blew across the park, brushing the trees and bringing a refreshing aroma of the park's many flowers closer to her senses; the breeze and aromas acted as a muted but orchestrated accompaniment to her testimony. Responding to nature's boost, she regained her peace of mind, straightened her body, folded her hands in front of her, and began speaking.

Across the street, Marc patiently sipped his five dollar cup of coffee wondering how much a cheese pastry would set him back. He wasn't hungry, he told himself, he merely wanted to know so he could calculate how much money he saved each morning when he had his 'usual' breakfast at home compared to eating here, say 365 days a year. His guessed a year's breakfast tab was close to $4,000.

From his vantage point, the conversation between Marina and the man from Washington had been equally shared until the last five minutes or so when Marina's facial expressions and body motions became more animated and her lips moved continuously, hardly pausing at all, with any interruption from the other side of the bench. It's likely she was telling him about the last night in Romania. Marc wanted so badly to be sitting next to her, even maybe across from her, just closer. But so far, it was all good. He'd keep watching; hoping for her sake that this would lead to finding and hearing from Sophia, then there would be no more half-eaten meals, no more nightmares for Marina: a return to normalcy, or as normal as possible in this time of Covid 19. His train of thought stopped as he lifted his head to watch the waiter lead several people to a nearby table socially distanced from his own. He waited until the waiter turned away from the newly seated customers before he made eye contact with him, then lifted his arm and waved him over to his table.

"Yes, Sir." The waiter asked politely. "More coffee?"

Smiling more at himself than the waiter, Marc answered affirmatively and added. "I'll have a cheese pastry also."

****

Marina finished her story sharing all the details from the phone call Sophia received at the club to Marina's telephone call to the Romanian Consulate in New York City. Crandall listened carefully, assisting her with small observations addressed more as clarifying questions on places and times, but also meant to slow her pace and to improve her memory for smaller details. Her story easily held his attention partly because he was trained to never rush a witness's account nor let his attention fade away from a witness's account because you might miss an important piece of information or fail to recognize a discrepancy in it. Today he had a more important reason to hear everything. He would be reporting her story and every detail of her movements in Romania to the man who sent him to speak to her. This man served other men who took their money and power seriously. Somehow this young woman unknowingly stepped into the dark side of their world. He knew from his experience with them that it was not a safe place for anyone to be, and certainly not a place for an innocent spirit.

Marina completed her account. She was exhausted from expending so much energy and tension in recalling fully for the first time the journey she has been on since her last night with Sophia. Headaches were not common for her but she was now visited with a whopper. Even her back and legs were tense and achy. Maybe it was the bench. She barely whispered her final words. "That's it. I'm so worried about her. I hope you can help, sir."

"Ms. Carlton," he began, "That is quite an ordeal that you have been through these past few days. The outline of the events as you describe them do have the familiar pattern of criminal action in its description: a hint of abduction, possibly foul play. I understand how you would come to be fearful for your friend."

"Thank you." Marina answered with controlled excitement, thankful a person in authority, and in law enforcement, believed what she had to say.

"But," Crandall said in a voice that had suddenly become more formal, "it's also possible that your friend took the phone call, decided to meet someone elsewhere, then later returned home, changed her clothes, forgot her phone and slept off the long, hard night, waking up long after you were on your way home. Possible?"

Her brief moment of excitement fell away like a lead pipe falling on her foot: fast, hard, and hurtful. Stammering, she looked wide-eyed at him and said, "You don't believe me."

"I believe what you told me," countered Crandall. "I just want you to know there can be another explanation for her disappearance that evening."

"But the blood spots on the boarding pass folder. How do you explain them?"

"I can't. We will want to take those for lab tests once we have more reason to believe your friend is missing."

"She hasn't contacted me. No one can find her." sighed Marina. "There's blood spots. Isn't that the definition of a missing person?" Marina's voice was rising, her body becoming tense as she spoke.

"It can be, Ms. Carlton." Crandall softened his tone. He didn't want Marina to lose faith in him and the DOJ. It is easier to handle a problem if you keep the problem under your control, until you have and a solution for it. He changed back to his condescending manner, he offered an apology and a promise of immediate action.

"I'm sorry if I upset you Ms. Carlton. I promise I will do everything in my power to help you find your friend. I will have someone from my D.C. office contact you tomorrow to make arrangements to have you deliver the boarding pass to the regional office here at the U.S. Customs House at 3rd and Chestnut Streets. They will have the local FBI lab run tests on the boarding pass. At the same time I will have our office request that the Romania Embassy provide us with a law enforcement contact in Mamia."

On the other side of the street, Marc noticed Marina's changes in body language. He put his fork down, pushed away his half-eaten pastry, and started to rise from the table before he stopped himself and remained seated. There was no threat of danger; the man on the bench didn't move at all. Marina's sudden sign of emotion startled him but she seemed to have regained her composure. But he suddenly lost his appetite and concentrated solely on Marina.

Speechless at both the apology and the promise of action, Marina sat nearly motionless, nervously running her fingers along her purse straps. She brushed her hair away from her eyes and waited for more words to be spoken by the Assistant Deputy AG. Crandall likewise remained quiet before he reached into his briefcase on the bench, pulled out a small pad and took a pen from the inside pocket of his winkle free suit coat. "I have a few questions about Sophia and how you both spent the days before your flight home. The answers might speed the investigation in Romania."

Crandall proceeded with his questions. They were largely related to Sophia and her family: where she lived, her parent's names, any siblings, what she did for a living, who her friends were, the names of people she met in Romania. The typical information an investigator would want to know when they went searching for a missing person. There wasn't much Marina could tell him. She told him what she knew but most of her information was years old. She was disappointed she didn't have more answers. In fact, unbeknownst to her, Crandall knew much more about Sophia than Marina knew, and only Crandall and one other person knew that getting the answers to these last few questions was the primary reason for his presence in Philadelphia today.

In a span of a few minutes, Marina answered Crandall's questions and Sophia's personal information was tucked neatly back into his briefcase. He thanked Marina for meeting with him and for providing information that he felt will lead to finding her friend safe and sound within a few days. They both rose from the bench, Crandall checked his watch and remarked that their meeting had been productive. He switched his briefcase to his left hand and lifting his right hand shoulder-high, waved slightly in place of exchanging any physical contact, a reflection of the new normal in the era of Covid 19.

"Goodbye, Ms. Carlton. I'm certain we will hear something positive regarding your friend, Sophia."

Marina nodded in return. "Thank you for coming here and for listening to me. I'll wait to hear from your office regarding the testing for the boarding pass." She smiled, added a parting remark, "Have a safe trip home, Mr. Crandall. Goodbye."

As soon as Crandall stepped into the dark blue government sedan that pulled alongside the square, Marc rose from his eagle's perch on the patio. The meeting's ending was perfectly timed as the restaurant's lunch regulars began to fill-in the 25% restricted-capacity seating mandated in the city. He crossed over the narrow side street to join Marina where she sat waiting for him at her original spot at the front entrance of the park.

****

As a cover for his meeting with Marina, Crandall told the driver to take him to the DOJ's Philadelphia office located in the U.S. Customs House building on the corner of Second and Chestnut Streets two blocks up from the Delaware River and on the edge of the city's historical neighborhood: Independence Hall, the Liberty Bell, Carpenter's Hall and others. The Custom House was convenient for his purposes today: it was only a dozen blocks from Rittenhouse Square and enabled him to keep his schedule intact. He would arrive there in time for lunch with a department colleague, meet with several department managers, and return at 6 PM on an Acela express train to Washington, DC. He was looking forward to his trip back home. He planned to sit back with a beverage, jot some notes into his laptop and submit them informally to the men who paid dearly for this level of government service.

Chapter 12: Turnpike

Approaching the noon hour, a full-sized rental car moved purposefully down the New Jersey turnpike blending into the flow of traffic. The driver with his sunglasses, Nets baseball cap, and a cardboard sign resting on the front passenger seat, was staying within the speed restrictions. It was the first thing he was told to do when he picked up the car earlier that day in Manhattan – stay under the speed limit. When the stranger who he never expected to meet again handed him the keys to the car along with the first payment of $400, he was given a short list of instructions. The instructions from this friend of a friend's friend who was willing to pay him a large sum of money to pick up a businessman were easy, only the last instruction was strange: tell no one about the pickup or destination; have no conversation with your passenger, speak only when spoken to, and do whatever he asks you to do.; leave your cell phone home, you will be provided a throwaway cell phone with pre-purchased minutes on it to be used only in an emergency; lastly, return the car to Manhattan and leave it locked on any side street. The final piece of business was the second $400. He was told someone would call him on the throwaway phone to tell him where to pick up the other $400 that same night. With $400 already in his pocket this was his lucky day, he was going to pull in $800 and he'd be home in Brooklyn before the day ended. It was going to be his best payday since the goddamn pandemic shut down most of his normal opportunities for quick cash. Hell, he didn't even mind having to wear the mask he was given in order to get into the airport. When this was over, he'd keep it as a souvenir.

In the wide backseat, stretched out with his legs touching the rear of the front passenger seat, Sergei was brushing up on his English. He spoke formal English well enough to hide his Russian accent so that on first meeting him many people would guess he was from a Balkan or German country. He always carried a handy mini-size Berlitz or Barron's language conversion dictionary, French to English, etc. that many international tourists carried in America. He didn't need one but it served more as a prop to make him appear to be a tourist or a travelling businessman. He had learned people noticed little things about a stranger, good or bad. So he used little things to make him appear less threatening in a strange country. An example was wearing a baseball cap in America, or carrying a bible, and when all else fails, feign timidity. Fit in. If you can't, use little things to lessen suspicion.

However, Sergei was a perfectionist in many ways. He was interested in colloquial English, conversational English where regional words were unique, and he liked knowing slang words that replaced proper English. America was flooded with such word usage, even abbreviations dominated American English. It captivated him. He saw it useful and he also recognized it as a coded language, that once-known, kept a student of the language more understanding of what the speaker was really saying and feeling. He insisted these two things were important to someone in his line of work, not understanding precisely what is being said or what is being felt in a foreign place can be costly. You can be endangered by the lack of communication even in the midst of gaiety and Sergei never wanted to be at any disadvantage. That's why he sat back now to read an American magazine and prepped up on his English for his current assignment. He set his watch alarm to tell him when the car was within five miles of the Richard Stockton rest area just before Exit 7A. He set the alarm as soon as the car was on the turnpike and headed south towards Philadelphia. He synchronized his alarm with the mileposts on the side of the highway, 60 miles equals 60 minutes: the John Stockton rest area was forty miles down the turnpike when he set his watch alarm for 40 minutes. As a precaution, he spoke to his driver, "Get off at the Richard Stockton rest area. It will be announced on your GPS."

It was late afternoon when the driver pulled into the rest area and headed for the space closest to the fast-food restaurants and coffee shops. The parking area was half-full with many spots available in the overflow parking lot located further from the food restaurants and gasoline refueling stations. Sergei re-directed the driver to park in the farthest corner of the primary lot intending to use the additional minutes it would take for the driver to make his roundtrip walk and return with their coffee to complete a scheduled phone call. He pulled a fresh twenty dollar bill from his gold money clip, one of the many U.S. currency bills a stranger had given him before he left Vienna. He remembered at that moment one of his favorite lines in a Marlon Brando film spoken by a woman who was living on the edge of society. "I am always so thankful for the kindness of strangers." He too was thankful to the many strangers who have stepped in and out of his professional life. Not for the same reasons as Tennessee Williams' lonely character but nevertheless he was often thankful for strangers.

He stretched his arm across the front seat waving the bill in his hand, "A black coffee for me. Whatever you want for yourself." He waited for the driver to begin walking towards the food area before he placed his phone call.

"All is satisfactory?" asked the male voice on the other end of the phone as soon as he answered the phone.

"All is good," answered Sergei, shaking his head affirmatively more as a habit to ascertain his own self-assurance than to placate the man on the phone who obviously couldn't see any of Sergei's movements or facial expressions. That was just as well since Sergei was tiring from his long flight and car ride and he never wished to appear to be less than at his peak when he was working. He and the man on the other end of the phone shared similar missions before and there was little reason to weary each other with repetition and reminders of their responsibilities or what to do in the event anything went awry. The conversation ended with time to spare before the driver returned with their coffee.

The coffee was a welcome infusion of caffeine that would bolster Sergei's alertness until he arrived in Philadelphia. Within minutes, the two men and their rental car merged with the thousands of cars that commuted daily between New York, Pennsylvania and New Jersey, in addition to the thousands that traversed the I-95 interstate highway between Maine and Florida. The destination was now more defined than "head to Philadelphia"; the car's internal GPS was set for the Sheraton Valley Forge Hotel in Valley Forge, approximately fifty miles away. Sergei reset his watch alarm to alert him of their arrival in less than an hour.

Chapter 13: Boiling Pot

The cloudless, late-morning blue sky made staying indoors almost sinful, so Marc and Marina found themselves several blocks north from Rittenhouse Square walking in quiet conversation along the Benjamin Franklin Parkway. Marc and Marina never intended to be on the Parkway at this moment. They were equally fond of this scenic open area where bicyclists, joggers, lovers, tourists, and native Philadelphians savored the foresight envisioned by the city's architects, past and present. After the stress of the meeting this morning, the Parkway seemed to be the most natural place to be where Marina could calm her senses. They found themselves on the sidewalk outside St. Peter and St. Paul Cathedral on 18th Street facing the Parkway as it stretched westward towards the Schuylkill River, an open boulevard fourteen blocks long, lined with trees, museums, and public-use buildings such as the Free Library, and the Franklin Institute.

Marina's anxiety slowly fell away while her eyes delighted in the inviting panorama of Logan Circle. The view included the decorative Swann fountain spraying translucent streams of water upward several stories high from its center and simultaneously inward from the mouths of the sculptured frogs and turtles arrayed in the outer area of its circular pond towards the classical figures in the center representing the three rivers that flow in and around the city: the Wissahickon, the Schuylkill, and the Delaware rivers. In the distance, silhouetted against the clear blue sky and placed regally on the top of a grand ascending staircase of wide steps stood the Philadelphia Museum of Art, the iconic centerpiece of the Parkway. The museum's Greek temple columns, mirroring the ancient Parthenon in Greece, offer a contrast of architectural splendor to the modern glass-coated steel skyscrapers surrounding the Parkway. Inside the museum a diverse collection of paintings and sculptures by artists throughout the millenniums share their fame alongside a re-assembled Japanese Tea House and a sacred Temple from East Asia, a few of the treasures Marina never tired of visiting. The newest celebrity art on the museum's list of attractions is one that first arrived on the top steps of the museum in 1982, departed, then re-appeared in 1990 and 2003, finally returning to the museum in 2006 where it's been greeting residents and visitors for fourteen years and is available for seeing, touching, and celebrating around the clock every day and night for three-hundred and sixty-five days a year, or as expressed in today's popular jargon, for 24/7/365. The celebrity art is the bronze Rocky statue sculpted by A. Thomas Schomberg for a sequel to a 1976 feel-good movie of the same name, a gritty profile of a club boxer in South Philly. Marina's and Marc's training regimen for their clients always included multiple sessions at the base of the intimidating museum steps but they began running the steps when they were in high schools for the same reason most Philadelphians and visitors from all over the United States and the world run the Rocky Steps - they want to recapture the gritty and triumphant scene in the film where Rocky conditions himself, heart and soul, to defeat the pain in his body and finish a strenuous four mile run from the Italian Market in his own neighborhood with a sprint to the top of the Art Museum. The climactic moment in the scene depicts Rocky, standing with his arms raised, looking out over the city below, triumphant in his moment of personal glory. It is a harbinger of the final scenes in the film. Rocky's ascent to the plaza at the top of the steps is symbolic of the individual struggle millions of people have overcome in their own personal fight against adversity, a fight they won despite the overwhelming odds against them.

The Rocky Steps are now more famous than the Spanish Steps in Rome and the stair-climbing challenge of the Empire State Building's 92 floors in NYC. The steps begin easy enough from street level at the Eakins' Oval Park in front of the museum, rising steadily higher as the runner completes each of the four stages, the climb coaxing aches in the joints and muscles before the runner lands on the wide plaza in front of the museum. A circular fountain awaits there, surrounded on three sides by buildings adorned with massive Greek columns wherein art treasures are arranged majestically within its walls. The fountain is a refreshing reward after climbing the steps, inviting visitors to sit and toss in a coin to make a wish come true before they enter through the museum's bronze doors. Marina often fields charges of blasphemy from her aunts and uncles and colonial history buffs whenever she shares her belief that the steps are the most popular tourist stop in the city surpassing century-old favorites such as Independence Hall, the Liberty Bell, Ben Franklin's gravesite and the Betsy Ross house. She never forgets her Uncle Walt's complaint that her comment on the steps' popularity was nearly as offensive as John Lennon's bold observation in 1966 that "the Beatles are more popular than Jesus Christ." She didn't contest Uncle Walt's contrary opinion about the steps; she simply hung on quietly to her own observation that the steps and the unflinching spirit of the film's underdog hero, Rocky Balboa, combine to depict for many people an Everyman who triumphs against great odds offering inspiration that the seeds of victory are often found in the effort a person puts forth in preparing for the challenge they face. As they continued down the Parkway, she couldn't help thinking it was like her challenge in trying to find Sophia.

Marc on the other hand was anxious to know what was said at the bench but he was sensitive to Marina's present mood of not having any appetite for sharing a word by word account of the conversation, so he said very little as they walked. Overall, this impromptu walk was good therapy. Gradually, the fresh air, green shrubs, trees, and summer flowers showing their last days of bloom, seemed to deliver renewed strength to Marina. They stopped in front of the relocated Rodin Museum on the Parkway. Marc purchased two bottled waters from a street vendor and steered Marina to a wooden bench under a clump of oak trees where a slight breeze gently drifted in from the City Hall end of the Parkway confirming his wisdom and timing, or luck, in selecting this specific bench.

Marina began the conversation in a soft voice, "Mr. Crandall was polite. He said he was in contact with the Romanian Embassy and he told me he understood my concern for Sophia and why I would be so worried for her." Pausing to take a sip of water, she continued, "He asked me to tell him everything I could remember of the events on my last day with Sophia, from waking in the morning to the moment after dinner when she and I were separated. Then he sat and listened, asking for a few clarifications as I told him everything."

"That's good." was all Marc could offer, not wanting to stop Marina while she was willing to share her conversation.

"Yes. That's good." She repeated Marc's words with emphasis, then with rising frustration and passion amplifying her voice, she said, "But after I finished telling him everything including not getting any response from Sophia to my texts and phone calls, his only comment left me thinking that he wasn't convinced she was in danger."

Marc placed his hand on her arm, as if to keep her from rising off the bench. "What did he say?"

"He told me he believed me but he said there can be another explanation for her disappearance."

"He's right." Marc said flatly, "There could be." Wanting to comfort her, he added with a hopeful tone, "Isn't that what you want to be true?"

"Yes, but how hard will he search for her if he doesn't think she is in danger, and if she is in danger, then every minute is important. That's why I'm afraid for Sophia."

"I know. I know." Marc wanted to soothe her frustration. Trying to calm her rising emotions he offered a more positive outcome. "Look. The man from the DOJ said he will have someone run tests on the boarding pass tomorrow and he also said he is going to contact someone in Romania tomorrow. So we should hear something in a day or two."

"I guess you're right." Marina replied, resigning herself to accept that they were doing what they could and maybe now she needed to trust higher authorities to take real action. She lifted her body up straighter on the bench, managed her first smile since the meeting and announced in her happy voice, "I'm hungry. Let's eat lunch."

They settled on a nearby Au Bon Pain café at 17th Street and headed there when Marina's cell phone buzzed, showing an unfamiliar number. She wouldn't normally answer a call from an unfamiliar or unknown number but the recent days now made every call possibly important to her. She answered it on the second ring.

"Hello?" she said, then paused to allow the caller to begin speaking. "Yes, this is Marina," she confirmed. "Oh, hi Carl." She was glad she took the call. She had been waiting to hear from Carl after he promised to connect her with his FBI agent contact.

"Today? Sure." Hesitating for a moment, she asked. "Marc is with me. Is it OK if he joins us?" Hearing the one word response, she replied. "OK. We'll be there at 2 PM, same place." She ended the call as they were approaching the Au Bon Pain cafe.

"That was Carl. He and his FBI agent friend will meet us at Le Café at two o'clock."

Marc frowned, "I can't. I have to meet a fitness client at the same time. Can you call him back and make it after three-thirty."

"No. That's not necessary. Going alone is not a problem. I'll be fine among my Le Café friends." She glanced at the digital time on her cell phone, and pointed towards the Au Bon Pain front door. "We have time for a quick lunch."

****

Carl and Doug Frister were already seated when Marina arrived at Le Cafe. Carl was his punctual self and he was possibly also a creature of habit seeing that he was sitting at the same table where she and Marc shared coffee with him a day or so ago. The days since her return home were few but they have been so long she wasn't certain what day it was.

Both men rose from the table as she walked over to them. Doug Frister, or Agent Frister, was not in the expected FBI uniform of a dark suit, white shirt, muted-colored tie, and black shoes. Dressed in casual tan slacks and a powder-blue oxford shirt and brown loafers, he resembled a college professor possibly in his mid-thirties, or maybe an office worker freed from the suit and tie in this new Covid 19 existence, maybe an IT technician, anything but an agent for the Federal Bureau of Investigation. Neither man had a beverage, confirming immediately to Marina Carl's promise on the phone that this was going to be a short meeting.

Carl spoke first, "Hi, Lady M. This is Doug Frister who I told you about the other day." He stayed with a short introduction. He was told it was a good practice in the private detective business to exchange the least amount of personal and business information in any public setting where inanimate objects and innocent-looking people soak up information that may be valuable to any inquisitive third party.

"It's nice to meet you, Mr. Frister." She replied. "Thank you for coming to talk to me about my friend. I hope you can find her."

"It's my pleasure, Ms. Carlton," the agent said as he and Carl waited to be seated until Marina sat down. "Carl gave me a brief outline of events that led to your concerns for your friend in Romania and how you've been unable to get any results from Romanian officials here in Philly or in New York City." First, let me tell you that isn't unusual. Here in the United States, in Philly, it is a practice to wait some days before launching a search for a missing person unless there is a sign of harm or forcible restraint involved. Granted this event should prove to have such behavior, the FBI still isn't assigned to protect or find foreign citizens, certainly not in their own country. With all that said, I want to help and possibly point you in the right direction if something bad happened to your friend.

Shifting in his hard-bottom chair, Doug began his interrogation, or as he liked to say, his discovery of facts. His initial questions were what was referred to in baseball as 'slow pitches', balls that are easy for the batter to hit: what is Sophia's full name, where did she live, what nationality is she if not Romanian, what are her parents' names, any siblings, how did she and Marina meet, and so on. In his experience, asking questions like these in the beginning put many witnesses at ease, made them feel comfortable because these questions can be easily answered and require little effort. The questions that follow are generally increasingly more stressful, demanding that the witness recall a more critical event or a key conversation. Using this approach, Agent Frister proceeded with his slow pitches to reduce Marina's anxiety and gain a measure of trust between them, besides he needed to know as much as possible about Sophia if he decided there was reason to go further.

The Special Agent quickly learned Sophia's last name is Glasinov, she is Russian, with a sister, Katrina, her mother's name is Anna, they lived just outside Moscow, her father didn't live with them, and Marina didn't know the father's name. Scribbling notes on a stenographer-size note pad, he continued with personal inquiries about Sophia even as the more important group of questions - who, what, where, and how of the evening's events were already forming in his mind. "How long did you and Sophia continue to write one another after high school?"

"We stayed connected after I went off to college. We wrote for a while, then her Moscow address was invalid. She told me later that she moved out to be on her own."

"So you stayed in touch with one another for several years but only through letters, is that correct?

"Yes, letters and email. We communicated less, mostly texts on holidays, birthdays. Until last month when she invited me to vacation with her. She texted me and called me several times in the last month. She told me not to call her, she knew it could be too expensive for me."

He interrupted her, "Do you have her cell phone number? And any other social addresses? Her current address in Moscow?"

"I have her cell phone number. That's all."

He looked up at her, pleased at that discovery. "That's great. Can you please give me that number "

"I can but she never called me back and I could never leave her a message. There was no voice messaging on her phone."

The agent stopped writing to look up. He didn't say a word but a slight knowing smile lit his face. He was getting more and more interested in Sophia.

Carl who was held spellbound by his law enforcement friend's casual but efficient pursuit of information was dry-mouthed as he knew all three of them must be. While the questions and answers continued to be exchanged from both sides of the table, he rose from the table to get three bottles of water. A few questions became intense and more dramatic but the agent's calming manner elicited clear, unemotional responses from Marina. What shocked Marina most during this interview was how little she knew about Sophia's life after completing their high school years. Marina's responses to Frister made her aware for the first time that during her week in Romania she was never introduced by name to anyone, leaving her to realize for the first time that she knew very little about her pen pal's friends, her work or her life. Nothing at all. They were too busy partying and sleeping. The lack of such personal details on Sophia was disturbing. During their high school years they shared absolutely everything about each other across the wide, deep, gray ocean that separated them. Letters and texts detailing common experiences and youthful milestones were exchanged, an occasional phone call was randomly inserted. None of it revealed much about Sophia's life. She remembered how excited she was to assume they would catch-up on each other's life in Mamaia with afternoon gab sessions around a pool or on a terrace overlooking the deep blue Adriatic Sea. Those sessions never happened. In the midst of this interrogation, she discovered she knew very little about Sophia.

Carl returned with a bottle of cold water for each of them necessitating a welcome break lasting only a few minutes. Agent Frister emptied his water in three gulps, a type of muscle-memory response from his past years competing in track and cross-country events. Carl slowly sipped his water, just enough to keep his lips wet while he lamented his missed opportunity for a cinnamon latte. Marina took several demure swallows, her fitness training discipline keeping her mindful to conserve her water through the remaining interview. The questions and responses shortened, signaling a nearing end to the interview. Doug revisited for clarity a few of the details Marina recounted in her return to the apartment and not finding Sophia there. Satisfied with the clarifications, he continued.

"Did you notice anything out of place in the apartment? Do you recall hearing or seeing anyone leaving the apartment at that time?"

Slightly refreshed by the short break, Marina was adamant that nothing was out of place other than Sophia's purse and shoes in the middle of the floor which Frister didn't find particularly alarming. She confirmed she didn't hear or see anything or anyone in or around the apartment. Knowing he was ready to end the interview, Frister took a moment to compliment her perseverance. "You've done a very good job in providing details and a timeline. This is all very helpful."

Sitting up, he stretched his lower back with in a slight twist and tightening motion, then placed both his hands on the wooden table, the left hand holding down the notepad, the right hand set to begin scribbling on the pad.

"The good news is we are finished but for two last questions."

Marina was pleased to hear the interview was over. It was good news for her tired mind and body but the manner in which he delivered this last sentence caused a slight wave of anxiety to enter her mind. His manner seemed to stiffen slightly and his voice became solemn, more serious. It was as though he was finished with being a friend who wanted to hear her story and commiserate with her, and suddenly became someone whose voice now sounded prosecutorial, not that he was pursuing her guilt, but as if he had discovered a lost key to a pad-locked treasure chest and sensed he was two questions away from its hidden location. She watched his face as the final two questions lingered on the edge of his lips much too long. Then he spoke in the same solemn voice, pausing between the two questions.

"Ms. Carlton, did Sophia tell you anything specific that she wanted you to keep in confidence? Did she give you anything to keep? A gift, a keepsake? A package to bring home? Anything?"

"No. She said nothing to me in confidence. There was nothing she told me that seemed to be important beyond reminding me to place my return ticket where I won't lose it. She shared no secrets. It was just fun and laughter all week. She was just so happy I was there with her in Mamaia."

"No parting gift? A souvenir? A small gift package, maybe?"

"Nothing was given to me. She did surprise me with a first class seat on the return flight but other than a whirlwind week of extravagant dinners, parties, and some sightseeing, there were no gifts, no shared secrets or confessions, if that's what you mean."

Agent Frister finished his scribbling, raised his head, "Ok, that's it, all good information. Let me go back to the office to see what I can do to find your Sophia."

Marina was relieved it was over. Two of these in one day. She now believed the good news was just around the corner. However, she did have one unsettling thought about today's interviews. Marina thought the final two questions Frister asked her were most curious because they were nearly identical to the final questions that Mr. Crandall asked. Questions that seem to have come out of nowhere, yet both men saved them for last, leaving her the impression that they were important questions and she asked herself if it was possible they could be reading off the same notepad?

Frister interrupted her suspicious musing "If you remember anything else in the next day or so, please call me or tell Carl you want to speak to me. I have my notes. I'll make a few calls. Is there anything you want to ask me?"

"Well, there is one thing." Marina quickly made a decision to address the duplication of closing questions with him now. "Mr. Crandall from the Department of Justice asked me those same final two questions this morning. Are you working together?"

Suddenly stiffening, Frister felt as if he had been jolted with a live wire. He recovered from the figurative shock in a matter of a few seconds before anyone noticed. At least he hoped no one noticed his sudden uneasiness.

"You spoke to someone from the DOJ's office? When?"

"Yes. Today. Here in Philadelphia. He came up this morning from Washington and we met in Rittenhouse Square. On a bench. He told me he was contacted by the Romanian Embassy and since he happened to be coming here today for a meeting in his regional office, he wanted to hear directly from me. I thought you knew."

"No. I didn't know." He looked over at Carl, then turned back to Marina and said, "My meeting with you was a returned favor for Carl in some chance that I could give you advice or assuage your concerns. Why didn't you mention the DOJ before we started?"

Setback by Frister's apparent discomfort, Marina explained, "Carl and I were on and off the phone so fast that I didn't think it mattered. Once I arrived here, I concentrated on answering your questions; the earlier meeting was out of my mind until you asked those last two questions."

"Why those questions?"

"Well, as I said, your last two questions were nearly identical – did Sophia say anything to me that might be important, and did she give anything to me. That made me think you were asking to see if I would give you the same answer I gave him.'

"Did you?" he asked.

"Yes."

"What did he tell you after the meeting?"

"He told me to go home. Let him find Sophia. Oh. There was something else. He said he will have his Philly DOJ personnel contact me tomorrow to pick up my boarding pass for lab testing."

Frister didn't respond immediately to Marina. He turned to face Carl and offered a farewell fist bump, telling him, "I'll call you tonight or tomorrow." Turning back to Marina, he smiled and said warmly. "It was a pleasure meeting you. I know all this is draining and very personal. I'll let you know something very soon. Goodbye."

With the interview ended, Marina felt relieved, saying simply, "Thank you so much for listening to me. Goodbye."

Carl and Marina stood at the table watching Frister as he walked out of the café.

Marina turned towards Carl and sighed. "Thanks, Carl. I appreciate you arranging this meeting. I guess we'll see what he can find out." She was tired; she knew she looked exactly how she felt.

"It's cool. I'm glad to help. Your story got his interest. Mine, too, Lady M."

He reached into his pocket for his mask. He tended bar at a club on the strip on 52nd Street in West Philadelphia and tonight was an early start and a late finish for him. His bartending gig provided a semi-organized structure for him, he had a schedule but it was a flexible arrangement among the bartenders depending upon whose emergency arose first, it allowed room to hone his P.I. skills. For now he'd head back to his West Philly apartment to freshen up before heading to the club.

Smiling, Marina, made him a promise, "I'll buy you dinner when this search ends."

"No dinner, Lady M." He bowed his head, motioned with a phantom fist bump. "I'll spring for a pizza. Hand-deliver it to your place myself. Whaddya say? Deal?"

"Deal" She answered. They exchanged quick goodbyes, Carl headed out the door; Marina checked with Fred to see how many hours she would be scheduled to work in the coming week.

****

Out on the sidewalk as he headed to the Federal Office Building at 6th and Arch Streets, Doug was replaying in his mind Marina's innocent telling of events. He had already filtered out some pieces of Marina's story, those pieces he perceived to be alarming information, and jotted them onto his notepad even while Marina was speaking. Now he placed them in his mind alongside the information he found last evening while searching inside the department's vast database. After receiving Carl's phone call last evening, he researched for recent activity and covert operations in the Eastern European block of nations, specifically in Romania. The database indicated there was a slight buzz in the air over the past week. He passed over this minor indicator at the time because there was always buzz occurring in the nations that bordered Russia, nations that were set free from the Soviet Republic since 1990, primarily set free to starve because the Soviet Union was bankrupt but these block of countries were never fully released from the influences and the intrigues of Putin's New Russia. But now this minor buzz grew a little louder when combined with the sudden appearance of someone from the Department of Justice (DOJ) being very interested in Marina Carlton who recently travelled from Romania in the last week. Nothing coming out of Russia's sphere of influence could be ignored as innocent and certainly nothing coming out of the DOJ headquarters at 950 Pennsylvania Ave. in D.C. these past three years can be considered good news for America. The current Attorney General had issued directives to pursue a recent string of bogus political investigations for the sole purpose of pleasing and protecting the current president's personal interests. These actions raised the public's concern that the Department of Justice's neutrality was compromised, that it had become a political tool solely under the control of the executive branch of the government. Agent Frister was not certain the Justice Department under the current AG could be trusted. Shakespeare may have phrased it best in his tragic play, *Hamlet*. "Something is rotten in Denmark." Frister wasn't a literary scholar but he could substitute cities and fill in the blank.

Chapter 14: Valley Forge

Forty minutes had passed since they resumed their ride back onto the New Jersey turnpike. The driver chose the Cars Only lanes so he could reduce the constant battle of changing lanes with the aggressive trailer trucks that dominated the Trucks Only lanes. The Cars Only lane also meant there would be less policemen and state troopers on that section of the highway. The driver liked it that way: cars and trucks separated. It was one of three things he liked about New Jersey; the other two were its low gas prices and its many coastal beaches. The GPS directed him to exit the Jersey Turnpike and proceed west on the Pennsylvania Turnpike to Philadelphia/Valley Forge, twenty miles ahead. The hotel was a mile away from the turnpike exit.

Overall, he admitted to himself, the ride was uneventful, and quiet, very quiet. His instructions remained unchanged: stay under the speed limit and attract no attention. He asked his passenger, Mr. Baskem, if he wanted anything on the radio. "No." was all he answered. So, no music. Mr. Baskem didn't speak. He didn't seem to be in a hurry. Other than telling him to put the hotel address into the GPS, he hadn't spoken since they stopped for coffee. He never stopped to take a piss, he ate nothing. He just stared out the window, wide-awake, he never nodded off to sleep, not once. He would occasionally check his phone. He appeared in the rearview mirror to be prosperous, wearing a business suit, fiftyish or so with neatly trimmed steel-gray hair. His one concession to his starchy manners was his removal of his suit coat that he laid carefully across the rear seat behind the driver. The driver noted warily that he never saw a smile cross Mr. Baskem's face, not even when he laughed once or twice while speaking on his phone.

Peering at the digital clock on the dashboard, he was pleased to see the numbers approaching fourteen-hundred hours which explained the increasing number of cars on both north and south lanes of the highway. He wasn't bothered by the traffic, after all he drove around the five boroughs of New York City at all hours of the day and night. In fact, the more traffic he saw the easier it was for him to stay alert: the dizzying array of the changing colors of cars and trucks, and the varying shapes and sizes of cars, trucks, SUVs, even motorcycles, sharpened his awareness, kept him from daydreaming. Soon, the best part of his day was about to arrive. In less than thirty minutes, he would say goodbye to his quiet passenger and head home, imagining during the two hour ride to Manhattan that he owned this fancy car. He'd put on his favorite music, stop for a coffee and a sandwich, enjoy the ride and be home before dark. He damn well might even get another business run in tonight to add cash on top of this easy $800.

A ringing alarm jolted the driver from him from his reverie. Sergei's watch alarm went off just as the car passed the large green road sign that told interested drivers the Pennsylvania Turnpike's Valley Forge exit was less than a mile ahead, three hundred yards later there was another large sign listing hotels off the exit: the Sheraton Valley Forge Hotel topped the list. The driver couldn't remember the last time he had an easier run. He would soon be another step closer to a good night's sleep or he'd have a chance to make more money before the night was over. Ka-ching! That's an American slang word he's heard on the streets.

He pulled the car off the turnpike, blended smoothly onto the connecting I-76 interchange and motored less than a half-mile before exiting onto N. Gulph Rd. The hotel was within sight immediately, it was less than the length of a city block away. He slowly approached the hotel's main entrance, put on his turning signal and waited patiently for the oncoming traffic to pass, then he drove into the hotel parking lot. At this time of the day the lot was less than half-full; many hotel guests were still conducting business elsewhere and newer guests like his passenger were yet to arrive. He pulled in front of the entrance with direct access to the hotel's front lobby.

"No. Not here." Sergei's voice was more formal now. "I have something I need to remove from the trunk." Looking out the rear driver-side window,

Sergei turned his head right, then left, then pointed to a far corner of the lot. "Park over there, under the trees."

Following what he was certain would be his passenger's final instructions for the evening, the driver moved the car to the chosen parking space that was as far away from the lobby as anyone could be without sitting out in traffic on the adjoining side street.

Sergei said, "Back in."

It was a familiar request from many of the driver's clients, some who were devotees to the idea that it was a safer option to back into a parking spot than to back out of one because many accidents occur in parking lots where drivers are often distracted or speed inside a parking lot as though they were still on a highway. Still other similarly employed persons like himself embraced the 'criminal's credo' as he had heard it called. Their street experiences taught them that the time spent backing into a parking space before performing many personal jobs and favors was well spent because it gained them the advantage of a quick exit if necessity demanded one. The driver did as he was told. Now with the car neatly settled in place and facing outward, Sergei enjoyed an unobstructed view of three of the four entrances to the hotel: the main entrance that he just relocated from, a side entrance into the east wing, and the rear entrance. The entrance into the west wing on the other side of the hotel was out of his vision but for his purpose tonight a three-quarters view was as much as he needed. No bird's eye or God's view of the fourth entrance was needed. He smiled coldly, wondering if newer technology would soon equip future agents with miniature drones, maybe the size of a small bird, maybe a mosquito.

"Mr. Baskem, is there anything else?" He was anxious to leave but he wanted his passenger to be pleased. He wanted no complaints. Only good words. Maybe, he would receive a cash tip. It's always possible. Mostly, he wanted to be finished and begin his trip back to New York.

"This is good. Just a few minutes longer. I'm waiting for a text message from a friend."

When the cell phone vibrated in his hand, Sergei glanced at the message screen. *OK* was all it read. Placing the phone in his pocket, he reached across the back seat, gathered up his suit coat, briefcase, and travel bag. "Yes. We are done."

The driver turned off the car engine, opened his door and walked around the front of the car to open the rear passenger door for Sergei but Sergei had already exited the car. He smiled at the young man, adding politely, 'Thank you for my safe delivery," and placed a fifty dollar bill in the driver's hand. This was the welcome bonus the driver had hoped for. "Thank you, Mr. Baskem."

Pausing for a moment as though he just remembered something, Sergei walked to the rear of car nestled under the leafy trees that were a continuation of a small forest that lined the four edges of the hotel property. He placed his suit coat on the car roof and said, "There is one last thing I need you to do for me. There is something in the trunk that I must take with me. It is a little heavy for me, but I am certain it isn't too heavy for you to lift."

"I would be glad to get it for you." The driver responded.

He moved quickly to join Sergei at the rear of the car. Now standing next to Sergei, he opened the lid of the trunk. The trunk was empty except for a dark grey painter's tarpaulin spread across the bottom. In a rear corner of the large trunk, he saw a large black plastic bag.

Sergei stepped away from the young man. "Yes. The bag. Can you place it outside on the ground?"

"Yes" he answered, then bending his body halfway into the trunk, he reached for the plastic bag. It didn't feel very heavy. In the next second a muffled thud burst from the Russian-made PSS-2 handgun in Sergei's right hand. It was the last sound the driver heard. A Sp-16 cartridge fired from point blank distance entered his brain leaving a small hole and a limited amount of blood. Still strong and an expert in such tasks, Sergei lifted up the man's dead legs and pushed the remaining half of the body into the trunk that had been well prepared to receive it. Calmly he lowered the trunk with a soft click and placed the gun back into its holster under his shirt. He took a quick glance into the trees around him, peered across the parking lot, and looked up at the windows of the hotel. There was no one to be seen. It was done. He put his suit coat back then he walked casually over to the hotel lobby entrance, stood outside and sent a short text from his phone. Now he was more fully alert than he had been during the whole journey from Vienna to this faraway place in America. He relished being professional and successful in his work and savored the full satisfaction that came to him from doing his work well. The last few minutes were good work and it was a good warmup for the harder work to come in the next day or so. He didn't enjoy killing anyone as much he appreciated his ability to do it so well for others who trusted him to be the best among the best. He was as human as anyone else. It was regrettable he thought to himself even while he was riding on the turnpike to Valley Forge that this young man would never go home or laugh or love again. It was unfortunate but it was a necessary action to ensure that there would be no interruptions to his primary task and to be certain there would be no witnesses who might lead anyone back to him before his task was done. The young man was going to die someday just as Sergei himself and everyone alive will die someday. The young man's time happened to be today. What was important to Sergei now was that everyone else must do their part. The car will be moved, the fifty dollar bill, anything connecting Sergei to the driver will be removed, and the body disposed of neatly, possibly delivered back into New York City, or disposed of, never to be found. Who knows? Who cares? Regardless, he is gone and so is Mr. Baskem. Sergei positioned his weapon more comfortably under his left armpit and waited for his ride to Philadelphia.

In less than a minute, a lone man driving a non-descript dark sedan pulled up to the front of the hotel entrance and stopped in front of Sergei. He shifted in his seat, leaned right from his driving position towards Sergei, lowered his passenger-side front window and said in a deep accent, through the lowered window "I have room for one only." and motioned to the back seat. Hearing the pre-scripted greeting, Sergei nodded, opened the rear passenger-side door and climbed into the car.

The new driver peered into his rearview mirror, taking in the professional attire and mannerisms of his passenger, and delivered a second scripted question. "Has everything gone well for you today, sir?"

"Yes. Perfect" was Sergei's reply. He was humorously entertained by this silly exchange of coded messages the two seasoned professionals had just engaged in. In this advanced age of drones, eye identification, sensors imbedded in bodies, the simple use of specific words or bland phrases, even recited poetry or song lyrics remained a tried and true means of identifying friendly contacts in dangerous operations. It was a common practice that Christianity in the budding years of its faith would use the shape of a cross on decorative jewelry, draw its simple crossed sticks on walls, or signal a cross with one's own hands to find like believers. Such coded words and actions were used to link Christian to Christian under the very eyes of their persecutors who were unaware of their coded significance.

Not finished with this ancient game, the driver continued speaking in a rather stiff manner as though he was measuring each word carefully. "Where do you wish to go, sir? I am at your service."

The world that Sergei lived in was full of people like this driver and the young man now lying in the trunk of the abandoned car: men and women who play their part in a shadow world where following the script was seriously important. Their livelihood, their lives, depended on following orders whenever their phone rang.

"As you were instructed." was Sergei's curt and confirming reply as he slid back into the rear passenger seat comfortable with a view of the road ahead and of the man who would drive him to Philadelphia. He was also positioned for a quick exit out of the car if he should need to do so. He recalled in his earlier conversation at the turnpike rest stop that his reservation was set in a hotel in center-city Philadelphia, a half-hour's ride from where he was now. The hotel was chosen because it is conveniently close to both his target and to his pre-arranged path out of the United States. Though the reservation was for five days, long enough for an international businessman to conduct his business and move on to the next leg of his busy journey, he expected to leave within two to three days. If he was there any longer he would be disappointed and so would those who were depending on him to put this problem away as soon as possible, yesterday would be much better for them.

Nevertheless, this was the final leg of a long travel day and he intended to relax and watch the late fall sun brighten the quiet visual canvas outside the car windows on either side of him. The distance from Valley Forge to center-city Philadelphia is twenty miles and with a normal amount of traffic on Interstate I-76's highway, he could expect within thirty minutes he would be driven past Love Park and its popular LOVE sculpture and City Hall, home to the city's municipal government. There would be few traffic lights between Valley Forge and his center city hotel.

His new driver followed the script and slowly pulled away from the Sheraton's hotel entrance and out onto the feeder road that deposited him and his passenger onto eastbound Interstate 76 expressway towards Philadelphia. Within minutes, the dark sedan merged onto I-76 just before the daily evening rush hours were set to begin. The driver zigzagged his car between competing cars and danced across inner and outer lanes until he finally settled into a line of moving cars in the outer lane closest to the Schuylkill River, a Dutch word meaning "hidden river". This hidden river flows in full view for a hundred miles from northwest of Philadelphia until it empties into the Delaware River at the southeastern edge of the city.

On this clear day, the late afternoon sunrays reflected on both the smooth surface of the river and on the highway and its colorful caravan of cars. These two passage ways - one natural, the other man-made - run parallel to one another, and from a bird's-eye view it appears they are in a continuous and eternal race to see which of them would reach the city's tall towers first. Sergei's eyes were fixed on the sparkling river but as the city drew nearer he was drawn to the left side of the river bank on which stood a number of brightly colored houses decorated with large Greek letters and images. Each house was fronted at its river edge with a dock with rowing boats stored in various manners. This was Philadelphia's Boathouse Row, so-called for its single row of sporting clubhouses decked out in brightly trimmed colors. It was often occupied and surrounded by a steady stream of male and female scullers from secondary, college and amateur rowing clubs stroking their watercrafts up and down the river, sometimes disappearing for seconds under the bridges that crisscrossed the river. This rustic river view found within walking distance of nineteenth-century colonial and twenty-first century Philadelphia provided a pleasant respite for Sergei

Once past the boathouses, the outline of the city's high rise buildings appeared and he saw the tall buildings closing in on him. In only seconds, the car turned off the I-76 highway and crossed a bridge over the river into the center of Philadelphia. The river and its glamorous views slipped away as the car was soon swallowed up in the city's rush hour traffic that famously lasted at least two hours every morning and afternoon. The car drifted into the traffic that moved achingly slow on the narrow streets below an increasing number of new skyscrapers. Sergei was not dismayed by the constant stops and starts amid the increasing traffic. It wasn't uncomfortable for him. He had travelled throughout the world and he had seen much worse traffic jams. He considered the snail-pace progress to be a free personal tour through the downtown area of the self-named City of Brotherly Love where his previous views of this city were only in newsreels and TV broadcasts showing the grit that haunts all major cities in the world. His car soon completed its circle around City Hall and proceeded down Market Street towards the Delaware River which served as the boundary between the neighboring states of Pennsylvania and New Jersey. Once past City Hall, the car wounded its way through the city's maze of one-way streets, finally gliding up a circular driveway, and stopping in front of a wide entry door manned by a uniformed attendant who opened the rear passenger car door and welcomed Sergei as he stepped out of the car. As predicted, the car arrived at its destination in thirty minutes after leaving Valley Forge.

"I'll carry my bags." Sergei said to the doorman, then he turned back towards his driver, nodded to him as if were saluting him, and without a word or any exchange of money, he entered the lobby carrying his briefcase and his single travel bag.

Sergei's steps echoed lightly on the spotless marble floor as he crossed the spacious three-story high lobby to the hotel reservation counter. A pleasant uniformed clerk stood attentively behind the waist-high check-in counter. Before Sergei could say a word, the clerk addressed him in a formal but pleasant manner.

"Good afternoon, sir. Welcome to Philadelphia." Then added, "Can I help you?"

"Good afternoon." was Sergei's response. "I have a reservation. Kohler. Walter Kohler."

The clerk tapped a few keys and pressed a few icons on his computer and announced the words that automatically appeared on the screen visible to him but hidden from the guest's eyes. "We have your room ready for you Mr. Kohler."

Sergei had no extra bags to carry and he didn't need any physical assistance to his room, nevertheless the clerk handed a room key disguised as a maroon credit card to a hotel attendant who appeared silently from behind one of the six-foot tall plants that decorated the lobby. The attendant escorted Sergei onto the elevator and up to the twelfth floor where he located Sergei's room, unlocked the door with the maroon credit card and proceeded to walk across the living room to draw aside the drapes on the large picture window, revealing a clear blue sky and a fading sun trying bravely to hold back the night that would soon fall over the city. The attendant completed his practiced duties which included checking the bed-

room, turning on the flat screen TV, and taking the courtesy bottle of water from the credenza and putting it inside the mini-refrigerator. Sergei
drifted over to the large picture window and gazed out at the view twelve
stories below him: a wondrous and surprising view awaited him, a look
backward to a piece of Old City Philadelphia. He was glancing down at
colonial buildings, cobblestone sidewalks, brick row houses with cast iron
steel tie-posts in front of each house and cast iron foot scrapers at others,
and at horse-drawn carriages trotting on narrow side streets and mingling
with twenty-first century automobiles on Market Street. He noticed a line
of people, young and old, waiting outside a two-story red brick building
with a bell tower and steeple opposite a large open grassy square. All the
people wore masks and were stationed dutifully six feet apart. The line
was marked by a bright neon-yellow rope hung from three-foot high porta-
ble stanchions that snaked away from the entrance. Curiously wondering
who these people in line were, Sergei asked the attendant, "What is this
brick building down below?

Walking over and peering out, the attendant answered with pride as
though the building was his own, "That's Independence Hall, sir. The
birthplace of America"

Independence Hall. Sergei knew about Independence Hall but he never
imagined he would see it in person and be so close to it. He would tell the
few friends he had about this close encounter with Independence Hall and
how Philadelphia was his last assignment. It was bizarre he would be in
the City of Brotherly Love, having just left Valley Forge and the nearby
encampment that America's first president and his troops suffered through
in the winter snow of 1777-78. Now he was in a hotel suite room overlooking the building where America's future was proclaimed in a written
pledge of separation from its king. It was bizarre because his reason for
being in this place at this time was to counter these accomplishments and
assist others in doing so by protecting the success of an incumbent president who sought to become a king in America and remove the freedoms
gained by the centuries-old proclamation.

Was it Fate? He didn't believe in Fate or in anything beyond his own reasoning. He was here, that is all. He would settle for coincidence. He was also tired and very hungry. He would take care of both needs – dinner first, he would rely on the recommendation of the concierge in the lobby, and after dinner, a good night's sleep. Tomorrow he will be rested and ready. Tomorrow he will do what he was sent here to do.

Chapter 15: Jack

Shortly after 6:30 PM that same evening, Agent Frister gathered his day's notes, slid them under the top pages of his working notepad and placed it on top of the various case reports he had spent the day reviewing when he wasn't on the phone gathering information or answering questions, and at the same time, supporting fellow agents' ongoing cases. He was busy. There was a lot going on across America these past four years. Chaotic was a fair description.

He opened the top right hand drawer of his desk and laid the papers inside the drawer, closed it and locked it. All that movement was repeated every office day when he wasn't on the street. Today had been a normal office day with the exception of his meeting with Marina in the coffee shop. He couldn't shake the thought that something was suspicious about an Assistant Attorney General meeting alone with anyone because their friend was missing in a foreign country, and in Romania of all places. Romania isn't even on the United States watch-list for any reason. To make the whole thing even stranger, the AAG met her away from an office, on a park bench. Such meetings were reserved for sensitive subjects. He knew something was really bothering him when his hair started to itch just after he finished his lunch in the cafeteria.

Whenever he felt unsettled about anything or anyone, even as a kid, his hair would itch. He'd rub the top and back of his head, not roughly, no scratching motion, just brush his hand or his drag his fingers through his hair. Over and over, not in manic strokes, but steady brushes. It was weird. He was worried when it first began but he decided not to tell anyone about the itchy feeling; however, he later did some book research on his own and read about strokes, brain tumors and other life-threatening afflictions. That's what young budding FBI agents do when they don't want others especially their moms and dads to be frightened unnecessarily. The quiet research was helpful. He learned enough to know he was thankful it was always his right hand and the top and right side of his head, never the left side: medical attention was always centered on the left side of the body, where the heart is located, as an indicator for a stroke. As he got older, he learned sailors and old ballplayers could tell when the weather might change, some even knew when it would rain or whether a storm at sea was near; he heard old wives' tales of seers sensing danger or doom. The itchy sensation never left him and it became something he learned to live with, never knowing when it would turn itself on. It was an automatic innate alert button. Even now, he unconsciously moved his right hand to the back of his head and stroked his hair just ever so lightly, then he laughed to himself that the most interesting thing about it was that his itchy hair was usually right.

He had already called home and told his wife he'd be a few hours late because he had some research to do on a new case. It was partly true, he had research to do but not on a case. He was going to research Marina's friend and hope he could find out why the Department of Justice would care so much about her or if there was any hidden reason she invited Marina to Romania. Maybe it was nothing more than a coincidence that Assistant Attorney General Crandall was in Philly immediately after the Romanian embassy called him. Maybe. But now he was too curious to look away. After all, in the past two years the Department of Justice had come under new management. Very little time had passed before it became common knowledge the DOJ hierarchy led by the current Attorney General of the United States was losing the respect and trust of its agents and attorneys across its operating subdivisions. It was an unavoidable by-product of the 180 degree turn the new Attorney General had taken in moving away from prosecuting all civil and criminal cases involving individuals and corporations favored by the current occupant in the White House. The lack of transparency from the Director on his reasons for prosecuting or not prosecuting cases lessened the DOJ's integrity in the eyes of Agent Frister and thousands of employees in the department's three major law enforcement agencies who were confused and dis-spirited by the DOJ's blatant disregard for the fundamental pursuit of justice.

Frister stepped out of his cubicle and walked straight to the bank of elevators that stood just a few feet from his daily perch. The proximity of the elevator was the only perk he could credit himself with having, and of course that was just dumb luck. As he exited for the day, he mixed in both a few half-waves, a batch of good nights, and a vocal see-you-tomorrow farewell. The office was still humming with activity, all the automatic lights were shining brightly from the open ceiling, with desk-top and laptop computers tapping at varying speeds dependent on the skill level of the individual manning the keyboard. It was both tiring and comforting to Frister, he knew first-hand that the FBI never slept.

Once out on the street it was a short walk: two blocks west on Walnut Street and four blocks south on 8th street, that soon brought him to a colleague's apartment where he intended to share his itchy feelings about the DOJ interest in Marina. If anyone knew what was going-on, facts and rumors, at any of the DOJ law enforcement and legal divisions, it was Jack, a veteran of many years in the Central Intelligence Agency. After leaving Marina and Carl at the café and while walking back to his office, he phoned Jack and asked him if he could stop by his apartment to speak with him about Marina's meeting with Assistant AG Crandall. Without providing any details on either of the two meetings, Frister wanted to share his unsettling thoughts and suspicions with Jack before his thoughts on them were buried under this day's work and his increasing workload. He knew Jack was that perfect someone: he was a mentor who listened then asked probing questions but only after he's heard the whole story. When he arrived, Jack was ready for him. Dinner was a surprising first order of comradery.

After drinking the last few ounces of golden lager from his glass, Frister pushed away an empty plate that fifteen minutes before held a healthy share of spaghetti and three meatballs. He patted his trim but full stomach with both his hands. "Where did you learn to cook like that?"

Jack laughed. He froze a forkful of spaghetti a few inches away from his mouth just long enough to reply to his dinner guest then deposited the spaghetti into his open mouth.

"A bachelor has to develop skills if he wants to keep his independence. Cooking is one of the most important skills to acquire, then food shopping, then laundry- washing and drying clothes. I stop at ironing. Fortunately, polyester solved most of my ironing and dry cleaning backlog."

Frister carried his plate to the kitchen counter and while facing the kitchen sink, he said over his shoulder. "Well, you better be careful, Jack. If word gets out that you do all those things you're going to make a wonderful husband for some clever and attractive career woman who doesn't cook or do laundry."

"I don't think that will happen." Was Jack's quick reply.

"Hell it won't. Yes sir. Ellen might have two or three attorneys in her office whot would be interested."

"No thanks, Doug. Not just yet. Cooking and washing is worth the price I pay for my bachelor life right now. There are lots of roses to pick from." He stood up, cleared the dining table of dishes, and with his next few words ended that discussion. "I'm in no hurry. Now let's talk business."

Two hours later, Doug was very pleased he confided in Jack. While sharing the details of Marina's story, he was forced to be more alert to pieces of Marina's story that he had paid less attention to during the interview at the café. What was also helpful were the questions and the several theories that Jack presented about who Sophia might be and why anyone in the DOJ would be so interested in Sophia… and Marina.

Looking earnest in his concern for his informal protégé, Jack cautioned him. "Doug, you want to be careful not to step on someone else's authority. This young woman hasn't formally requested any FBI assistance for finding her friend and you don't have any grounds for opening a case on your own. Not yet. Maybe never."

"I know that. I'll follow the leads you gave me."

"One more thing. If you go further, and I know you will, you will be running an investigation that is paralleling a DOJ case."

"I know."

Frister knew this was taboo in federal law enforcement, it was taboo at all levels of law enforcement. Every agent knew that stepping into another division's case or another jurisdiction's case without being invited into it meant certain grief at varying levels. It wouldn't be as bad as breaching a gang's neighborhood, a drug dealer's or a pimp's territory, but it was damn close. There'd be no gunshots but there would be lots of hard feelings and a loss of future support and cooperation if you ever needed some. It's even possible that not everyone would have your back or give you a head's up when bad news is in the wind. That's why it didn't happen often. When it did, it likely happened for the same reason Frister is willing to do it now. Something was wrong. So Doug was going to continue just a bit further, then let go before trouble was inevitable.

Shaking his head and frowning, Jack must've read his mind and tutored his friend further. "It's not according to Hoyle. You and the FBI report to the DOJ. Remember that. OK."

There was silence. Neither man said a word. Both stared downward.

Jack lifted his eyes, smiled at his friend, relaying in his own face what they both knew he had said to Frister in both his few spoken words and in the words he left unsaid: proceed with caution, get in and get out. He made a fist, stretched his arm out to its full length towards Doug, and said with light sarcasm in his voice, "Let's share a manly fist bump in this time of chaos." Doug lifted his arm up, reached out and lightly tapped Jack's closed fist with his own fist. "Thanks, Jack, for listening and for the shared thoughts." The meeting was over. Jack walked with Frister to the door and said, "Good night, Doug. Tell Ellen I said hello and tell her I apologize for stealing you away for three hours." Then he added in a serious note. "Be careful. This could be bigger than we both think. I hope it's nothing."

****

At the same moment Agent Frister stepped out of Jack's apartment and onto the dark sidewalk, a stirring movement from a classical overture played on a cell phone on a continent away, awakening a long-time acquaintance of Sergei Gazunov. The awaken man was normally a light sleeper and much accustomed to early morning calls but it had been a busy few days and his body complained achingly to him as he pushed himself to sit up quickly. He saw the name on the alarm details and in minutes his prearranged call was sent onward to Philadelphia.

Chapter 16: Carl Joseph Lewis

Carl stepped into his apartment in West Philadelphia. He was tired and his aching feet and weary legs were dragging him just far enough to get him home. He had just finished working his butt off on his once-weekly extra-long night at a local bar on 52nd Street. It was part of a swing shift arrangement that brought in most of his income since he returned to life outside the steel bars, barbed wire, electrified fences, and 24/7/365 video cameras. He was fortunate to have this job especially now after the virus shut down most businesses, keeping millions of people from working for the past seven months. The double-shift always left him beat but he was brought down tonight after listening to Marina share her story with Doug before he came to work. When Marina first told him about Romania, he volunteered Doug's assistance to be helpful, thinking it was just a minor search operation easily done with Doug's FBI access to data and technology. Now after hearing the whole story, he sensed there was something deeper and darker happening, he saw it on Doug's face when Marina told him that someone from Washington met her earlier in the day. Doug was walloped by that bit of news and they exchanged eye contact instantly, briefly signaling to each other they knew an alarm bell had been sounded. The smell of fish transcends all languages and appearances: if something doesn't smell, look, sound, or feel right, it likely means something is wrong, or as a stiff ivy-league private investigator might say, something is amiss.

He admitted to himself it was even more than that today, it was all the increased bullshit that was taking place around the country: the coronavirus, the millions of people out of work, police violence, city violence, and now an election that has the country divided and on edge, primarily due to a president and his political goons who continue to do anything to get him re-elected. It began in 2017 the day after he was inaugurated with his immediate obsession for a second term which hindered any real American progress for four years, governing to benefit only himself and his obscenely rich and crooked friends and contributors. Eight months into this

pandemic and his administration and GOP congress have no plan to survive it, to end it or defeat it, other than waiting for the wind to blow the virus away, and maybe with the virus, the many dreams and the two-hundred and ninety thousand loved ones that have been victim to the virus and
the president's poor management of it. None of this shit was a surprise.
After all, he trumpeted chaos and disorder on America since he announced
his candidacy for president in 2016. It was inevitable that America would
be fucked up after leaving this man in control for any length of time. Carl
was certain he could do better. Hell, anyone could do better than this president. What did his own Secretary of State call the president? Yep. A fucking moron.

In the midst of all the lunacy, he knew he was luckier than most people for
once in his life. His stint in prison allowed him to be uninterruptedly educated. That was good. But upon release, what followed was a nearly hopeless period where he felt like a dead man walking: no place to live, no job,
with friends who were in more trouble than he was and who had less than
he had. He discovered through these experiences that other men and
women like him who were released after serving their sentences were
forced to wear an invisible ball and chain for the rest of their lives as
though being black wasn't enough of a visible burden in white America.
He discovered paying your debt to society wasn't enough, they wanted
you to accept their slave wages for the rest of your life. Was he angry?
Yes. And he would remain angry far beyond his days on this earth. His
luck changed when he latched onto this bit of work at The Carousel Bar.
He didn't need a folder full of proper papers signed off by some office
dude in a probation office. Most of the real cash he earned was under the
table and so he got to keep all of that money. Yes, he was finally gaining
on the world, and with money in his pocket he setup a side action as a private investigator. He insisted on using the word detective once he realized
he was smart enough and careful about who he worked for and what he
was willing to do. It was slow going but it was working. The bar was his
living money, the P.I. bit was his future. After all who else was going to
hire him for real money once they knew he was an ex-convict? Yet there

were plenty of people who accepted his experience in prison as an unofficial college of hard knocks degree, he also received silent recommendations for being street-smart and savvy to what is happening around him. They assumed he knew every crook, con artist, every nook and corner in the darker side of the city and neighborhoods. He knows some, he's learning more every day from the action at his bar and from being at ground zero in the center of a West Philly nightlife that provides new entries into his own walking encyclopedia. He's been told, "Carl Joseph Lewis, CJ, PI, knows more than the police and public investigators." That's mostly true, Carl agreed. He knew a lot but he was sure about only one thing - Carl Joseph Lewis made one mistake five years ago and he wasn't going to make any more mistakes. He wasn't going to spend the rest of his life begging for low-paying jobs because of one mistake he was forced into making as a young man. So he worked his P.I. gigs when he wasn't at the bar; his swing shifts gave him flexibility and allowed him to spend breakfast downtown at Le Café not far from the police headquarters and City Hall. These two buildings offered better sources of information for him, definitely more current information, than all of the books, documents in the National Archives in Washington, D.C. and all the pages in Philadelphia's Free Library could offer a room full of research students. But not tonight. Tonight, or today since it was already past 2 AM after his long night at the bar, he intended to watch a DVR World Series baseball game or last week's Eagle's football game.

Bracing himself, he walked into the kitchen, laid his collection of keys on the second-hand kitchen table, opened the fridge, took out a beer, twisted off the cap, and tasted its coolness. Already feeling renewed, he entered the living room and leaned over the coffee table to pick-up the TV remote, then pressed the on-button. He was bummed right away at his fellow co-tenant - his 50" smart LG TV - who was poised and waiting to deliver more bad news to him in glorious HD 1080 pixel color definition and stereo sound. The source of this disappointing news was the never-ending barrage of tweet-shit that emanated from of all places in America, the White House. This president's twitter quotient was vastly higher than his

IQ. Today's barrage of tweet messages were focused on his recovery from contracting the coronavirus at a gathering of like-minded thinkers who refused to social distance or wear masks. At least thirty-five attendees reported they contracted the virus that is ravaging the world and particularly, our world – America, the United States of America, and he and his elitist enablers don't wear masks or social distance. He couldn't help saying out loud what he was thinking. "That's sure no fucking way to lead a country, you asshole."

Carl's sense of pending doom was only relieved in knowing November 3 would come soon and the current president would be gone. He only regretted he could not vote because Pennsylvania's voter suppression laws denied convicted felons the right to vote even after they've served their time. So Carl took the most effective action he could take. He picked up the TV remote and turned off the annoying coverage and searched for some local sports. At least he knew his Sixers couldn't lose another game this year. Why not? Because their season was over! The Boston Celtics, Philly's arch nemesis swept them in four games in the NBA's Covid Bubble Tournament in Orlando, FL. Even that dagger to the heart was easier to bear than the daily chaos emanating from the White House. The pandemic was out of control but somehow all of the pro sports managed to have a Covid 19 version of their season. Television was flooded with sports because all the leagues were playing out their seasons at the same time delivering a glut of hometown teams competing with one another at the same time for fan attention through the summer and fall when the only club normally playing in Philly would have been the Phillies who recently failed to make the playoffs even with playoffs expanded to sixteen teams. Carl didn't bother with the Flyers and he paid sparse attention to the Eagles. It was all a fucking mess. That's what his cellmates might say or they'd call it something much worse. His final decision was to go to bed.

The next morning Carl rolled out of bed. Nothing good had happened overnight. Nothing! More intelligent beings from another galaxy didn't land in the White House Rose Garden in the wee hours of the morning and muzzle and kidnap the man without a brain. And the coronavirus didn't fly away on a breeze, it was still menacing America and the world. Carl shrugged it all off. He was counting on a double café latte with cinnamon, and a warm crumb bun with butter. "God," he said to himself, "don't let Le Café shut down."

Chapter 17: Ground Zero

One out of two is not so bad but it's not great either. Sergei's single intention after arriving in Philadelphia was to accomplish two immediate goals: enjoy a relaxing dinner, then spend a good night's sleep before embarking on his assigned task. The first part of his evening was a success: a tasty dinner at the City Tavern recommended by the hotel concierge. The City Tavern is one of the city's finest colonial-era restaurants whose authentic eighteenth-century American fare suited Sergei's interests in discovering the historical flavors of the cities he visited. The restaurant's authentic colonial decor accented with table servers and attendants dressed in eighteenth century garb recalled a dining establishment several centuries removed where early Americans from Europe would gather for traditional pairings. Sergei settled for a bountiful home-style pot pie, boiled potatoes, apple pie, and coffee not topped with whipped cream. To his delight, the tavern, though modeled as colonial, had a full bar stocked with a wide range of beers, whiskies, cordials, and most surprising to Sergei, several choices of Russian vodkas. He selected Stolichnaya, though he would prefer to enjoy a bottle of Beluga or Jewel of Russia's Ultra blend, more expensive and lavish choices perfect for his first evening in America if he were celebrating with a colleague. Even so, he seldom dined with anyone because he worked alone. He was what his friends in Russia would call, an odinokiy volk, or a biryuk, a Lone Wolf. Often he would return years later to such places as this on his vacations to enjoy them in quieter circumstances though he knew he was unlikely to ever return to Philadelphia. The United States of America was one country where Sergei visited only for business and his business was always un-American. It was the nature of his employment.

The tavern was a short walk from the hotel so he was glad to have the opportunity to stroll quietly along the Independence Mall area, first past the famous Liberty Bell that rang out America's first call for freedom and liberty from a king far across a wide ocean, a world far away. He understood the bravery and courage in those colonial men; in his lifetime his parents and grandparents matched that same courage in Russia's great revolutions. As he neared his hotel he strode over to the cobblestoned sidewalk and narrow streets alongside Carpenter Hall and Independence Hall which was originally the Pennsylvania State House. The State House was the only building large enough to accommodate the leaders from the thirteen colonies, all men at that time, who debated what actions to take and who would jointly author America's vaunted Declaration of Independence, writing it in the humid and musky upstairs rooms while debating it downstairs during the hot humid summer in 1776. As buildings, this State House was much less than the grand buildings and palaces found in the major cities in European countries. It was small and bland, lacking any combination of charm and opulence expected in the old world of kings and queens, achieving more attention for its history than for its attraction as architecture. In fact it would be nearly invisible if it was placed beside the palaces where earlier monumental decisions were made, or more correctly stated, decreed throughout history by kings, emperors and tyrants. Nevertheless, Sergei knew it is revered, honored, and respected by these Americans, as is its single bell that would be so easily lost in the massive bell towers in the cathedrals in cities around the world. "Yes" mused Sergei. "Here sat men who reasoned life to be valued only so much as it can be lived under the certainty of liberty." He understood such sentiment, appreciated the magic in words such as liberty, freedom, equality; how powerful they were but there must be a priority for order, conformity, a place for leaders and followers. Besides these words are too costly when you try to give them equally to everyone. In his country, these same virtues are promised but never delivered, the price is always too high. So it is best to live and learn: the sun comes up, then goes down; the rain comes, then goes. You live free and enjoy life when you can.

When he arrived back in his room he received a coded text message on his phone informing him to expect a call within the next fifteen minutes. His experience with such calls in the past taught him to set aside all his plans and freeze his actions because a call received this far along in the execution of a plan usually meant new information was available or the mission was to be aborted. He wasn't fazed nor annoyed by its appearance just disappointed that his anticipated good night's sleep was delayed. He had come a long way from fretting over every change in plans when he was a novice almost four decades ago. Experience taught him things always work out somehow: some assignments turn messier than others but it was rare when he returned without completing his mission. Sitting back in the soft cushioned armchair, he recalled only one mission where he wished he would've received such a call to abort, even praying a call would come.

He must've stared at his phone a thousand times for the last forty-eight hours before proceeding with that mission but his cell phone never made a sound and he did what he was tasked to do. He was a good performer, a highly-valued performer, he was trained in both tried and true skills and taught to use new technology and newer weapons to solve problems in every part of the world: controlled explosions, lightning quick executions – knife, pistol, rifle, even garroting, and in recent years there were quiet and lethal means: poisonings, undetected agents invoking heart attacks, strokes, paralysis, and sudden death. He often thought he would write a book, a training book, or a memoir. In America, in the western orb, he could make money, maybe there would be a movie. Who would play him? Every actor he knew was now either too old to be him at 22 or could not move as graciously as he could now at 58. It was also true for deciding which women he would choose to portray the women in his life, and there were many women he fondly remembered. He didn't know today's actresses. He only knew the women would have to be gorgeous, flashy, sexy, and always willing. He would expect four would be needed to be fair to his story. Yes, at least four. But who would be Anna, his first love and the mother of his daughters. He thought there might be no need to tell the whole story. He would decide later. Yes, he could write a book but it would have to be smuggled out of his country like Pasternak's, Solzhenitsyn's and others. After all, it is no secret to anyone in his country or anywhere in the world that his country does not accept the truth in any form. No, he concluded after his meandering self-discussion, it will never be written. His stories and his life will be blown away in the eternal winds that blow dust, sand, flesh and bones, and memories from land and sea and history, making room for newer stories and other lives to follow. He was content as always to do his job so he sat and waited for his call, finding it difficult to stay awake.

He didn't have to wait very long and he was relieved the conversation was brief. As always, there was little for him to say so he listened, asking few questions and understanding what new information and instructions he was given.

"So you see Sergei," the voice on the phone explained, "This girl's search for Sophia complicates the mission but it does not change the target nor the urgency to act as soon as you can. In fact it is imperative that you act soon, the sooner the better. Our in-country contacts will neutralize any interference from their FBI long enough to allow you to silence the girl and bring back the prize." Pausing long enough to let these two goals stand boldly at the end of the sentence, the voice continued in a more solemn tone. "However, should anyone interfere with you completing your objectives, remove them as you see fit and necessary to complete the mission. Be cautious as we don't want unnecessary noise and diplomatic troubles but you know Sergei the prize is too valuable to allow it fall into anyone's hands other than yours." The voice stopped, waiting for Sergei to reply.

"I understand what is needed to be done." was Sergei's stiff military response, only his salute was missing.

The call ended with a muffled goodbye from the caller. Satisfied to have alerted Sergei that U.S. law enforcement agencies are also investigating Marina, the caller placed his phone on the night table and slipped under the expensive covers to sleep for the few hours remaining before daybreak. He was confident in Sergei's ability to manage his mission but mostly pleased to have been released of all blame should it fail.

In his hotel room, Sergei was finding it difficult to sleep as he lay awake wrestling with a plan to find Marina alone in her apartment where he was certain she had placed the prize in safe keeping. The added interest in Marina from others complicated his mission but it also heightened his sense of excitement of the challenge in front of him. He knew he must be quick but patient. He would not panic, nor be hasty. He had been in similar situations before. Stay calm, have a plan, be prepared. Now he would sleep. Tomorrow he would do what he was sent to do. It was *prostoy*, as simple as that.

Chapter 18: Unraveling

An overcast morning greeted all of Philadelphia and its surrounding communities, foreshadowing the rain that was predicted to fall from mid-morning through the early evening. Its accompanying gray and cloudy skies provided an added degree of gloom to the dark moodiness of the past week since Sophia's disappearance. Marina had reason to be despondent because she had not been contacted by the local Department of Justice office or any follow-up from its Washington DC headquarters regarding the promised testing of her boarding pass. Agent Crandall assured her the boarding pass envelope would be picked up by the DOJ's local lab but it was still lying in a larger manila envelope on her bedroom bureau where she had placed it when she returned from the meeting in the park. She was hopeful someone was going to test the blood splatter on the envelope very soon. It would be helpful to be certain if the blood was from her, or from Sophia, or unexpectedly from any unknown person. Anyway, that's what she was told would happen but she was still waiting. And things were getting complicated. Now she had both the FBI and the DOJ promising to help her after the Romanian embassies and consulates were unable to locate Sophia. It was apparent there was no interest or urgency from Romania in locating her, possibly because she was not Romanian.

Fortunately, she was able to sleep uninterrupted this past evening. At first, Marc insisted he was going to sleep on her couch for as many nights as necessary or at least until she had one night without a nightmare of being assaulted or pursued. No, she told him. She was fine and she planned to read, then go to bed early. That's what she did, escorting him to her apartment door, then kissing him goodnight. Her plan was successful. She slept soundly with no bad dreams. She woke up refreshed ready for singing birds and plenty of sunshine, hopeful for a new start to a new week; maybe even some good news on Sophia. But when she woke her morning glass was only half-full: she settled for a good night's sleep and rain.

****

133

Elsewhere Doug began his day even earlier. He didn't sleep well. His mind was replaying the conversations with Jack. He finally gave up trying to capture the 1 or 2 hours of sleep that he especially enjoyed whenever he'd awaken too early but still had the luxury of falling back to sleep. He always considered that hour or more of sleep as an occasional bonus. Today he wasn't planning to sleep any longer this morning, there was too much on his mind. He removed himself quietly from bed without disturbing Ellen. He didn't have to be too stealthful. After the first few years of slinking into and out of bed due to his shifting hours on assignments, his wife barely noticed his comings and goings if they occurred during her normal sleep pattern between 11 PM and 6:30 AM. Still he treaded lightly in his bare feet down the stairs, then quietly tip-toed into the kitchen where he placed a coffee pod into the Kuerig, waited for it to brew into his prized FBI porcelain coffee mug, pulled it from under the dispenser, entered into his home office at the rear of the house, and softly closed the door to his home office behind him. Installing the office door became necessary when his work hours at home were extended due to the Covid 19 pandemic. The door provided privacy and also represented a barrier not only to Ellen but to any friend or family member who might otherwise wander in unannounced while he was on company business.

Following Jack's suggestions, Doug immediately began researching international news articles published within the past several months on Russian activities and changes related to Moscow and the Kremlin including unclassified U.S. government reports on recent changes in Russia's military and government offices. Jack told him there was considerable recent CIA buzz concerning a string of sudden retirements, unexpected resignations, and rumored disappearances at the highest levels of the former soviet state not publically announced but identified by CIA operatives. All of the changes were following a pattern since the disintegration of the soviet empire in 1995. They were all closely connected to the new rulers in modern Russia: the multi-billionaire oligarchs and the FSB, Russia's Federal Security Service organization, the successor to the former KGB arm for state spy operations, led since 1998 by Russia's president Vladimir Putin. These insatiably rich oligarchs were enabled by corrupt political leaders to engage in criminal means to grab Russia's vast resources and all of the major state-owned companies when bankruptcies and confusion descended on the soviet government in the 1990's. Protecting their illegal operations and eliminating competitors through false imprisonments and even untimely deaths, Putin became president in 1995 and also astonishingly rich as he ushered in a criminal empire in Russia. The price for maintaining such control and power is to constantly enforce loyalty and silence through intimidation and oppression. Thus, Russia had come full-circle since its revolution in 1917 when its pre-Lenin rulers were czars and czarinas whose disregard for its citizenry was displayed openly with violence and is now replaced with a new Russian ruling class of oligarchs, protected by a police state, who are even richer and greedier than the czarist regimes, and equally dangerous to any opposition.

Of particular interest within the past three months was the reported resignation and the presently unknown whereabouts of a long-tenured and trusted member of the FSB, a confidant of the Russian president since both served in the former KGB, now restructured in name only as the FSB. This individual like many such members of Russia's political establishments was a familiar attendee cavorting with young women in the boisterous party scenes in Moscow and its sister cities. Jack's attention was heightened when Doug mentioned Marina's friend's name, Sophia Glasinov.

Doug carefully copied these articles onto his cell phone and his company computer. The hair on his head hinted to him that his hunch about Marina's encounter with the DOJ was approaching a larger hunting ground. His informal investigation was leading him deeper into the likelihood that Marina's friend was kidnapped or in a worst case scenario, murdered. If so, Marina may have been the last person other than a kidnapper or a killer to have seen her alive, and if the findings so far in this research on the similar rash of disappearances in Moscow are confirmed, Marina's life could also be in danger. Why would she be in danger? He didn't know yet.

Or maybe he was letting his investigative genes carry him too far in his imaginings. Nevertheless, he needed to talk to Jack again, then Marina, then based on what Jack suggests, he would have to alert his local FBI director. Right now, it was too soon. There didn't seem to be any immediate threat of danger to anyone on this side of the ocean.

****

"I want it to be effective today.' Jefferson Crandall politely demanded of the man on the other end of the mid-morning phone call. "You will have Agent Frister enroute to Redding tomorrow morning or even this evening if possible." Crandall's most commanding authoritative voice filled his office and travelled through the air in nanoseconds to the FBI official holding onto a cell phone one-hundred plus miles north in Philadelphia. He continued forcefully, "You can tell him he'll receive his instructions when he arrives in Redding." Pulling the phone away from his ear, he listened to a few words from the FBI official, then interrupted him. "He's needed on a short but urgent assignment. Maybe a few weeks, it could be a little more or less." It was unpleasant enough for Crandall that he was being micro-managed from the highest level of the department to handle the Philly problem as it was now labeled but he was also being personally instructed to handle it gingerly and effectively as if he was a novice. Additionally, he was told to do it alone, use no one else. Just remove the agent from Philly to a short-time assignment as far away from Philadelphia as possible until he received further instructions.

Crandall was not normally involved in the transfers of personnel between DOJ divisions. So now he was burdened with making calls to underlings who were several positions below him. It grated him, but it was an order not a request. Now as he prepared to end the call, he added a few final comments of importance, "Tell him the senior officer in Redding will welcome his assistance and provide specific details when he arrives. Also, keep my name and this office out of any discussions." He started to say goodbye, but stopped. "Oh! Call me later this evening as soon as you have completed the transfer." Hearing the acknowledgement from the other end of the call, he signed off with a last comment. "I'll speak with you later. Goodbye."

He pushed himself and his chair away from his desk. He stood up, stretched, took a deep breath, then he let all the captured air out in one large exhale. "That's done," he said. He proceeded to walk around one side of his desk, looked at a framed photo mounted on his side wall a few inches beneath his university law degree. In the photo he is smiling and shaking hands with the 45th president of the United States in a happier time. Looking away, he sighed, saying out loud, "Jesus Christ. It's just one disaster after another."

****

Back in the Old City section of Philadelphia, Sergei rode the elevator up to his room after finishing the hotel chef's recommended 1776 Liberty breakfast complete with three slices of bacon, hash brown potatoes, and three eggs cooked once-over lightly, two slices of toast, and two cups of black coffee. It was a generously hearty meal to begin his day. He knew Americans liked a hearty and not necessarily healthy starter meal in the mornings with time permitting of course. He decided this morning was a good day to enjoy the Liberty feast. It was possible he wouldn't be in America long enough for a second opportunity at such a breakfast. He expected to be an ocean away from Philadelphia before daybreak tomorrow.

Chapter 19: Watched

It had been eight days since Marina boarded the plane in Mamaia. It seemed much longer; every day since then had been exhausting. As much as she tried to return to normalcy, her sense of dread for Sophia only grew stronger and so did her uneasy feeling that she was also vulnerable. It wasn't that she expected the same forces that may have touched Sophia could reach her, after all she was thousands of miles and an ocean away from Romania but she reasoned if a sudden danger happened to her friend or to any woman or man, it could happen to her. She understood it is an innate human response to feel threatened whenever danger or a mishap damages another person, especially one nearby. It reminded her that life is tenuous, and more so when there is no immediate answer to how or why an event occurred: a tree falling on a car, lightning striking a person, even a car accident, all are life-shattering but a disappearance, a violent death or attack without rhyme or reason, infects everyone with an increased and immediate latent fear of the unknown. All of it made her realize no one is able to defend themselves when they are unaware they are being stalked and targeted. Today, she was determined to move forward while others searched for Sophia, she was thankful her schedule required her to work the mid-morning shift at the café.

Marina decided to leave her umbrella in her apartment, instead donning a floppy rain hat and a stylish rain slicker. She moved sure-footed through the light rain, skipped her way over small pools of rain water, and arrived at Le Café just after 9 AM. Free of gloomy thoughts, she was pleased to be out of her apartment and happily pre-occupied with filling customers' orders for coffee lattes, café au lait, expressos, bear claw pastries, and breakfast sandwiches. The many smiles, laughter, small talk, even the occasional gripes and complaints about warm coffee and skimpy dessert sizes, were welcome.

"Good morning, Marina. I heard you are working through lunch today," was Nelson's greeting when she entered the café. "It will make my day better."

"Aw, you just want someone to talk to, Nelson." Marina kidded as she put on her Le Café apron and cap. "I'll bet anyone will do."

"Not true." He laughed at her, thrilled as always whenever she spoke to him. He proceeded immediately to whistle the theme song he reserved only for Marina, his familiar rendition of "Here Comes the Sun".

She smiled, then changed the subject, she asked him, "Where's Peggy? Is she on or off today?"

Before Nelson could answer, Fred bellowed from the rear of the counter, "Called in sick". He walked over to her and said, "I was hoping you could fill-in and stay until the dinner hour. You'll get an added thirty-minute break after the lunch crowd."

There was no hesitation. "Sure. I have no fitness clients today." It was perfect timing for her. Marc was busy all day and into the evening with his training classes and personal clients. She would call her Mom and excuse herself from a planned dinner tonight. Busy, busy was a partial cure for her just now. It was turning out to be a good day for her, a day to start her small journey back to normal.

The constant stream of customers thirsting for varying levels of caffeine fixes continued through the next two hours. The three baristas, Marina, Nelson, and Sarah, the newest and youngest employee, emptied the brewing vats and the dessert cases several times before lunch. The continuing threat of the virus was mindful to everyone as masks were required for entry into the café and social conversations between the café staff and the customers were minimal, most limited to transactions with a few exceptions from café regulars. This hectic pace is the likely reason Marina failed to notice the gentleman who was seated along the left side of the wall farthest from the delivery counter. Dressed in a dark blue oxford shirt, dark slacks and black shoes, no one could be blamed for mistaking Sergei for a local plainclothes policeman or an off-duty Federal agent. It was surprising he wouldn't have been forewarned that his choice of wardrobe might not be considered to be 'blending in' and in fact it might actually attract attention from some people. Regardless, he thought the partially zippered non-descript dark brown jacket he wore to camouflage the PSS-2 Russian handgun holstered under his right armpit completed the final accessory for his disguise. He was wise to abandoned his suit and tie for this reconnaissance.

Sergei was relaxed and leisurely enjoying his third cup of coffee this morning, opting out of purchasing one of the pastries temptingly arrayed inside the display cases. He was reflecting on the exactness of the information he was being fed from his in-country supporting team. The details of Marisa's personal life were exact as if they knew where she would go, when, and with whom, almost as if she told them beforehand what her plans for the day would be. He didn't know how they got it right but it was making his job easier, at least so far. Le Café was busy with a constant flow of people moving in and out so most people might conclude it wouldn't be a safe place for a person in his line of work to conduct surveillance but the reverse was true. The activity and the large number of customers offered many distractions as people cycled in and out of the café, hurrying about, in fact most customers were paying no attention to those around them. He thought of Dimitri, a colleague and professional pickpocket from his boyhood years, how Dimitri would salivate over the daily income to be gained from both inside and outside Le Café. For Sergei, the constant motion inside the cafe, the hustle and bustle as he had heard it called in American films, offered him ample time to locate a good vantage point to see his prey and comfortably watch her perform as though she was auditioning specifically for him for the role of his victim. In fact, the most productive piece of information he gathered this morning was provided by his victim herself. He heard her answer directly to her supervisor that she would work into the dinner hour. He didn't know what exact time that would be but he knew now where she would be for the next five or six hours. He wasn't disappointed he would have to wait. His career was largely built on successfully managing a waiting game. He would wait for the opportunity to isolate her. That was best. If it wasn't possible to isolate her, he would just have more work to do. For now he would wait.

He knew from the moment he sat in the palace a week ago when he was told to go to America to find her that he would be challenged to do more than remove his target. A straightforward assassination was a playful challenge for him. But this assignment was more complicated. Here he must go into the lion's den, speak with the doomed, and recover the prize, assuming the prize was still in her possession, and so far the flawless information he received to date confirmed the prize was with her. So it was not enough to silence her; he could do that in an instant on a crowded street, in a marketplace, or at her doorstep. The challenge was to keep her captive and alive long enough for her to give him what he was sent to retrieve or tell him the whereabouts of the prize. His task was a three-headed monster: first he must gain possession of the prize, second he must kill the young woman, third he must deliver the prize to his client.

So he would wait, not here for that would be foolish and risky to linger too long and be noticed by Marina or anyone of her friends or co-workers before he is ready to reveal himself. His Covid mask was a perfect added measure of safety from both the coronavirus and from being recognized as a familiar face before he is ready to strike. Even today's rain and cloudy gloominess assisted him. He always considered bad weather to be helpful for his work. "Gloominess favors the darker deeds and its doers," was Sergei's often-shared opinion. At least it was his experience. There was less visual alacrity or mental awareness displayed by his victims when the weather was poor and visibility hindered. A melancholy haze coupled with the element of surprise administered to perfection by Sergei had always been too much for his targets to overcome.

He finished his coffee, adjusted the thin strap under his jacket and rose from the table looking away from the serving counter. He planned to return in a few hours before her shift ended and follow her to her apartment where he would wait somewhere in the shadows, staying dry until darkness arrived to serve as his collaborator.

Chapter 20: Reassigned

"You can't be serious," Doug was nearly yelling at his supervisor. "Tonight? You need me to leave immediately? I…" Stammering for his words, Doug was trying to remain calm, he knew spur of the moment changes occurred in his department and agents and co-workers were expected to comply with changing circumstances but flying to California on a moment's notice without an explanation other than you're needed out West prompted his outburst. He expected sudden assignments to be reserved for real emergencies but even then you were told what the duty was and why you were rushing off. This was a call for assistance in California with no instructions for what he would do out there and why he was selected. No, he couldn't go now, not with his most recent investigation just beginning but he wasn't in a position to tell his superior about it right now. He didn't have enough hard facts to share with his office and worse he would be reprimanded for conducting an investigation on his own into an on-going investigation being handled at the senior level of the Department of Justice. It was bad timing for him and for Marina.

The supervisor was surprised by Doug's strong resistance to the news of his reassignment. Doug was always accepting of his assignments. He told Doug it was temporary; it wasn't in a danger zone; he wasn't being shipped to somewhere in the Deep South or stuck in a car on the streets of East LA. He liked Doug and he knew the young agent's response was unusual. He lifted himself from his padded leather swivel chair and stood looking down at Doug, he measured his words and tempered his voice in order to bring the conversation down a few decibels.

"Doug," he began, "evidently it's too hush-hush for them to share with me. The request, no, more precisely, the order was funneled from headquarters and you were specifically requested by name, yours was the only name mentioned."

Now moving from behind his desk, the supervisor placed his hands on his hips and approached Doug. "Leave your desk as it is, go home, pack up, and then call me from the airport. We'll have the e-ticket ready for you at the baggage check-in ticketing counter when you arrive at the D terminal."

Still flustered, Doug asked, "For how long? How long is the assignment?" His mind was already calculating the interference this assignment would have on his investigation on Sophia's disappearance.

"For as long as it takes. You know how it works, Doug." was the supervisor's flat-tone reply.

The discussion ended the only way Doug knew it would end. He was flying to California. He stopped at his desk long enough to collect his notes and a few folders on existing cases, then he left an office voice message announcing to callers he would be out of the office for a few days, asking callers to leave a message and telling them he would return their calls, otherwise please call the main switchboard, and he provided that number. Now he rushed home to pack clothes, toiletries, and several books for relaxing on the long flight and for the evenings spent in his hotel room in Redding, California. He would call Ellen when he was seated in the passenger lounge prior to takeoff. She was becoming immune to these occasional last-minute absences. It would be a short call if she was in the middle of a meeting or a disposition.

As for Marina and Sophia, he thought of a short range solution while he was preparing for the flight. He'd ask Carl to keep a protective eye on Marina. Carl was in the café meeting so he already knew as much as anyone except for the new information from Jack and the additional research Doug uncovered last night and earlier this morning. Carl would be perfect. After all, he's a private investigator: Carl, P.I. is on the case. It sounded funny but it was accurate. OK, Carl, P.I., let's see what you can do. He would call Jack later after he was settled in Redding. With all this activity occupying him now, Doug was becoming more accepting of his sudden reassignment. Maybe, he thought to himself, this was for the best. In the day or so he was away, Marina may have her answer from the DOJ or maybe her friend in Romania will call her and end all the worry and fuss about

146

her disappearance. If not, he'd pick up where he left off. He supposed a day or two wouldn't matter that much. That's what he was thinking just before his right hand reflexively brushed his hair back on the right side of his head, and moved to the top of his head to lightly scratch his hair with his fingers. He froze for that moment and stared at his desk. Something was subconsciously bothering him. Was it the DOJ's interest in Marina? or her friend's disappearance in Romania and its possible connection to a recent CIA report on the disappearance of high-level member of Russia's FSB? Maybe it was both, or it might just be lice. He laughed out loud at himself. Lice?

****

Carl answered the phone right away and Doug's conversation with Carl was reassuring. He shared as much information as he could about the additional research he did last evening and explained the career complications for being involved in Marina's search for Sophia at the same time the DOJ headquarters in D.C. was doing the same investigation.

"My role in Marina's search for her friend is informal at this stage." He began. "I spoke to Marina as a business courtesy to you." Doug was explaining this to Carl as much as he was practicing the explanation he might have to give to the authorities who would question him if such a need ever arose.

"Yep. I got it." answered Carl. "I'm cool with the chain of command. It's like a gang's turf, or a drug dealer's block in a community: there's yours and there's mine. You stay on your own side unless you're invited in. Correct?"

"Correct. Except the DOJ owns all the territories and that includes the FBI. Using your drug analogy, the DOJ is the cartel, the FBI is one of the cartels subdivisions. OK?"

"Fuck, yes. I got it." Carl shook his head, and added curtly. "You can be shit-canned or worse for this, right?"

147

"Right." Doug answered firmly. Carl's summation was short and swift, it described Doug's fate in one kick-ass word. Fucked. Doug could be fucked if he didn't drop the case. But something told him to stay on the edges of it, just don't lean over too far. It could be fatal.

Doug continued, "My fear is for Marina's safety. I don't know if anyone would harm her, or at the most maybe intimidate her, but until I have more facts, I'd appreciate you keeping an eye on her outside of her work or in the company of friends or family, mainly watch her when she's alone, maybe an occasional check on her apartment." Checking his watch, he added. "Call me with any suspicions, or if you see any actions or persons you think look irregular."

"Will do."

"Carl, do you carry a gun?"

"Of course I don't carry a gun, man." Carl answered tongue-in-cheek which Doug could not see through his cell phone. "I'm an ex-con. I'd be back in the white man's cold-steel boarding house faster than Trump could grab a woman's pussy if anyone found a gun on me." He paused, then to give Doug some comfort, he said, "I have access to several defensive protection devices if that is what you are asking me."

"Fine, that's what I was asking. OK. I have to make another call, Be careful. Thanks."

"You, too. Stay cool."

Doug's next phone call was to Marina. He wanted her to know two things quickly: first, he wasn't going to be in town for a few days but he was still researching information on Sophia; and second, she should expect to see more of Carl who was helping him in his capacity as a private detective. He told her he didn't want her startled if she sees Carl in places where she would not expect to see him. Carl was going to be his eyes and ears while he was away. Let him wander around, he told her. One important thing he and Carl agreed on was a code word, a word to signal her need for help if she was caught in a situation where direct conversation with either of them was not possible. The word they selected is pizza.

"Pizza?" Marina laughed. "Why pizza?"

"No specific jaw-dropping reason for pizza." He told her. "It's just a word. It's short, common, and non-assuming. Just remember it. Pizza! Got it?" Doug explained that she was to use it as a signal to mean she was in danger, that she needed help but couldn't call out.

Doug explained further to Marina. "Carl knows it could appear from you in a text, an email, a tweet, spoken on a phone, printed on a napkin, on a wall, scratched in the dirt. He will also use the word if he needs to signal to you if he believes you might be in imminent danger."

Doug provided all of their phone numbers, email addresses, Twitter and Instagram information to each of them. Naturally, code words and emergency access sounded ominous but the Boy Scout slogan, Be Prepared, was a tried and true strategy for success.

After laying out the precautionary plans, he told her there was nothing for her to be alarmed about, code words and some light surveillance were standard procedure for most FBI cases. This last self-assurance was a little lie but he learned long ago a little lie is the best tool to soften the edges on the truth. Finally, he told her to call him directly if anyone from any branch of the DOJ or any other law enforcement of government agency contacted her.

****

Within three hours of receiving orders to head out to California, Agent Frister strapped himself into an Airbus A321 flying straight through to San Francisco where he could transfer to a local air carrier for a quick flight to Redding, or he could pick up a rental car and drive the two-hundred miles to Redding. He received a text message from his supervisor shortly after he arrived at the airport telling him they were expecting to see him tomorrow in mid-morning at the local office in downtown Redding. He felt like he was back in Army ROTC again, Hurry up and wait. It was absurd, ten hours ago they needed him out of Philly and into Redding; it was clear a rocket-propelled jet couldn't have delivered him fast enough. Now he's just about there and he's told he isn't needed until 10 AM the next morning. Well, it doesn't matter now, he's on his way. The added time, however, did give him a choice to get a room in Frisco or wait until he arrived in Redding. The time difference between east coast and west coast meant he would pick up three extra hours today, providing a small bonus of time for a lazy evening, a good meal, maybe even a movie on cable TV. He couldn't get much work done on his east coast cases today: he lost five hours enroute and adding the three hour difference meant any calls other than emergency calls had to be made by 7 or 8 PM west coast time.

"Something to drink, sir?" a voice interrupted his travel calculations.

"Yes." A smile appeared on his face for the first time all day. "A double bourbon on ice, please."

It was time to chill. He shifted his weight a little, tugged at his shoulder to reposition his department-issued Glock 27 firearm. With his mandatory traveling buddy settled in place, his immediate plan was to finish his beverage of choice and fall asleep, not waking until he landed in San Francisco.

****

In the city Doug left behind, Marina ended her long shift at Le Café. Although she was tired after being on her feet for the last six hours, she relished the distractions brought on from pleasing her customers, cleaning coffee machines and counter tops. It freed her from being pre-occupied with the past week's continuing drama and contributed to moving the day swiftly along. She clocked in her day's work hours in the back office, waved good night to the remaining staff, and walked out onto the sidewalk. The unseasonably warm air refreshed her, providing a calmness around her; she took a deep breath and began walking at a casual pace towards her apartment. Even the weather was beginning to cooperate, the rainy day had morphed into a partly cloudy and mild evening with the sun beginning to set behind the taller city skyscrapers that surrounded her. Her stylish raincoat made her seem overdressed; she carried her rain cap in her left hand and balanced her backpack off her right shoulder allowing it to hang loosely at her side. Today had been a pleasant surprise; the day turned out better than she expected it would. It was almost a normal day, at least what she would consider a normal day for her before Romania. She was at peace and didn't notice the man in a dark jacket following two blocks behind her on the opposite side of the street.

Chapter 21: Checkmate

Sergei could've waited in a corner near Marina's apartment: he knew where she lived and that she would be coming home shortly before dark. However, his M.O., his method of operation, or in plain English, the way he did things, was tried and true for him. Whenever possible he liked to be certain of his playing field, to see for himself that things were in order. He wasn't comfortable relying solely on others if he could avoid it. Tonight he could avoid it so he decided to arrive at Le Café early enough to watch her leave from point A, where she was when he left her this morning, and follow her to point B, to her apartment. He didn't want to stand blindly on a corner several blocks away expecting her to show up and when she didn't appear suddenly realize he lost her somewhere in between points A and B. He also wanted the additional self-assurance that she wasn't followed by anyone who wanted to protect her or harm her, certainly not before he secured from her what he was sent to America to retrieve. He didn't want to be surprised by anyone who might show up outside her apartment unseen by him. What a disaster that would be. He couldn't deny he was becoming more suspicious and a bit paranoid about the steady stream of information he was being given from his project team. The information flowed abundantly like a small stream after a heavy rainstorm and it was more accurate and timely than what he would normally receive from his sources on previous assignments. There didn't seem to be any gap in someone knowing this girl's movements from one moment to the next. His professional intuition told him her movements are being tracked and whoever is tracking her is strangely feeding the information to his team. Who else knew he was here? Did that someone else know why he was here? Was that good news or bad news? In his experience it was bad news. He considered a trap was being set for him, to be sprung when he approached the girl. It's possible but he was confident his team would stop everything at the least suspicion of interference and send a message to him to disappear. He also conceded it would not be the first time that two separate parties with different reasons had aided in the successful outcome of one of his missions. Regardless, he was here: it was his job. He continued tracking his prey, knowing beforehand, like the seasoned predator he was, where his prey would soon nest.

The street lights began their nightly bloom throughout the city as Marina turned the corner onto her two-way street now crammed with the final hour of the evening's work traffic. The twin lines of cars snaked their way through the City of Brotherly Love's narrow center-city streets, finally exiting the downtown business center and merging onto feeder roads, then highways and some over bridges to nearby suburban communities and others to the more distant daily commuter destinations in New York, New Jersey, Delaware, and even Maryland and Washington, D.C. Walking home was at least one bonus in Marina's choice to make her home in center city: she wasn't yet involved in having to work harder to get to and from work than she did actually working at her job. Ten minutes was the maximum travel time to or from Le Café and her transportation costs were limited to a pair of sneakers every six months and an occasional wool knit cap for the winter. Her fitness training commute was even shorter with all her clients living nearby, in fact it was now approaching zero with the training sessions dwindling again with a recent spike in coronavirus cases as the virus continued complicating everyone's life.

She entered the small foyer of her apartment building and in thoughtless habit she unlocked her mail slot. It was rare she received more than an occasional bill, unsolicited offers for 0% credit cards, and retail ads. Lately, it was mostly campaign leaflets and candidate postcards with the presidential election only a few days away. She gripped today's mail in her left hand, unlocked the entry door to the three apartments, and with little effort climbed the two levels up to her third-floor apartment. She was thankful for her fitness training and youthfulness; they were fair tradeoffs for the reduced cost of a third floor walkup that provided privacy away from the street and the added luxury of having no footsteps above her.

She was home and looking forward to another quiet evening alone. Last night had been a good trial run for her, she slept soundly, expecting more of the same tonight. She and Marc had planned to have dinner tonight but he texted her at Le Café just before noon to tell her he was filling in as an emergency babysitter for his sister's three-year old daughter. He was smitten with his first niece and she imagined no arms were twisted to get him to volunteer when the teenage sitter called in sick. He said he'd come over afterwards, around 10 PM or so. No, she told him; it wasn't necessary. She would have a light dinner, a salad and a yogurt, lounge on the sofa with a book and she planned to be sleeping before ten. She was tired but mentally refreshed by the physical activity at work instead of the exhaustion that accompanied the anxiety she had been under the past week. Tossing her rain coat and hat onto the standup hat rack, she loosened the laces on her soft-sole, cushioned nurse-style working shoes, then flopped onto the convertible sofa/daybed in the small cozy living room. She rested for a few minutes hoping to accumulate a next burst of energy to piece together a perfect mid-week short-notice dinner for one.

Outside on the street, Sergei observed how Marina's neighborhood was congested with permit-tagged cars parked on both sides of the street; how the curbs in front of the houses on both sides of the street had trees planted in a pattern whereby every front door was gifted a tree: an oak, elm, or walnut. It was ironic Sergei thought, he'd expect to see such conformity in a socialist country but not in, of all places, America. The difference of course was these trees weren't mandated in accordance with a national edict as would be the case in his homeland. In his country, he didn't consider trees to be in anyone's personal possession except for those fortunate elite comrades living on large properties. Trees in his countries' public areas, cities, towns, and villages were systematically arranged in a rigid formation and proudly designated as a People's Party Park blandly named after a recently deceased comrade of local renown but of little national interest.

The temperature had fallen as the sun faded below the horizon. He anticipated this and changed his clothing this afternoon, selecting a standard uniform of dark clothes reflective of his profession and sensibly more dif-

ficult to be seen at night even in a lighted room where the lack of color offered more protection for him from the attention of the naked eye. His
jacket was warmer but not bulkier, providing a perfect shelter for his
weapon; his dark pants, dark socks, and the black rubber-soled wingtips
shoes he preferred for night duty completed his costume so he could move
unseen across dark open spaces. The piece de' resistance was the knife he
strapped strategically around his left calf a few inches below his knee. Finally, there was his black coronavirus cloth mask, the climatic piece of
disguise now worn openly by saints and sinners alike, a beneficial by-
product of the pandemic's upswing.

An hour passed and he'd seen no one follow her as she walked from work
and no one appear outside her apartment since she arrived home. There
had been little pedestrian activity on the streets, nearly everyone who entered the street on foot transited all the way to the other end or entered
other residences on the street. One or two persons went into Marina's
building but they looked harmless, there was nothing suspicious about
them. He had waited long enough. It was time to complete his part of Operation Omega. Stepping from the shadow of a large tree, he casually
crossed the street to her apartment building where he entered the foyer,
surveyed the individual mailboxes to confirm her name tag and apartment
number matched his previous information, then he operated his latest hi-
tech burglar device which easily opened the door. Now he had access to
all three apartments though he was interested only in the one occupied by
M. Carlton. Opening the apartment door would be child's play. Access
wasn't his biggest concern, having the element of surprise was more important. He was pleased to see each person occupied one entire floor
meaning each landing offered only one door, there were no two doors facing one another on each landing. It was a level of privacy that was an attractive advantage for the occupant and tonight an additional benefit for
him and his mission. Barring a sudden intervention of bad luck for him or
a generous dose of good fortune for Marina, he would complete his mission tonight and he would be going home.

****

In the hour or so prior to Sergei entering the downstairs foyer, Marina watched her favorite local news station and devoured a comfy meal she rustled up for herself: a salad, yogurt, and a glass of water, then followed it with a soothing hot shower. She quickly threw on a one-size-too-big Widener University monogrammed sweatshirt and a pair of baggy workout pants hanging on a hook on the back of her bathroom door, crisp clean cotton pajamas seemed too formal in her present frame of mind. She just wanted to kick-back and relax, to lose herself in someone else's drama, and finally drag herself to bed. She slipped on a pair of worn black flats her more stylish friends had shamed her to retire, telling her the Beatnik era stopped beating nearly six decades earlier. Marina's loyal-to-a-fault gene promptly kicked in, she responded by reinventing them as dress-down scuzzy slipper footwear for indoor use only. Gliding silently into the kitchen, she brewed herself a cup of green tea and turned off all the lights in the apartment except the recessed light over the kitchen sink. The television was always on when she was awake even while she was in the shower. It was her television family that filled her apartment with human voices, kept her company, obstructed loneliness, and substituted as a security blanket for her. She also enjoyed watching television with all of the lights off; telling her closest friends how the darkness isolated her from her surroundings, creating a time machine to transport her into the story's locale, drama, lightness or romance experienced by the characters on the screen, drawing her closer into an emotional bond with heroes, heroines and villains. She embraced those characters she liked and feared and loathed others.

As always, she positioned herself on the end of the couch nearest the entry door, diagonally opposite and farthest away from the 32" TV nestled against the wall on the far side of the room. She placed her tea on the end table next to her and removed her beatnik shoes. Lifting her bare feet onto the couch, she browsed through her vast collection of Grey's Anatomy taped programs and predictably selected a favorite episode she had watched umpteen times. It was remarkable how she never tired of living the lives of the staff at Seattle Grace Hospital over and over again. The network series began in 2005 when Marina was ten years old. She discovered the show in her early teen years and slowly adopted the GA family into her expanded family, particularly Meredith Gray and the sometimes arrogant Dr. Alex Kerev, imagining herself as Meredith with various romantic possibilities. She had considered a medical career as an early life choice for herself until the curriculum requirements exceeded her willingness to sacrifice sports and social gigs for academic perfection. Besides, each season of her own life made her understand GA's drama was no life for her. Nevertheless, this was her TV equal to comfort food: viewing its reruns didn't lessen her interest in hearing every word and not wanting to miss any scenes. Lost in concentration, there couldn't be a better remedy for forgetting the real world and its troubles.

Perhaps, the darkness and her total self-absorption in Meredith's world were the reasons she didn't hear her front door unlock. It is unlikely Sergei would agree, he was confident no distractions would've made any difference. He was where he intended to be.

Chapter 22: Intruder:

Perfect. Sergei was having good fortune tonight. There was very scant light seen under Marina's apartment door and sufficient sound was audible from a television inside, a perfect combination of darkness and sound to cover his entry into the apartment. Not knowing how the furniture was arranged was a small inconvenience. He was unsure where the TV was oriented as its placement played a significant part on whether he would gain any element of surprise. He was prepared to silence her immediately if he must but his intention was to talk to her, to reassure her he only wanted to talk, he would promise not to harm her. He must find the prize, then he would do what he needed to do. He listened carefully at the door, hearing both voices and music, muffled and distant, drifting from across the room to the door where he was standing. That would mean the television was on the opposite end of the room and Marina was against the wall nearest the door, only a heartbeat away from him: the slightest cough from him now would echo loudly into the room. In his mind, he saw her sitting comfortably in a chair or on a couch against the same wall they were sharing now but she was looking away from him. He continued listening. There was no movement at all, no sound from anywhere other than the TV. He readied his door opener tool and unsnapped his holster but stopped when he heard a small noise and a shuffle of feet inside, followed by a movement of an object, a soft yawn and movement back onto a chair, a couch. The television never ceased its synchronized mixture of dialogue and music. Now all movement ceased. He was confident she was just inside the door facing away from him.

He slipped the small all-purpose tool into the opening between the door and the door jam, unlocking the door with a slight click. Holding his breath, he waited with patient stillness, then gripped the door, pushed it lightly to find the darkness he had hoped for, and observed a long length of wall to his left that continued down a hallway; on his right side, extending from just inside the doorway was a short two to three foot section of wall that ended abruptly revealing an open archway and an average size living room, the sounds he heard outside the door were now accompanied by flickering light from the television screen at the far corner of the living room. He couldn't see Marina but he now knew exactly where she was, just on the other side of this three foot wide wall. He couldn't have configured the room any better for his present needs. He had enough space to slide unseen inside the doorway, hug the narrow section of wall, and surprise his prey: Marina Carlton, the young woman who his client and his friends never met or heard about before last week. She must die to keep them and their billions of dollars safe. It is a pity. He had seen worse things; he had done worse things.

Enough. He timed his sudden movement into the room with a pause in the program's dialogue. A split second or two of silence descended on the room as their eyes met. She froze, her mouth agape, she started to project a scream from deep inside herself but his movements were lightning fast and eerily silent. He was over her, blocking the light from the TV, his gloved hand now held firmly over her mouth. He whispered, "No." adding in a commanding voice, "Don't scream."

Marina was still locked in the pose she assumed in the split-second it took for the shadowy figure to descend upon her, nearly landing in her lap. She was sitting upright, half-on, half-off the couch, restrained from speaking and unable to move as a second hand kept a strong grip on her shoulder. Then, as if the intruder read her mind, he lightened the pressure from both of his hands and spoke again.

"I will not harm you." He said in the same clear, calm voice. "Please be quiet. I will explain who I am and why I need to speak with you" Exchanging eye contact, both of them understood the unspoken alternative. Sergei removed his hands from Marina, she remained still and did not speak or cry out.

Regaining some composure, Marina fought against her rising fear and told herself to breathe and listen. She had no choice but to listen. She hadn't been physically harmed, at least not yet. This man sounded educated, his accent seemed European, smooth, continental but not distinctively from any country she could precisely pinpoint, His face was masked so only his eyes were visible, they were dark eyes, intense but not glaring with menace. Certainly she was terrified but his instant withdrawal of aggression and his calm manner provided some instant comfort considering her predicament. She remained terrified but she didn't want to panic. You're not in control, Marina, she told herself; he is. Let's hope for the best.

At that moment, Sergei moved backward a step or two from Marina hoping to instantly reduce some of the explosive tension in the room; he wanted to begin a conversation without hysterics. He echoed his earlier promise. "I will not harm you. There is something important you have in your possession that belongs to a friend of mine."

With tears welling up in her eyes, Marina said half gasping and choking back fear, "I don't know what you mean. I don't know who you are." Shaking her head back and forth, she pleaded." You must be mistaken. You have to be …."

"No, I'm not mistaken." Sergei's voice cut her off. "You are Marina Carlton. You work at Le Cafe, train persons for body fitness. Correct?"

The facts were like stab wounds in her first effort to convince herself and this intruder that he was mistaken; that she is not whomever he is looking for. The sound of her name coming out of his mouth crushed her spirit. He knows her name and more. How?

Struggling to control her voice, wanting to scream, to cry, wanting to release all of her raw instinctive responses to the incredulous situation she found herself in, she managed to blurt out what puzzled her most. "I don't know you. How do you know me?"

"I have a friend in Romania." Was Sergei's short answer and it was the answer she feared hearing the most. Somehow a ghost had flown across a wide ocean to give life to her haunting nightmares. She realized instantly his presence here was no mistake, he was in the correct place. Still she had

161

nothing to tell. That was her saving fact: the truth was going to free her from this living nightmare. This shadowy ghost will return to its airy dwelling.

She believed it not because it was the best she could hope for but because it was the reasonable outcome once she convinced him she had nothing to hide, nothing to withhold from him. He would leave her to her TV drama though she knew no matter how this evening ended she would never watch another episode of Grey's Anatomy. Her mind did not rest here, for as she reasoned her way closer to a pleasant ending, her spinning thoughts focused on the man's announcement that he was from Romania, or he had a friend in Romania. She couldn't exactly recall but he did say Romania. If so, he could be involved in Sophia's disappearance and therefore he was a dangerous man. The same questions were being repeated in her head. What was he doing in her apartment? How did he find her? She couldn't help thinking in the midst of this craziness how her grandmother and great aunts would blame home infestations or an appearance of a single crawly creature on the tile floor on a brown paper bag brought home from the supermarket. They'd protest it wasn't their fault the unwelcome creature found its way into their home. Maybe so but like this man from Romania who was an unwelcome intruder who found his way into her home, like the roach in a bag from a supermarket, he was still here. She didn't really know what her grandmother did about the bug or roach or whether any of it ever really happened but she knew this two-legged roach was more threatening. Crazy, zany, scary thoughts continued to bang into one another inside her brain, competing with conflicting messages for Marina's confused judgement.

Still standing, Sergei pulled an upholstered chair from against the same side of the wall where the television stood; he dragged the chair to the center of the room stopping a safe distance from the couch where Marina sat with her arms folded in front of her. She was stricken with fear and unsure what would happen next. Sergei reached across her and lifted the TV remote from the end table; he aimed it at the images on the screen, shutting off the television. A sudden silence dominated the room. Marina sat stiffly, breathed lightly, and folded her hands formally in her lap. Sergei walked over to the chair, sat down and removed his mask.

Chapter 23: Caught

"We've met before." Sergei announced boldly. "Do you remember? It wasn't so long ago."

Stunned by this startling declaration, Marina was speechless. After letting the words sink into her brain, she could only repeat his words, not as a fact, but as a question? "We've met before?"

"Yes. That's correct."

"That's not possible." She replied, challenging him as she retreated into denial. It was incredulous.

She said it again, "It's not possible." Yet, in the first seconds of the house invasion, she heard and felt something familiar in the man's voice and calm manner but her flash of recognition was abruptly forgotten as her primal instinct for self-preservation and escape chased away any thoughts other than flight, on getting instantly away from him. Now with his face fully exposed, she linked face, voice, and manner together. She didn't have to search long or go back too far in her memory before she found him. He was correct. They had met before, not formally, in fact they hardly spoke to one another but they had met before.

Sergei watched her face closely, he was perceptive enough to see the exact moment when she recalled their chance meeting. This is what Sergei wanted from her, to have her accept he was telling her the truth; he wanted her to accept him as being truthful, his words; it was important she believe him to be truthful so she would accept his words as factual, and soon his promises as dependable. In any profession there are useful tools that contribute to a successful outcome. The appearance of being truthful, of being trusted, creates a path where control in short term and long term relationships is easily surrendered, particularly in times of stress. The trust quickly gained by salespersons who sell automobiles, houses, financial investments are universal examples. Sergei understood this tool and he used it to sell himself as being trustworthy up to the moment he betrayed it.

Marina's face lightened, she spoke cautiously. "We met in the passenger lounge, waiting for the flight to Bucharest." She saw him in her mind, the distinguished man seated with wireless earphones. He was helpful. Kind.

Sergei continued. "Yes, at the airport in Mamaia. Your destination was here in Philadelphia, correct?" Not waiting for her response, he added a more defining detail of the conversation. "You thought you were at the wrong gate when the agent announced a departure for Bucharest."

"Yes." Marina replied, recalling how disorganized her state of mind was when she arrived that morning at the airport shortly after Sophia disappeared, how she was smothered with concern for her friend. The idea she might miss her flight home terrified her. The man's reassurance that she was on the correct flight was very settling for her.

Sergei was pleased with her calm, cooperative responses; he didn't want to be aggressive if he could avoid it. Certainly, she was still confused and frightened but the frenzied look in her eyes was beginning to fade as she digested his knowledge of her and his connection to Sophia. On the other hand, Marina now knew this man wasn't a random intruder, not a crazed serial killer who could not be swayed from obeying his inner demons. He wasn't random at all, he found her for a specific reason so there would be a chance for a conversation, an exchange of some kind, and hopefully a resolution where he gets what he wants and she remains whole and safe.

"Now here you are home in Philadelphia and I am here with you." His voice changed slightly, not into a menacing tone but in a professorial manner dressing his voice in an inquisitive tone a teacher or a trial lawyer might acquire to lead a student or witness forward in order to obtain information that would profit the teacher, inquisitor or his client. "Can you guess why I'm here?"

"Yes, because of Sophia." Marina felt a chill run across her shoulders, an unusual occurrence in an apartment that was always too warm even in the winter. "Are you looking for her?" she added.

166

He expected this question and answered earnestly, "No. I know where she is. I'm here to speak with you. I expect what you tell me will help Sophia."

Gaining some control over her mind and body, Marina seized as good news the fact that someone knows where Sophia is. Would he tell her where her friend is and why she was taken from her apartment? Most importantly, is she safe? Why did this man know so much about both of them? She had so many questions to ask. She wanted to know where Sophia is but she was also desperate to have this man leave her apartment. At this moment, she needed someone to rescue her. Why didn't she listen to Marc? If only she had let him stay with her for a few more days. All this was going through her mind before she gained control of herself. She heard a voice inside her head comfort her. "OK this might be your best chance to learn where Sophia is." Immediately a flood of questions gushed from Marina's mouth, all of them raced to confront Sergei, each question lining up like loyal minions hoping to elicit answers to satisfy their mistress.

"Where is Sophia? She hasn't called me. Why can't I reach her? What happened that last evening? Who are you? Why do you care about Sophia? What do you think I am supposed to know or what do you think I received from Sophia?"

Sergei sat stone-faced as the litany of questions ricocheted around the room, echoing off the four walls around them. He took his cue and began his practiced response to her deluge of concerns. "As I said moments ago, Sophia is safe. The series of events began when Sophia was informed her life was in danger on the evening before you left Mamaia. It was subsequently arranged by important people to have her return to Moscow where she could be protected from harm. As a cautionary action, she was advised to cease all communications with anyone other than her immediate family. This blackout is beneficial to her and it remains in place." He paused purposely to allow Marina to absorb his words. He wanted her to accept his account of events on her own. He knew once she accepted these events, she would have reasonable answers to Sophia's sudden disappearance, her present location, and why she hadn't received any responses from Sophia in a week, and thereafter, the rest of his story would face little if any resistance. He was not a formal psychologist but he had become a student of human beings in his life journey: among his many observations of homosapiens, he was often a witness to a person's or a community's easy willingness to accept a distorted truth and more so when the lie is what the listener is desiring to accept.

Marina wanted to scream out loud but Sergei's cold manner and controlling deportment convinced her it would be futile and any resistance would likely lessen her chance of escape. She battled internally to hide her fear and her distrust of this stranger. It was ludicrous to believe anyone would break into her apartment to tell her that her friend was doing fine somewhere in another country; it was an absurd act even if secrecy was a major priority. She knew she was in danger. It was critical to buy time, any additional time that might present an opportunity for her escape, for a miracle, for anything that would get her away from him, or vice versa, him away from her. Cooperate, she decided. She would cooperate until she found a way out. To begin with, she needed to find out who he was besides being a man from a passenger lounge in Romania. Why was he in Mamaia?

"Who are you?" She asked him directly. "Why were you in Mamaia at the same time with Sophia?"

Sergei was tiring of this game. This was the last question he would accept from Marina. From this point forward, he would ask all of the remaining questions, and he had reduced the number of remaining questions to two. Admittedly, he admired Marina's spunk. It was a quality he'd seen her display once before, years ago. It was to her credit that she held her composure and was now trying to turn the tables on him. He recognized her attempt to lengthen the conversation, to slow him down, to buy some time, while in turn, he was patiently speeding towards an end to any further aimless conversation. The FSB, at least the former KGB, would welcome a young woman with such innate intelligence as an ally or a foe. Now it was time for him to raise the pressure on Marina and gain possession of the prize his client values more highly than any number of lives it would cost to collect it. Marina, he agreed, was an impressive young woman, it was not surprising to him that she and Sophia would be friends: he regretted she must leave this world of opportunities so young.

With visions of Sophia floating softly through his mind, he answered Marina's questions in the manner of a bored clerk repeating a list of practiced responses to an application for a parade permit. "I was there only on the day you saw me in the passenger lounge." He began. "I traveled there to warn Sophia. We spoke on the phone late in the evening, we agreed to meet at her apartment. Later that evening she was taken to a home outside Bucharest before being escorted the next morning to Moscow. I returned to Moscow alone."

As Marina started to ask another question, Sergei cut her off in mid-sentence.

"Stop!" Sergei talked over her, his voice now commanding her attention and raising her anxiety level ten-fold. His face and voice were suddenly hard and threatening, his body tense, it was though a new person had instantly replaced the man who sat in front of her. The air in the room seemed to get colder. He raised his hand high, his palm facing outward, looking for a moment like a traffic cop at a busy intersection.

He continued. "Question number one: I want to know why Sophia invited you to Mamaia and what she told you about the Omega Project? I don't want to hear a long story. Just tell me why she invited you to Mamaia? What did she tell you? Who else did you tell?"

"I don't know what..." she began to speak but she was interrupted a second time.

"Question number two: Where is the data she gave you to smuggle into America?"

Data? Omega Project. Marina's mind was floundering in confusion. This was crazy stuff. None of this had anything to do with her. "I don't know what you're talking about." She protested. "Omega? Data drive? Smuggle? Sophia gave me nothing, told me nothing about her job; she didn't even talk about boyfriends, nothing. It was all party and fun."

Sergei stiffened. It appeared like his mission was about to get ugly. He would give her one more chance to avoid any pain but his patience was exhausted. It was at that moment, his thoughts were interrupted by a loud knock rumbling from the surface of the apartment door, followed by a loud male voice.

"Pizza man"

The combination of the loud rapping and a loud male voice startled Sergei and Marina. Marina's heart jumped a millimeter or two higher than the rest of her body. Sergei froze, he shifted to both a defensive and an attack mode instantly.

"Pizza man here. Carlton for one large pizza." The male voice hesitated. "Sorry it's late. You get a free pizza next time."

"Kristos!" was Sergei's single thought. He's going to wake up the building. Pulling Marina off the couch, he shoved her towards the entry door and whispered, "Tell him to go away. Do it quickly. Don't let him in or I will kill both of you. Now, right here at the door."

"Lady, it's the..."

"OK. OK. I'm coming," was Marina's nervous response. She could feel her body shaking as she walked to the door. Sergei stood behind her on her right side fitting snugly against the long hallway wall. Marina couldn't see Sergei's left hand wrapped securely around an Israeli commando knife. Her last thought before opening the door should have been 'am I going to die with a pizza and a pizza delivery man', but her last thought was much simpler, 'this is a mistake, it isn't my pizza'. She was certain of that. She'd never had a pizza delivered to her in her life.

"Open it slowly." whispered Sergei. "Tell him to go away."

With her hand trembling, she turned the doorknob and slowly pulled the door inward, pinching Sergei tighter against the wall. As the door opened wider, she saw a tall black man but no pizza in his empty hands. She looked up to the man's face and caught her breath. It was Carl with his fingers to his lips signaling her to say nothing.

"OK. Here's your pizza" he nearly shouted. Then he slipped one arm through the open door and grabbed Marina's arm pulling her out of the apartment and almost instantaneously pushed the door inward as hard as he could, pinning Sergei to the wall. In a split second he had Marina out of the apartment and out onto the hallway landing, then he pulled the door towards him with all his power, slamming it shut. Turning towards the steps, he said under his breath, "Let's get the fuck outta here." He led her furiously down the two flights of stairs, half jumping, skipping steps, until they were through the main door he had previously jammed open with a stick. Once they stepped onto the outside curb, they raced across the street and disappeared into the darkness.

Chapter 24: Pizza Man

The subway system in Philadelphia like most subway systems in major cities around the world is an often-unappreciated lifeblood for the millions of people it carries within and outside its metropolitan area. On any given day more than a half a million passengers ride on Philadelphia's underground and surface cars and depend on the system and its movers and shakers, its conductors, engineers, and its ticket takers and others to get them all delivered safely and on time to their individual destinations. Carl was one of those riders who knew and valued the importance of the subway, the city's underground lifeline. Tonight he was especially thankful he knew the system forward and backward. He knew he could get Marina to an underground station before this man could get onto the curb outside the apartment; he also knew where he was going and how to get there underground, something his pursuer didn't know and if he did know any of that, he wouldn't be able to maneuver his way down into the station and onto the trains with even the slightest percentage of speed as fast as he could. Carl was certain he and Marina would soon be miles away from center city and the man in a matter of a few minutes. This round, he thought, definitely belonged to him on points.

Carl was correct. Sergei was stunned by the Pizza Man's attack. Carl's quick action with the apartment door surprised Sergei. The speed and violence of the door hitting him so forcibly was so unexpected that it caused him to lose his balance just slightly enough to have the knife he was holding cut a gash in his left hand when he was sandwiched between the door and the wall. Even the sudden noise of the door being quickly slammed shut affected him. He had noticed his balance and location of sound was a growing inconvenience more often since he lost hearing in his left ear a year ago. Until now, it hadn't interfered with his normal activities in any way. He was embarrassed and angry more than he could recall in a very long time, possibly never so embarrassed. Nevertheless, he didn't chase Marina and her Pizza Man down onto the street. He didn't want to be seen

by anyone and he wasn't familiar with the city, with this urban battle-
ground. Instead, he turned away from the closed door, walked over beside
the television and looked out of the window thinking he might see two
people fleeing down the street, maybe get a glance at the Pizza Man. He
had a hunch he'd see him again; he hoped he would. He saw no one on the
street below. Now he decided he had only a few minutes to look in the
small apartment for the prize; he could settle with Marina at a later time.

He started his searching in the bedroom. He always questioned why most
people felt it was safest to hide anything of value in their bedroom. It was
uncanny how often that was true, yet it was the first place most burglars
would search if they had access to an empty house. In his occasions to do
so, he was normally very neat with his searches; he prided himself in his
belief that whenever he did have to search anyone's room, those persons
never realized he had been in their room, never rummaged through their
garments, their possessions, they never gave a thought anyone had been
there. He wanted to be as professional here and leave no evidence of his
searching but he couldn't afford the luxury this time. He had to get out of
the building before neighbors came out or the police arrived to investigate
the small commotion, so he ransacked the small apartment as swiftly as he
could not wanting to pass up the possibility the prize, this golden apple,
might be sitting only a few feet away. It was fortunate for him she had a
spare amount of furniture: one dresser drawer, a single queen-sized bed, a
small jewelry case, a night stand, and a nearly bare clothes closet. There
was no safe box, no hiding places to be inspected. All of these proved to
be dead ends. The large luggage piece in the closet presented the likeliest
hiding place, the travel tags from Romania were still on the bag, lying beside it was a much smaller travel bag with a long shoulder strap. He
dumped the travel bag onto the closet floor, its contents splayed at his feet,
but nothing resembled a computer device. He dragged the larger luggage
piece out of the closet, furiously tossing clothing and shoes onto the floor,
running his hands along the inside perimeter of the bag. Still nothing.
Then he saw a small purse-like cloth bag, a woman's makeup bag, in the
top half of the luggage compartment. He smiled as he unzipped the bag,

turned it upside down and shook its contents onto the bedroom floor. He slowed his pace a bit and carefully spread the lipsticks, the square cases, the mirrors, hairbrush, tooth paste and teeth flossing cases. His moment of expected triumph faded. There was nothing resembling a data disc, a flash drive, no digital device disguised as a pen. Sergei rushed through a final check under the bed, in the bathroom cabinets and shelving, rifled through the pockets of coats and jeans in the closets. Still nothing. If it was here it was securely hidden and he didn't have the time to linger. He was disappointed but now he knew he didn't need to come back here. He must find Marina again and very soon; force her to tell him where the prize was, if possible make her get it for him; then he would silence her whether Sophia told her anything at all. It was the only way he could be sure no one else found out about Omega. This would be no different than what he had resigned himself to do with his Sophia, his 'doch', his daughter.

After finishing his search, Sergei waited just inside the door listening for voices or sounds from any of the persons who lived in the other two apartments. Convinced no one was out in the common areas and positive it was clear for him to leave, he stepped outside Marina's door, closed it softly and tread softly down the stairways and out onto the pavement. The darkness and the low wattage lighting combined with the damp weather and cooler temperatures to keep most people off the surrounding streets. Now, the pandemic forced the closings of most commercial stores, restaurants and bars leaving the neighborhood looking and sounding like an urban ghost town. Without filled garbage cans and plastic bags lying outside the rear of the city's eateries, even stray dogs and alley cats weren't visible in the alleyways and on the streets. Once he turned the corner from Marina's block, he realized he had no reason to worry about being seen so his concern shifted to his hand. He regretted not keeping his knife in his sheath but as the saying goes, hindsight is easier than foresight. He needed a silent weapon; he couldn't know such a freakish moment would occur. He wasn't damaged to the extent he would stop pursuing her, his wound was going to require some home repair when he returned to the hotel but the pain and some spilled blood was his least concern, his biggest injury was to his pride: he was bested by a Pizza Man.

While he continued to make his way to the hotel, he was puzzled by the sudden appearance of this Pizza Man. His best self-defense has always been his instinct for self-preservation and this primal force was beginning to tug at his mind, prodding him to bail out on this assignment. His intuition, rather his real-life experience, told him this Pizza Man was not a haphazard occurrence. Someone either knew he was stalking the girl or someone was protecting or monitoring her for reasons important to others. These were danger signs to him. If he were not so committed to pleasing The Man and if this mission hadn't already personally cost him so much of his soul, he would leave tonight as he had originally planned. His biggest concern was his failure to claim the prize after coming so close to possessing it. The 'Biryuk', his colleagues called him, but now this Lone Wolf was going to need help. He refused to call and ask for help, he was too proud, besides he might have to explain how the girl got away from him, and he knew failed missions were scrutinized to the smallest detail, so much so that everything would be known even the size of the pizza. He's seen it happen so many times in the past; a few times he was the person who asked the questions. Under intense persuasion and with few exceptions, the strongest person would tell everything. No, he would go it alone one more day. Marina's escape was problematic but recovering the elusive prize would be complete redemption for him.

Incredibly, he was now further away from finding her than ever before. From this moment onward, she had the advantage over him. She knew she was hunted which meant she wouldn't return to her apartment or go to work, she would hide. The obvious question was where will she hide? He had no idea where to begin looking for her, at the same time, his head began to ache from his mind's repeated self-criticism. For some relief, he lifted his eyes up from their mindless task of watching his slow moving shadow on the pavement and found himself staring at a golden haze of

outdoor lighting falling upon Independence Hall, the city's symbol of freedom celebrated around the world and the grassy mall laying silently in
front of it. Sergei interrupted his painful musings, he supposed freedom
would sleep safe tonight under this protective glimmer but tomorrow it
could be less certain. Now less than a block from his hotel, he was com-
forted knowing he would clean his wound, order room service to deliver a
meal and a bottle of Stolichnaya, then he'd decide what to do next.

Chapter 25: West Philly

Within minutes of escaping from her own apartment, Marina was sitting beside Carl in a nearly empty subway car on the Market Frankford Line headed away from City Hall. She held tightly onto Carl's hand fearful she would suddenly be separated from him and fall back into her intruder's grasp. Her fear would be abated if she knew how fierce Carl was in his determination that he would not lose his grip on her hand as he pulled her through dark alleys, across wide streets, and down into the nearest subway concourse. He knew his way around this part of the city both above and below the streets. He was a child of the city and he knew the subway routes and interchanges much better than most riders. The subway cars were a poor man's imperfect getaway car: perfect when they ran on time, not so perfect when they lagged behind schedule. It made life interesting when you needed to stay a step ahead of the man chasing you. Carl knew first-hand the importance of bad timing; he never forgot how a late train cost him five years of his life and how it continues every day to complicate his future. They were fortunate tonight as a string of metal cars pulled alongside the westbound track just as they hurried down the steps beneath the fifteenth street subway concourse. They stepped into the car as the door closed immediately behind them.

Of course, Marina was no stranger to the subway. She rode the cars from time to time dependent on their convenience and her destination; she was familiar with the impersonal environment, the throngs of crowds and the daunting emptiness at other times, and always the noise, the screeching wheels, the rollicking motion and the occasional bumping sounds of metal upon metal. The subway was a second or third choice of transportation for her, a giant public substitution when all other transportation options failed.

The subway system was Carl's family car, station wagon and party bus. It was a bloodline for him and the millions of people in and around the Philly metropolis. At various times in his life it was a playground, a social connector, a ride to work, and now an escape from a very dangerous man.

Carl was in charge down here. Once he boarded a car he could close his eyes and tell you which station the car was arriving at, how long it will take to travel from one stop to the next and how much to adjust the time for express trains, locals, and weekend and holiday schedules. The subway's smell of dampness, stale air, endless human traffic were among many familiar markers that accompanied life in a big city, it was the natural product of the system carrying people above and below the city streets for more than a century of performance and service.

That was why he relaxed immediately after the train moved away from the station. They were the last people to enter the last car as the line of cars pulled away. He knew they would arrive at his stop on Fifty-Second Street in twenty-five minutes. They were safe for those twenty-five minutes, he knew there would be no threats from anyone outside the car who might be chasing them. They might be on the next train but not on this train. This was his world, he was in his element. He now had this time to think, to plan. Whoever the man behind the door was, Carl knew he would be at a disadvantage here in the subway and he would definitely be a bull in a china shop in his neighborhood of sisters and brothers in his West Philadelphia neighborhood. This was why he was taking Marina to his apartment: if the man appeared outside Carl's apartment, he'd standout like a sore thumb glowing redder than Rudolph's nose the longer he stood there; he'd be as obvious as a swan in a pond full of ducks.

There was much to think about as the line of metal cars carried the two of them under the river, through 30th St Penn Station and onward to begin its ascent onto the massive stilted steel structures that lifted the train thirty feet above street level in West Philadelphia. He rested his back against the hard plastic seat, looked at Marina and finally let go of her hand, speaking to her for the first time since freeing her from her captive.

"Are you OK?" he asked quietly, keeping his voice almost to a whisper, afraid she might be feeling so brittle that even the slightest sound could cause her to fall to pieces.

"I'm good. I'm OK." She answered in a low voice, at the same time she looked around the car seeing no one seated near them, then seeing a few persons at the far end of the long two-section car. She raised her head, smiled and said, "Thank you so much for saving my life." That was all she could manage. There were no tears, nor any fear in her voice, just relief and thankfulness to be here, to be safe. Carl saw her struggle to breathe deeply before she poured out more words with deeper feeling. "I'm alive, and away from him. This was the miracle I was praying for. Then the knocking…I was confused, then I was afraid that I, that we would both be killed. He said he'd do that." Her head and shoulders dropped as if someone had cut the strings that someone else was using to hold her head up.

Reaching his arms around her, Carl drew Marina closer to him. To the strangers on the train or to anyone who at this moment might have peered into the moving car, it would seem a sweet moment, to see a young couple out for the evening, coming home, maybe in love, certainly happy to be together. It would appear so ordinary, this embrace, to strangers not knowing it was a gesture of comfort by one and unbridled gratitude from the other, exchanged after a moment of great danger for both of them. No one could know that of course, nor see, nor expect it to be so. Carl's thoughts were different – he was thinking how this scene must occur so many thousands of times a day somewhere, what appears to be a vision of a loving exchange is in fact a response to human conflict and fear.

As scheduled, the subway cars screeched to a halt at their destination almost exactly 25 minutes after leaving downtown. Grasping Marina's hand again, Carl led her out of their metal cocoon onto the station's concrete platform. Marina's first reaction was to see herself suspended thirty feet above Market Street looking down on pedestrians and cars moving below her. The massive steel structure with its intimidating steps winding down to the sidewalk was old, painted recently but old, reminding her of photos she had seen of the Eiffel Tower, countless over-sized beams and girders, fastened with steel nuts and bolts, bringing to mind a 1940's film noir look with dark corners and shadowy images under the streetlights. She had never been this far west in the city for several reasons, chief among them were she never had a reason to come here and she was warned trouble was easily found here on the 52nd Street Strip if you didn't know where to go or who to see. This part of the city was busy with a large number of small businesses, restaurants, and bars. The businesses extended outward for several blocks in all directions with people streaming in at all hours of a day. She was aware the community was predominately black, populated by families with low income, and in too many households, there was no income at all. Seeing it for the first time made her aware how vital this bustling community was to the city. No one would describe it as the most attractive area in the city and it didn't have the safest streets in the city but that was not surprising in a community where a quick buck is sometimes the only choice to earn a living. This was Carl's neighborhood where he grew up, played some ball, attended school and lived a good life; he danced with pretty girls and shared sex with some of them. It was an unremarkable but acceptable life until he was pinched in a drug raid while carrying his personal dose of crack cocaine. It cost him his future and any possibilities for a normal life. Possession of a drug was a felony. Unable to afford lawyer fees, it landed him in prison. He learned later a felony would prevent him from becoming the president of the United States even if everyone voted for him. It wasn't a big disappointment for him, it wasn't on his list of favorite careers anyway. He wanted to be a cop when he was a teenager. That was now impossible. He was a member of a not-so-exclusive club, an ex-convict who couldn't expect to be anything ever again, hell, he couldn't even vote. Tonight, however, it was the safest place he could take Marina. Tonight, she was his guest in West Philly, "the soul of Philly."

"This is my Love Shack. All of it." laughed Carl when he closed the door behind them as they entered his studio apartment. Studio apartment was a polite real estate description for his two-room apartment with a sofa-bed in the living room, a bathroom/shower, and a small kitchen area equipped with a stove, sink, and a mini-refrigerator.

In a faux ceremonial voice, he bowed slightly and said "Welcome to my piece of paradise, Lady M. I offer you my home. Sit anywhere you'd like," and laughing again, he added, "But there's not many choices."

Marina sat on a cushioned chair. She was shivering but she wasn't cold.

"What would you like to drink? I'm having a shot or two of bourbon. I suggest you have something strong, then I'll set up the room for you to sleep."

"Just water for me." Marina replied, then she changed her mind, thinking she needed something to stop her shivering. "No water. Maybe tea. Do you have tea?"

Carl moved over to the cabinet above the sink and took out a box of Tetley tea bags, waved it at her. "I have tea but no teapot, I just heat the water in the microwave. OK?"

"Yes, that's fine."

While the tea water cooked for a minute, Carl uncorked his bottle of Bullett and used his trained bartender's eye to pour a double shot into a juice glass. Tonight's adventure called for a double dose of his all-purpose elixir. He'd sip it slowly and reflect on his decision to stop by Marina's apartment for a short surveillance and how incredibly providential it was. The first sip was perfect.

"What do you like in your tea, Lady M?"

"One sugar, just a little milk, please"

He placed the tea on the small tray next to the chair, then sat on the couch/bed with his drink in hand. Marina sipped her tea allowing the rising steam and the warmth of the cup to enter her body. Before Carl could say anything more, she asked, "What brought you to my apartment? How did you know he was in my apartment?"

"FBI agent Frister asked me to watch over you while he was away on an assignment, he wanted me to check in on you periodically. He had a bad feeling about the fella from D.C. So before going to the bar to begin my late shift tonight, I decided to pass by your apartment, to check the streets for any loiterers. When I arrived, I noticed a man step out from the shadow of a tree and enter your building. He didn't come out. In a few minutes the flickering lights from your TV went off. I noticed two figures in your front window, both seated, not moving. That's when I went upstairs, listened at the door. You were talking to someone and the other voice was a male voice with a foreign accent. The rest was just acting on instinct, remembering the code word Doug told us to use, pizza. That's why I was there." He took a short breath and finished. "Thanks to Doug. God did the rest."

"Thanks to you, Carl." She repeated her words on the subway car. "Thank you for saving my life."

After finishing his bourbon, Carl pulled out the daybed, replaced the sheets and convinced Marina to try falling asleep. He placed a small Army Surplus cot for himself in the narrow hallway between the front room and the bathroom. It wasn't his first time sleeping in the hallway.

Once he had Marina settled, he stepped into the bathroom and called his bar, telling him he had an emergency, knowing he wouldn't have to offer much in the details of his emergency. They were cool with it; after all they all had emergencies of one kind or another. His next call was to Doug in Redwood, CA where it was three hours earlier.

Chapter 26: Doug and Jack

The cellphone was resting on the oval dining table in the kitchen area of his hotel mini-suite when he received the call from Carl. The standard ring tone told him instantly it wasn't Ellen or anyone from his Philly office, he had created individual signature rings for his personal and work contacts. Rising from the couch, he padded over to the table and connected the call. Before he could say hello, he heard Carl speaking in a low hurried voice.

"Doug, this is Carl. You're not gonna believe the shit I'm about to tell you."

Surprised by his opening greeting and by the sound of urgency in his voice, Doug stopped Carl before he could say another word. "Where are you calling from?"

"Philly. My place."

"Does this call involve Marina?"

"It definitely does. It's all about Marina."

"Is she OK?"

"Yeah, she's fine and she's here with me, but it was a close call."

"She's with you? Where are you? What happened? When did…"

"No. Stop, dude." Carl interrupted. "Wait. Just wait. Let me tell you what happened. It will be quicker than me answering your questions one at a time."

Doug's immediate silence was the signal for Carl to continue. "First Marina's unharmed. We're at my apartment. She's sleeping in the other room, actually it's the only other room in my apartment. I'm calling you from my home office, seated on the toilet. Are you ready to listen?" Hearing Doug's affirmative response, Carl began sharing his story. "You can interrupt me if you're confused."

185

Carl took a deep breath and began, "I was on my way to work tonight and I decided …"

Carl finished his recollection without any interruption from Doug who was impressed by the straightforward presentation without wordy descriptions and emotions most witnesses add that only lengthen and often muddy their recounting of events. This was classic police work, just the facts with precise details provided where they were most needed. Nothing was left out from the pizza break-in through the escape with Marina to West Philly.

"Holy shit" was Doug's reaction when Carl finished talking. "That is crazy. That man is likely a professional assassin." With the words pizza man ringing in his ears, Doug gushed, "You are wild and smart."

"And lucky." inserted Carl.

"You are smarter than lucky, Carl." Then reaching across the dining table for a pen and paper, he said, "Can you keep her safe with you until I can get someone over there to move her under full FBI custody?"

"Hell yes!" Carl boasted with a broad smile Doug couldn't see from three thousand miles away. "She's safe here. No one else knows she's here and if anyone with skin lighter than me showed up in this part of West Philly at this hour of the night, they'd glow like the Rockefeller Center's decorated Christmas tree and stand out with a strong scent of sorry-but-you-don't-belong-here all around themselves." He laughed at his weak attempt at humor and repeated his firm assertion more as a promise this time. "Yep, she's safe here."

Doug realized he didn't want flashing lights or a caravan of black SUVs racing into West Philly this late at night, he was certain it would draw attention and possibly alert the wrong person or persons who were after Marina. He wanted a low key approach to getting her safely into FBI custody. He decided he would call Jack. This assignment was in line with his friend's past CIA experience of relocating targets to friendlier surroundings before anyone knew they were gone, a low-tech twenty-first century version of a Star Trek transporter beaming a person from point A to point B, in this case, moving Marina to FBI headquarters.

"I'll have Jack contact you with the arrangements." He told Carl, adding. "You remember I told you about Jack?"

"I do." Carl remembered Doug's reference to Jack as being connected to the CIA. It made Carl uncomfortable at the time. Carl's opinion of the CIA was jaded, what he knew of its history was its inconsistent role as being the good guys or the bad guys. He decided to keep that opinion to himself. He'd just be cautious around Jack; he'd treat him just as he treats meeting policemen for the first time, he'd hope they'd be helpful but he'd remain suspicious of being able to count on them, never relying on it to happen.

Doug wanted to emphasize caution to Carl. "I'd like the handoff of Marina to be as soon as possible. Jack will use the same code word I gave you and Marina to use before you speak with or meet with anyone." Glancing at his watch and adding in the three hours difference in Philly, he told Carl not to expect Jack's call until sometime after 6 AM Philly time. He calculated it would take that much time for him to stir Jack and allow Jack a few hours to organize support and set up a rendezvous location; he also didn't want Carl or Marina stepping outside again tonight or in the dark morning hours before 6 AM.

Satisfied that all the bases were covered for Marina's safety and expecting a smooth transfer in the morning, Doug prepared to end the call.

"Carl, that's about all I can do from out here but there is one last thing I want to tell you. You know it, of course, but I need to say it and I plan to tell other people in high places." He waited a few seconds to amplify his respect for Carl and said. "You saved her life. You know that. You may not realize it but you have also saved more than just her life."

"Thanks." Carl was proud of his actions and humbled by Doug's acknowledgement; he was still replaying the images and words in his mind. "It was hairy, man. I did what I could."

"I know. Now try to get some rest if you can. I'll see you tomorrow. Goodnight."

"OK. I'll try. I'll expect a call from your friend Jack. Goodnight."

Within minutes, Doug was speaking with Jack and giving him every detail of Carl's confrontation with Marina's intruder. Jack was already suffering anxiety, anger, and frustration as he was watching a previously taped football game between his hometown Eagles and their rival New York Giants. He uses his DVR to tape all of the local sports team's games, then views them when he isn't physically chasing after bad guys and bad girls, or searching the internet on his top level security clearance computer for the latest information on America's most dangerous enemies inside and outside the nation's borders. So tonight he didn't mind the late hour interruption. On the contrary, he welcomed the relief from suffering through another 2020 edition of his home team's spiraling downfall week after week since their nightmare record of 1-3-1 catapulted them into first place in the weakest division in the NFL. Jack was scarred by the Vegas odds-makers who projected the Eagles would win the NFL East with as ugly a win-loss record of any playoff team in any sport, an embarrassing predicted compilation at 5 and 11. So, instead of being annoyed, Jack wanted to respond to Doug's opening greeting of 'Hello, it's Doug' with a resounding countergreeting of Halleluiah. He didn't have the slightest idea why Doug called him but he was certain nothing could be as awful as this game. He was soon mesmerized as he listened to Doug relay Carl's soon-to-be a classic escape story, it was far more exciting than his 2020 Philadelphia Eagles.

Doug ended the story with Carl and Marina arriving at Carl's apartment.

"So now you know what I know. As I told you a few days ago, this began for me when Carl asked me to listen to his friend's story about her girlfriend who went missing in Romania. After our conversation the other night, I began following your leads and advice and discovered some very interesting information on recent activities that appear to be connected to the girl's disappearance. They are tinted with big time intrigue surrounding very powerful people."

"Are you telling me you think the coffee barista is being pursued by an international assassin?"

"I am."

"What would make them interested in her?"

"I don't know but they are interested in her, Jack."

Jack was wide awake now. He was running Doug's story back through his brain. Who would send a professional assassin to kill a college student who lives in Philadelphia? Why?

"You said the intruder told the girl her friend is safe in Moscow, correct?"

"Yes. Moscow."

"What is the missing girl's name? It sounded familiar to me. Was it Gazunov? Did you say her name was Gazunov?

"Not Gazunov. It's Sophia Glasinov."

"Gazunov. Glasinov. Hmmn. I find that interesting. They are two very similar names and maybe in Russia they are as common as Smith and Smythe or Brown and Braun in English. Nevertheless, there is one additional piece of information in your story with respect to the names. The name Gazunov is a name many senior members of intelligence agencies around the world would recognize instantly. Sergei Gazunov is a professional Russian operative who is credited with stealthful assassinations throughout Europe and the Mideast and rumored to have conducted others in South America but none in America, at least until now. He is a seldom used weapon but when he is active, he has been extremely effective."

The litany of information flowing from Jack continued and was giving Doug a clearer picture now of the danger Marina and Carl were facing. Sophia and this man might be connected but how does that include Marina. He remained quiet, wanting to hear more from Jack.

"Of course. We know about Gazunov's successes but no one ever broadcasts his failures." Jack continued. "His reputation and elusiveness are often compared with Illich Ramirez Sanchez, a ruthless, leftist political assassin-for-hire better known by his pseudonym, Carlos. Carlos terrorized European democracies for several decades beginning in 1975, he was the subject of a twenty year international manhunt before he was captured and placed in a French prison where he is still awaiting a natural but lonesome death."

With Doug's attention now fully engaged, Jack went on sharing more background on Sergei. "The difficulty in capturing or neutralizing Gazunov is the constant protection he is given from the second or third most powerful nation in the world depending on your opinion of Russia and China in the world order. Sergei is similar to the mythological dragon that leaves its lair to strike with fire and devastation, then returns to its safe place to be guarded by poisonous and vicious six-headed wolves with enormous strength. He only leaves to spread his fire when summoned, then returns to await his next call to duty".

Jack went on to describe what he saw as the two major differences between the two assassins: their political dogma and loyalty. Carlos was raised in Venezuela in a world of luxury and educated in the Marxist universities prominent in Moscow in the '70s, Russian schools funded to indoctrinate students from communist nations across the globe. Therefore, it was not surprising Carlos would be committed to Marxist organizations, to large and small nations, and militant groups. However, he worked passionately with one caveat: his clients must be able to afford his price, his loyalty was dependent on personal gain: his services went to the highest bidder. His primary loyalty was to money and to the luxuries money could buy. He was addicted to living an expensive life.

Sergei on the other hand was raised in a colorless suburb of Moscow under the strict confines of Khrushchev's Soviet Union where an individual's adherence to sacrifice and service for the State was foremost. It was not surprising that his loyalty was given to the State and by default to the one person who represented the once glorious power of the Soviet Union, the current President and Prime Minister of Russia, Vladimir Vladimirovich Putin. Sergei's loyalty to the State was strengthened with the bond he and Putin forged after they both served in the notorious KGB, the Soviet Union's primary intelligence agency. In the passing years, Sergei's political philosophy was rooted in his loyalty to one state, one man. Sergei's extreme loyalty and his KGB skills became a secret weapon Putin used to secure silence from dissidents, for the removal of competition, and the offering of discreet favors to powerful men inside and outside Russia. This partnership ended with Gazunov's retirement from the KGB in 1991 but it was short-lived. He was soon given a position as a consulting specialist with the FSB (Federal Security Service), the Russian replacement for the Soviet era KGB. Following Putin's self-appointment as FSB Director in 1998, he became Putin's number one fixer for the past twenty years. Hearing all of this background on Sergei raised the hair on Doug's arms a bit. He was ready to speak when Jack said exactly what was on Doug's own mind.

"Doug, if this is Gazunov, this is very big. Too big for just you and me."

Trying to choose his next words carefully, Jack placed his thoughts on his mental whiteboard before sharing them out loud. He recalled a recent CIA monthly report from Russia. He was hoping he wasn't going to sound looney or out of control.

"Doug, within the past three months the CIA has reported the unannounced resignation of a long-tenured and trusted executive officer of the FSB, the security organization that replicates the KGB. His current status in CIA circles is highlighted with the ominous declaration of CWU, current whereabouts unknown. He has been a confidant of Putin since both served in the KGB. This individual like many such members of Russia's political establishments is also a popular attendee cavorting with young women in Moscow. You will be interested to know this fellow's social circle includes a young woman named Sophia Glasinov."

"Jesus Christ!" was Doug's unrestrained reply.

"Yes. This sudden interest in Marina is heating up into a firestorm." Jack replied in a solemn tone. "Gazunov works for only one person. If Gazunov is the man who attacked Marina tonight, he is here to solve a problem that involves the Kremlin." Both men remained silent for a few seconds until Jack offered his opinion of what he saw lying before them. "This is about more than a missing girl". Jack assured Doug. "My guess is it already involves America". He asked Doug. "Where is Marina now?"

"That's why I called you, Jack. She's safe in West Philly. But I called to ask you to take her to the FBI headquarters tomorrow morning. It's too late tonight and I think it's too risky in the dark. You know the story, Jack, but no one at headquarters knows any of this. You can explain it to the chief. You have the rank. He'll listen to you. I'll call my senior in the morning and get his authority to fly back to Philly tomorrow."

"Where do I pick her up? Where in West Philly?"

"You're not picking her up. Carl's going to bring her to you. It will cause much less commotion than a few black SUVs double-parking on 52nd St in West Philly. We don't want to wake anybody who isn't already still awake from the night before."

"OK, Doug. Pick a spot between West Philly and the office."

"What about the Boathouse, maybe near the Azalea Garden, say 7 AM. The area should be empty, maybe a few boaters but the chilly weather should keep people sparse and the morning work traffic will cover the limited operation."

"OK. The Azalea Garden, at 7 AM."

"Jack. One last thing. I want you to call Carl with the final details. Use the code word pizza. Any problems, any changes I need to know about, call me. Thanks."

Jack hung up last. If he waited a second longer before moving the cell phone from his ear, he would've heard a single soft click, like a faint ticking sound from a wall clock. If he been able to hear that low tick, it might have made a difference in avoiding the disaster that followed the next morning.

Chapter 27: Unexpected Help

The recording device shut off automatically when Doug ended the call. Jefferson Crandall's private order issued only two days ago to monitor Agent Frister's personal and business phones proved to be the right decision. In the past four years as the rift widened between the FBI and the DOJ executive office in D.C., mistrust between the agencies surfaced creating a suffocating presence of 'Big Brother is watching' inside the offices and conference rooms of the nation's top law enforcement communities. Crandall and his superiors increased their surveillance of regional offices by enlisting the services from those few FBI employees whose sympathies sided with the current administration. A list of Frister's key contacts was provided to Crandall by one such employee in the Philadelphia FBI office with a recommendation to place additional phone taps on the first four contacts, Jack's phone was contact number three.

Within minutes after Doug and Jack's conversation, Crandall's cell phone rang interrupting his evening ritual of browsing the newspaper while half-listening to Fox News. He listened to the caller carefully, grunting lowly, and taking pencil notes as the voice on the phone relayed a summary of the conversations he had intercepted. Crandall asked the caller to repeat the summary and told him to prepare the transmission to be coded and forwarded to another private number. He added a last command before ending the call without a goodbye.

"Monitor both phones all night and let me know if any other calls take place to and from either of those phones." Adding emphasis, Crandall ended the call in a strong voice. "We want to have the latest information on that meeting time and location."

Pressing the keys on his own cell phone, he muttered to himself, "This mess keeps spreading. There'd be no early night tonight." As soon as the phone he called began ringing, he put his frustration aside, hopeful he sounded calm. A voice answered and Crandall said brightly, "It's me. I've got an important update on Omega, something you need to hear now."

****

Sergei called his contact when he returned to his hotel room. He gave him a quick summary of the evening's events and assured him he'd find the girl again and make one more attempt to get what he was sent to find. He didn't think it was necessary to share all of the details of the bungled attempt. It was left unsaid but both men on the phone were disappointed in the delay.

His contact offered a muted measure of encouragement "We are confident in you, Sergei. Tomorrow is as good a day as any to be successful." Then he said goodnight, "Spokoynoy nochi."

"Spokoynoy nochi, moy drug." was Sergei's polite response."

Sergei learned at an early age not to rely on people and things to brighten his spirits or bolster his courage when bad days surfaced or misfortune found him vulnerable. He considered bad days as an inevitable cycle of life. What he required now was simple: a good meal to nourish his physical body; his spirit and perseverance were his own personal challenges and responsibilities and food and drink never failed to restore him. And so it was the meal and the Russian vodka delivered from room service satisfied Sergei's tired body and weary mind. He had much to do so he limited his vodka consumption leaving a half bottle of vodka staring back at him, beckoning to him whenever he passed by the mini-bar. He soothed himself with his self-assurance that he would drink more than his share of Russian vodka when he returned victorious to Moscow.

He decided to nap on the couch in the large sitting room; he wasn't going to get much sleep anyway and he wanted to be ready to move very early in the morning. Though he still didn't know where he would begin, he was hopeful the same source who provided unsolicited information in the past few days would do so again and soon. He selected a reputable 24-hour television news station, that didn't include Fox News for he and all of Russia knew the Fox network was unreliable for factual reporting, even Russia's state-controlled networks reported more truths than Fox News. He settled on CNN. Sergei considered a reliable news source as a necessary piece of communication for him whenever he was on assignment. His assignments were often connected to matters of state and men and women in high places; therefore, the world news kept him alert to events that might impact his ability to perform or travel to his destinations. At home, in between assignments, he could afford to watch whatever he wished whenever he wanted. He could even do what he hears the younger generations say they do, he could binge watch whatever he missed while he was away. Binge. What a strange word for television programs, but it fit of course. Binge was a reference to excessive behavior. Binge drinking, gambling, eating, and so on. Is there Binge sex? Likely so. He dwelled on that thought.

He received his call before midnight.

"We have information on the girl. She will be delivered tomorrow to a CIA agent."

"That's not good news."

"No, but she will be on the street, in a park, to be transferred at 7 AM. She will be vulnerable. We know where and when."

"What else do you know? Tell me everything."

****

Jack made the final arrangements for transferring Marina from Carl to FBI headquarters. The transfer will take place near Boathouse Row, he gave the exact time and place to Carl. Jack told Carl to call him immediately if any other questions or any confusion arose. The primary goal was to keep Marina alive and to transfer her safely to FBI custody: it was a matter of life and death and it was the next step in solving the mystery of why she would be so important to the people who sent Sergei to kill her.

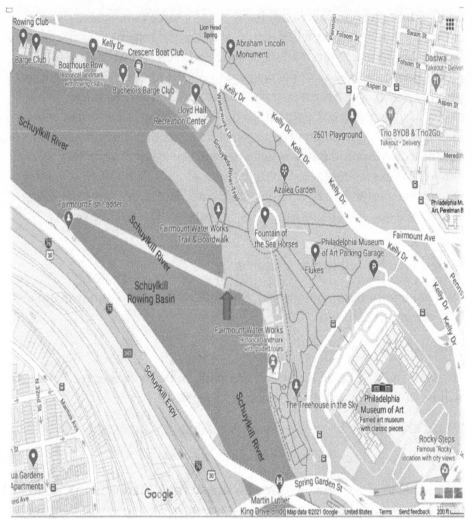

Kelly Drive, Boathouse Row & the Waterworks (<u>large arrow below fountain</u> indicates location of gazebo and promenade)

Chapter 28: Boathouse Row

"Is it safe for me to call my friend Marc before we go downstairs for the Uber ride?" Marina asked as she put on the jacket Carl insisted she wear to keep her warm against the morning chill.

"Yes." Carl answered. "Call him. Just tell him you're fine and you'll be home soon. Tell him I'm taking you to the FBI building; that you'll call him back when you get there." Remembering Doug's insistence to be extra cautious, he added. "Tell him nothing else. OK?

"OK."

It wouldn't be correct to say Carl and Marina slept well. It was a short night. She slept on a lumpy sofa-bed and he slept on a thin mattress slapped on top of what even a snake oil salesman might be hesitant to call an army cot. The addition of several nerve-testing phone calls and the rising tension from the danger hovering over them left them exhausted but glad the long evening was over. Carl brewed a pot of coffee on the decades-old Mr. Coffee machine a friend gave to him. A fresh hot cup of coffee was the extent of their breakfast; they were both too nervous to trust food would stay in their stomachs long enough to be digested properly.

Marc was awake when he received Marina's call. He was an early riser believing most work is accomplished in the first half of a day. Marina spoke before he could say anything, telling him only what Carl told her to say.

"You're at Carl's?" Marc couldn't believe what he was hearing. "How did you end up at Carl's apartment?" Then switching thoughts, he asked her. "Why are you going to the Federal Building at 7 AM?" He was worried and puzzled. The last time they spoke she was planning to chill out with some TV and a thrown-together dinner.

"I'll tell you all about it when I'm downtown." She countered "I am fine. I can't talk now. Don't worry. Just wait for my call. "

"In an hour or so?"

"Yes. An hour or so. Maybe sooner." Then with more warmth in her voice, "I'll see you soon. Goodbye."

Marina shutdown her phone as the driver arrived. When Carl opened his apartment door it was a few minitues past 6:30. They were meeting Jack at 7 AM.

Jack had phoned Carl only an hour or so earlier. He introduced himself using the code word pizza, confirmed who he was, his connection with Doug, and told Carl they would meet at Azalea Garden, a popular open area along the banks of the river midway between Boathouse Row and the rear entrance to the Philadelphia Art Museum. Carl knew the location well, it was practically in his back yard. Jack's instructions were precise and brief, "pull off of Kelly Drive at Sedgley Drive, drive towards the river, the Lloyd Recreation Center is on the corner, continue through the first parking lot, at the end of the parking lot you'll see the circular Fountain of the Four Horses, and for point of reference you will see in the not-so-distant background, elevated on a hill, the rear entrance to the Philadelphia Art Museum. The transfer spot will be to the left side of the circular fountain at the front of the entrance to the Azalea Garden with its wooden benches and pergola. Wait at the benches. Don't be too early. See you at 7 AM."

Carl followed Marina into the backseat of the Uber car. There was no need to say anything to the driver other than good morning, he already knew the destination, it was the primary information exchanged between both parties before the driver and the passenger agreed on the contract: how much will the ride cost to go from point A to point B, and how soon will you arrive at point A. It is a fundamental service contract yet it seemed so revolutionary and innovative when the car service hit the streets of America in 2009.

They sat silent as the driver headed to Kelly Drive. The sun was beginning to rise from the east over the city, tiny rays of sun tinted the sky gently pushing away the overnight darkness and showing the promise of a beauti-ful late autumn day. Yesterday's rainfall was already forgotten except for the few puddles and damp sidewalks that marked its passing. The forecast was for a highest temperature of 53 degrees but at this hour of the morning as they stepped outside to get into the car it was close to 40 degrees and chilly.

It was ten minutes before seven AM when they arrived at the Azalea Gar-den benches by the Four Horses fountain, just a short walk from Boat-house Row. They appeared to be early. It was a tribute to Carl's devotion to punctuality, a trait he acquired from his dark campus days inside the steel bars and concrete flooring of his college of hard knocks. His mantra was simple: if you're late, you lose.

Marina was no stranger to this section of Fairmount Park. She often ped-dled along its many bicycle paths throughout this part of the city. The Drive's many outdoor attractions were close to her apartment and she of-ten used the park areas along the river for her client fitness training ses-sions. Formerly called the East River Drive, Kelly Drive's bicycling and jogging paths and pedestrian walkways follow the river from the rear of the Art Museum north past the Waterworks complex and the Fountain of Four Horses, passing in front of the multicolored rowing clubs that com-bine to give this piece of the city its signature name, Boathouse Row. The paths along the river are sheltered from sun and rain by an abundance of trees and acres of scenic woodlands nearby in Fairmount Park. Only a short walk from the end of the Drive on the west side of the river via the Girard Street Bridge is the Philadelphia Zoo, a major attraction and a source of pride for the city

Marina sat on a park bench, folding and unfolding her hands in her lap while Carl paced back and forth in front of her – both of them exhibiting nervous tension. They waited beneath the pergola, alternating their gaze from the grassy banks of the river in front of them to an opening between the hedges that separated the fountain from the parking lot the Uber driver drove through to access the fountain. It was the most direct way to drive

201

into and out of the fountain and the Azalea Garden. Beyond the fountain rose the Waterworks complex and the rear entrance to the Art Museum, further in the distance were some of the city's newer skyscrapers.

Behind them on Kelly Drive, the number of cars speeding and passing the boathouses to and from center city were fewer than normal. It was usually a busy artery between center city and the western suburbs during the morning and evening rush hours but the coronavirus had reduced the traffic to less than half its normal flow. This was primarily due to the city and local business efforts to safeguard people from the coronavirus by shifting many commuters away from the offices and stores downtown and back into their own homes. Twenty years ago, possibly as few as ten years ago, this would have been a monumental task with a minimal likelihood of success but rapid advances in virtual and remote technologies and the increases in broadband speeds in the recent past contributed to a smooth transition of workplaces to homes and remote office locations. This reduced the threat of viral exposure to millions of people in the general workforce, proving once again technology may create anxieties and disruptions but it more often brings benefits and timely blessings. This was one of those blessings. A lesser noticed benefit of the deadly virus was a by-product of the low traffic volume on Kelly Drive this morning: the reduced cost at the gas pumps. Going nowhere uses less gas; less demand for gas produces lower gas prices. Economics 101.

Unseen by Carl and Marina, but watching and waiting for the Uber car to drop-off its two passengers in front of the pergola, was someone else who also embraced punctuality: Jack, Doug's emergency fill-in. Jack watched as an attractive dark-haired young woman and a tall lean black man exited the Uber vehicle in front of the wooden Azalea Garden sign mounted on a post next to the pergola. He sat in his car in the back row of the small parking lot linking the recreation center and the fountain. Following the "back-in, don't back-out" dictum, Jack's car faced the fountain and the Azalea Garden. He arrived at 6:30 AM while it was still dark and finished off his black coffee and a McDonald's Egg Mc Muffin. He wasn't a fancy coffee drinker, his coffee routine hadn't changed in his twenty years in the Company. Though he was partial to the darker and heavier coffee brews he sampled on his duty assignments in Europe and in the Mid-East, he always defaulted to his black coffee and Egg Mc Muffin at home. He was loyal; it was good enough for him when it was all he could afford so many years ago and it was still the best breakfast value for his money. Hell. Hundreds of millions of people all over the world drink McDonald's coffee and wolf-down McMuffin breakfasts. He looked down at the digital clock on his dashboard, it was 6:48 AM. He'd wait a few more minutes to make sure an unwanted visitor or two didn't show; he knew if anyone was going to intrude, he wanted them to show before he did then he'd have the final element of surprise. It was a professional safety practice, every good agent used it. He made one last gesture to acknowledge his riding partner, the Glock 19 who never left his side, and confirmed it was comfortably seated in his holster. He was ready to rescue the fair maiden and defeat the evil wizard, the flame-throwing dragon, the evil empire or whoever the villain is this time.

The sun was rising and Jack's experience was that daylight always lessened the degree of danger that surrounded any clandestine meeting. With one less worry about someone lurking in the shadows, this transfer would take only a few minutes. As soon as he placed the young woman in the car he'll call his backup team waiting in two SUVs in the park on the other side of the Drive to give them his all clear to join him here and follow closely behind him on the short ride around the Art Museum and down the Parkway to FBI headquarters on 6th and Arch Street. While he waited the three or four minutes it would take for the SUVs to join him at the fountain, he planned to call Doug. He smiled at that thought. Yes, he'd get a small pleasure calling him now. He could hear himself saying to his groggy, sleep-deprived friend. "Good morning." Then announce, "Early wake up call for Agent Frister." It would be 4AM in California. That would even the score between two friends. After all, Jack had been awake all night.

Pulling his Covid mask out of his pocket, he stepped out of his car and walked from the parking lot into the fountain area, then he strode to his left where Carl and Marina waited for him. They saw him right away. Marina stood up, took a step toward Jack but Carl moved in front of her, keeping her behind him until he was sure it was Jack.

Chapter 29: Ambush

"Pizza."

Carl relaxed when he heard Jack say the single word clear and direct with conviction as though it was the answer to the final clue on Jeopardy. He didn't hide his relief. He could breathe easier, the cavalry had arrived.

"You must be the Pizza Man." were Jack's next words, said with less formality. "You're already famous in our very small circle of G-Men." Switching his attention to Marina, he introduced himself, "Hello, Marina. I'm Jack, a friend of Agent Frister who's given me the pleasure and the important responsibility to take you to the FBI office downtown. It will take us fifteen minutes or less to get there."

"Hello, Jack. Thank you." She responded in a low voice, looking like a pre-teen in Carl's jacket, many sizes too big for her.

Carl, having watched Jack appear from the parking lot but not seeing a vehicle, asked him with his own brand of sarcasm and wit, "Did you walk here? Where's your car? I thought there'd be more of you, man."

"Nope. I didn't walk." Was the answer to the first question; the answers to questions 2 and 3 followed. "My car is in the lot behind me, in the last row closest to the river. I'm alone but my backup is just behind you across the road, out of sight. They'll be here as soon as I have you both in the car."

"Do you want me to come with you?" Carl questioned. He didn't expect he'd be needed downtown and he intended to call for another Uber ride to take him directly to his workplace at the bar so he could help clean-up after missing last night's shift.

"Yes, I need you to come with me. Doug believes you can add valuable information on the case." Jack returned to a more formal tone. "He also thinks your safety is compromised."

205

Showing Carl his formal ID card, Jack pointed back towards the direction he came from, "My car is over there. It's the black one." He guided them around the fountain and back into the parking lot, keeping both of them in front of him. As they approached the car, Carl stopped about twenty feet away and told Jack he needed to make a quick call to the bar.

"This will only take a minute." He assured Jack. "I just want to tell them I'll be in later than I thought."

"Sure."

After Jack placed Marina in the back of the car, he walked around to the driver side of the car, opened the door, then stood and waited for Carl to finish his call. Carl's call took only fifteen seconds but it was fifteen seconds too long.

Sergei knew the time and place of the transfer. He was given the rendezvous details only minutes after Jack confirmed them to Carl. He was also warned there could be several carloads of agents for support, maybe not. He figured he'd take his chances. If things weren't to his advantage, he would do nothing, he'd walk away. There would be no reason for anyone to stop him, he'd just be a tourist out for an early morning walk along the river. But it wasn't his bad habit to give up easily on any assignment and he was getting desperate to succeed on this one, he was also certain they would find him if he stayed in the area any longer. It was now or never.

Like Carl and Jack, Sergei believes the early bird gets the worm. He also knows not every sacrifice reaps a reward, but it can increase the odds for success. As soon as he had the transfer point and time, he phoned his in-country contact to request the same driver who delivered him to his hotel a few days ago. He was Sergei's ideal choice: professional, tight-lipped, and knew what was expected from him. He and the driver arrived at Boathouse Row in the dark, before anyone else. They cruised around the fountain area, surveying the parking lot until Sergei selected a hiding place amid some trees with the river behind him, an ideal spot where he could see the Azalea Garden and any traffic that entered the fountain area from Kelly

Drive. His driver sat waiting inside a car in the small parking area in front of the Waterworks complex and restaurant, across the field on the far side of the Sea of Four Horses Fountain, about a hundred yards from where Jack stood waiting for Carl to complete his call.

The pieces now fell in place, it was perfectly orchestrated. The agent practically delivered the girl to him. The tall black fellow's delay gave Sergei an advantage: the agent was distracted and his back was to Sergei. So Sergei stepped out silently from behind several trees and bushes at the edge of the parking lot and fired one shot from his silencer-equipped pistol. Jack never saw Sergei; he never heard the bullet leave the gun barrel. He was struck instantly feeling a hard thud, then an explosion of fire erupted inside the back of his head. He began falling slowly as his instincts and arms tried to keep him upright, all this was in vain as his brain's last signals told him the worst possible thing had just happened to him: he was going to die, and worse, his effort to protect someone from harm had failed.

It was Marina's scream that caused Carl to jerk his head in a whiplash motion from his phone. He saw Jack collapse outside the car with the driver's door hanging open but he didn't know what caused him to fall. Instinctively, he motioned to run towards the car when he saw a gunman aim at him, saw the quick flashes and felt two bullets strike him. His last view of Marina as he looked up from the gravel parking lot was seeing the horror on her face as she was being dragged out of the car.

With the exception of Marina's scream, there were no other sounds transmitted by Sergei's sudden attack. If anyone heard Marina's scream from inside the car, they dismissed it. Among the few people in the area, no one reacted. There was no visible sign that anything was out of the ordinary: Jack's body was hidden between his own car and a Hyundai SUV with a bike rack likely belonging to a bicyclist already peddling east or west along the river. Carl's body now lay partially hidden beside the hedges that separated the parking lot from the fountain area.

Sitting in the back of Jack's car, Marina witnessed him fall, then saw Carl's body react violently to the bullets striking him. She was in shock and immobile. Sergei walked to the rear passenger door opened it, reached in, grabbed her hand and growled, "Get out!" He recognized the signs of shock as she didn't move or speak, as she just sat there, covering her eyes with her free hand. He pulled her roughly out of the car. "Come with me!" He held the gun at his side while he used his other hand to push her in front of him, away from the parking lot and out onto the grassy field along the river. Before he arrived at the Waterworks he wasn't sure how he would end his final meeting with Marina, only that he knew it would be their last one. While waiting behind the trees in the chilly pre-dawn air, he surveyed the area along the river and found a convenient setting for his final discussion with Marina, a thirty foot tall gazebo in a classical Greek architectural design with columns stood as a sentinel overlooking the river. It sat at the end of a long concrete promenade that stretched along the river's edge from the rear of the Art Museum and the Waterworks complex. The promenade was enclosed with a classical spiral balustrade and was a favored scenic location for the millions of people each year who visited this peaceful stretch of Kelly Drive and Boathouse Row. Sergei's reason for selecting the gazebo wasn't as romantic; he appreciated it for its convenient location and saw it as a literal drop-off point. The promenade jutted out a short distance from the center of the gazebo to its abrupt end facing west across the river, its decorative waist-high railing was the only barrier separating anyone standing there from the torrent of water flowing rapidly over the waterfall, twenty feet below. Regardless of how their conversation ended, Sergei planned to send Marina into the water below. It would delay the discovery of her body and provide added insurance if the bullet wound didn't kill her fast enough though he considered that to be highly unlikely. He also prided himself on his personal mantras for Assassination 101: location, location, location: he would put the bullet where it can do its deadliest damage. It would also allow him to join his driver and be out of Philadelphia quickly, out of America before the day was over.

He was thankful for the kindness of strangers for the details of this last minute rendezvous could only have come from someone having inside access to local FBI communications: either by tapping phones or having an insider in FBI headquarters who was passing on data with impunity. It wasn't important to Sergei where the information came from, only that it was accurate and it put Marina back in his hands. He was given a second chance at silencing her for good and he still hoped to find the location of the prize before he added another dead body to this mission.

Bam! Bam! The loud noises erupted from the direction of the Drive. It sounded like gunfire to Marina. She was startled then realized it was a car backfiring. Sergei was also startled and noticeably confused by the direction of the sound. Able to hear only with his right ear, he turned to his right away from the original source of the sound thinking they were gunshots coming from the parking lot. Not seeing anyone, he stopped walking and looked away from Marina. This distraction provided precious seconds for Marina to escape from Sergei. Her fitness training and youthfulness gave her the advantage she needed to distance herself quickly before Sergei turned to see her running ten yards away, racing across the field towards the Waterworks parking lot. Marina noticed a lone car in the parking lot with a man sitting in it. Maybe, she thought, it was someone who could help her. It was her only chance to get away from Sergei.

Running after her, Sergei called out to her to stop, threatening loudly that he would shoot her. She ignored his threat to shoot. She was faster and more agile than Sergei, and she began weaving side to side as she ran to make it more difficult for him to hit her. She was also convinced if he wanted her dead, he would've shot her at the same time he shot the agent. He must want her alive, maybe only long enough for him to have a final chance at finding the item. She knew whatever the item was, it was more important to him than she was.

As she increased her distance from Sergei, the man got out of the parked car and waved towards her. Oh, thank God she thought, she's going to make it. As she drew closer, she saw he wasn't waving at her, he was signaling to someone behind her. Without losing stride, she looked over her shoulder to see Sergei waving back to the man and pointing at Marina. No, this can't be happening. "My God. No." was the desperate prayer she whispered. She turned away from the man and the Waterworks and looked towards the river. If she could reach the river bank, she could dive into the river and swim down to the museum or swim directly across the river to West Philly but he could end her dash for life with one expert shot as she moved in a straight line to the edge of the river. She stopped immediately not knowing which way to run. In those brief seconds, a puff of dirt exploded next to her feet. It was a warning shot from Sergei's silencer. She froze; she was caught, trapped again.

Sergei, puffing for breath, reached her but said nothing. He marched her back towards the river accessing a section of the promenade and balustrade that stretched between the Waterworks back to the gazebo. They ascended the steps to the promenade and walked onto the gazebo, stopping just under the expansive golden eagle dome supported thirty feet above them by twelve columns. The morning sun was fuller now, moving higher and westerly as the minutes ticked on, making it difficult for Marina to see Sergei's face after he managed to position her facing the sun and he had the river behind him and the entire park area in his view.

"There is not so much to say now." he began. "You can look around and see your friends lying on the ground. I am intent on having whatever Sophia gave to you. It can mean life or death for you at this moment."

"But I don't have anything from Sophia," she pleaded. "She gave me nothing as I told you before. Nothing." She repeated her words again, more earnestly. "There is nothing for me to give to you." Staring at Sergei's gun, fighting back tears and gasping for air, she wondered if she could jump off the gazebo into the cold water below her. Instead she implored him. "You have to believe me."

Growing more impatient, Sergei raised his voice. "I don't believe you! I want what you have. Give it to me or tell me where it is. Or did you already give it to someone?" Hearing his own voice rise, Sergei calmed himself. "Do you understand how much I want the item? I will trade it for your life. Give me the object and I will save your life and Sophia's life."

Marina was surprised. "Save Sophia's life? You told me she was safe. Safe in Moscow."

"She is safe only as long as I collect what she gave you. My client will trade the object for her life once it is in his hand. I will trade it for your life once you give it to me. It is simple."

Only seconds passed though it seemed so much longer as Marina tried to think of an answer that would buy more time for her. But time to do what?

"OK" she conceded. "I do have it and I will tell you where it is but first you must tell me why it is so important to anyone and why Sophia would give it to me."

At last! He must be careful now that he is so close to the prize. He stared at Marina. So, this young girl does have the prize, she had it all along. How impressive she is, he said to himself. Sophia would be proud of her friend's courage. He decided he would make what he and his colleagues called a Russian Trade, he would tell Marina some of what she wants to know in exchange for everything he needs to have, but it will not matter what he tells her because she will soon take that knowledge into the river with her. For now, he must keep her trust a little longer.

"I will tell you only about Sophia. The other things do not concern you and they are too dangerous for you to know." He hesitated, then released a torrent of words he must've held inside for too long, thankful to be willing and able to release them from a dark place in his mind.

"Sophia is my *doch*, my daughter. You know her beauty and her personality but she is also intelligent, capable of achieving whatever she chooses to master but she chose a different life than I expected. Her beauty attracted attention and favors; she became fond of the fast plush life and soon she became a favored escort to men much older than herself, even colleagues of mine. Everyone loved Sophia including oligarchs and FSB officers, particularly one senior FSB officer who was a trusted confidant to the most powerful and richest men in Russia. Her mistake was one that so many young women make, she fell in love with the wrong person at a worse possible time." Holding his words back for a moment as though he decided he had said enough, he nevertheless seemed compelled to continue.

"The unnamed FSB officer became less welcome inside the higher circles for a number of reasons, jealousy for Sophia may have been one reason. It was soon discovered he kept a hoard of classified documents and compromising photos and videos of his circle of friends as a source of blackmail insurance against the inevitable time when friendship and loyalty will not be remembered or rewarded. He was betrayed and removed suddenly only a few months ago. It was my duty to end his career, and in doing so, break my daughter's heart. However, he was a brave man, maybe a foolish man, because despite the extreme efforts to convince him to divulge the location of the data, he died painfully without revealing its location. It was soon agreed he gave it to someone he trusted. The consensus of opinions was that Sophia was that person. With the consent of the highest authority in the government, I volunteered to speak to her, to get any such information from her. My reason was selfish, I wanted to keep her safe from an ugly end."

Mesmerized by the story but conscious of her pending doom, Marina began slowly drifting from under the dome towards the farthest end of the promenade that overlooked the waterfall. If she could get closer to the edge, she might be able to leap over the waist-high balustrade into the river just above the falls and swim across to the other side or take her chances going over the falls. Sergei was so intense in exorcising this fresh memory, he mindlessly kept pace with her slow dance along the railing as he continued speaking.

"I called her when I arrived in Mamaia. We met and talked. There was disagreement and denial. I drugged her with a swift injection, then drove her to Bucharest for transfer to Moscow for FSB interrogation. She is alive but she will die if I return empty-handed. If the prize lands in the wrong hands, it will destroy powerful men in Russia and America."

Signaling an apparent ending to his story, Sergei stopped, then he said almost as though he were wishing it were so. "It is expected Sophia's lover wanted her to get the information to your government in exchange for his and her safe passage to America. You were her means to get it into America." His story was finished. Now it was Marina's turn to complete her part of the trade. They were both overlooking the waterfall, standing only inches from the balustrade.

Sergei took a minute to recover from his revelations then spoke in a calm but demanding manner. "Now, where is the prize? I am hopeful it is in your possession now."

"I don't have it with me."

"Where is it?" Sergei almost shouted in frustration.

"It is in my makeup kit, in my apartment." Marina lied and Sergei knew it.

"That is not true." He replied, anger rising in his voice. "You are lying." Sergei knew at that moment she was never going to give him what he sought either because she was also a fool or she didn't have it. "I looked in your makeup kit and in your luggage. I emptied the contents on the floor. There was nothing from Sophia."

It was time to end this now. He had been here longer than he planned, ten minutes had passed since he stepped out from behind the tree. Maybe she didn't receive anything from Sophia, it didn't matter now; she knew more than she should know. With one silent bullet and an unceremonial toss of her body over the railing, he will complete at least half of his assignment. If there was information to be found here, someone else would be sent to find it. He raised his gun towards Marina, took careful aim and announced in a flat mechanical voice. "Enough. I am at the end of my patience. It is unfortunate my daughter sought you out as her way into America and away from her home in Russia. She was wrong. I will tell Sophia you said goodbye."

Chapter 30: Rescue

Before Sergei started speaking his last words to Marina, her barely noticable slow dance had lulled him in step with her until both of them had moved alongside the balustrade overlooking the waterfall. Marina had decided to jump over the railing, then froze in place at the sight of the gun barrel only a few feet from her face but she instantly recovered knowing her attempt to escape would prevent her from seeing the flash from the gun and the bullet race towards her. She marveled for a brief moment at her strange thought that she now understood why it might be true that ostriches hide their heads in the sand when danger approaches. She placed both her hands on the railing.

With his back to the grassy field and Kelly Drive, Sergei readied his finger to pull the trigger when he felt a bullet smash into his right shoulder causing his hand to loosen its grip on his gun, then a second bullet smashed into his right leg. Turning quickly, he saw Carl who he left for dead in the parking lot, fire at him again. He tried desperately to make a full turn and return fire but his injured leg refused to cooperate, the pain was too great to hold him up, he lost his footing and he fell heavily against the low railing with his full body weight pulling him over the railing. Unable to grasp the railing to regain his balance, he tumbled into the fast moving water below.

He voiced no sound at all, only his gun dropping harmlessly to the promenade shattered the silence as Marina watched his body hit the flat surface of the river, then disappear for a moment with a splash under the brown water, his arms and legs frantically surfaced taking turns reaching up to escape from the rushing waters but to no avail. Soon he was being thrashed about in the fast-flowing river until he was finally tossed like a flailing salmon over the falls.

Marina turned away from the water, then looked beyond where Sergei had been standing. There she saw Carl under the gazebo's dome, holding a gun at his side, limping painfully towards her.

"Are you hurt?" he called out to her.

"No, I'm not". She answered solemnly, grateful and stunned by her change of fortune in so few seconds. "Thank God for you." That's when she saw that the left side of his face was streaked with blood and more blood was leaking from his torn left pant leg onto his once white designer sneakers. She rushed towards him and helped lower his body slowly onto the promenade, he rested his back against the railing, facing away from the sun rising higher above the river. He still held Jack's gun gripped firmly in his hand as though he expected Sergei to rise from the river.

"I thought you were dead." She whispered, as though saying it out loud was a curse on the living.

"That makes two of us, Lady M." Carl forced a smile as he straightened his left leg. He lifted it over his right leg and did his best not to unleash a streak of profanities; he raised the heel of his left shoe onto the tip of his right shoe, in an effort to elevate the wound and slow the loss of blood.

"How did you find us?" Marina was drifting between belief and disbelief that she was alive, and not drowning in the rushing waters or slumped in a lifeless heap on the cold promenade.

Carl was in pain but he welcomed the chance to hear what he did to stop the killer and save her life. He wasn't sure how all the pieces fitted together. "I was hit twice and the second shot struck me on the side of my head, it knocked me down but not unconscious. I decided to become a dead man. There was no other defense." He stopped talking while he recalled his own thought that he would die as he lay by the hedges, then he continued. "I laid there and watched you both move across the field to the gazebo. I touched my head, there was blood but the wound was shallow. It was a grazing wound. I knew I then I was going to live, all the rest fell in place." He looked up to the blue sky, shook his head from side to side and said softly to himself. "But I didn't know if I'd get here in time."

Within seconds two black SUVs with red flashing lights raced through the fountain's circular driveway onto the grassy field between the Waterworks and the gazebo. Screeching to a halt, car doors were suddenly and violently swung open and two men in each of the vehicles ran towards them, guns drawn. Two agents came carefully up the steps leading to the promenade where Carl and Marina were seated. Carl was still holding the gun he had taken from Jack's waistband holster. Both agents raised their weapons and aimed at Carl.

"No. No. Don't shoot!" Marina cried out. "He's with me, he saved my life. Don't shoot!"

Carl immediately dropped the gun.

Marina continued. "The man you want is in the river. He's in the river."

In the short distance from the gazebo, a third black SUV was parked in the middle of the parking lot. Two more agents were tending to Jack but it was too late to do more than protect his body from the elements and from the curious pedestrians and commuters who were beginning to gather there. Jack had died instantly from Sergei's single shot. In only minutes, Kelly Drive and the entire area between Boathouse Row and the Art Museum was closed to the public and all the vehicles parked in the area were restricted from leaving. The Waterworks parking lot where Sergei's driver had patiently waited for him was empty.

Chapter 31: Headlines

The headline *Federal Agent Killed at Boathouse Row* was already old news when it was broadcasted on the front page of the next morning's Philadelphia Inquirer. Within hours of the shootings, news outlets across the country were covering the attempted abduction of a federal witness and the murder of a government agent in broad daylight in a popular tourist area in Philadelphia. Doug Frister hadn't even arrived in Sacramento's airport for his return flight to Philadelphia when he heard the tragic news on his car radio. He was heartsick and crushed when he heard the first accounts of the shootout. There were additional details on the number of persons shot and killed. What a disaster. He couldn't think straight for the first ten minutes or so, he was shocked. Every assignment has its risks and this one was expected to be risky, but he never believed it would lead to this. An ambush in broad daylight on Kelly Drive was a clear example of the adage that the best laid schemes of mice and men often go astray. Doug arranged the transfer with Jack for the sole purpose of avoiding danger to anyone and to keep the presence of an international assassin in Philadelphia out of the public's attention, out of anyone's attention until they could find the assassin and pick him up before he vanished into thin air like one of those rabbits in a magic act. It was to be a low-key operation, but something went terribly wrong. His mind continued to reel and spin with him second guessing himself and having doubts on his own judgement: what went wrong? What did he do wrong? He barely made it to his departure gate in San Francisco before he received a call from his Philly supervisor who filled him in with the horrible news that it was Jack who was killed. There wasn't much added information on his death other than he was ambushed and died instantly. Doug learned later from his fellow FBI investigators that footprints were found a short distance away in the damp grass leading from a clump of trees to Jack's parked car. The only good news he received was that Marina was alive and safe in FBI custody, and his friend Carl was being treated at the University of Pennsylvania

Hospital where he was in satisfactory condition and under police protection.

Of course, there would be an investigation on protocol, on the lack of backup at the transfer point: questions on why were the other two government vehicles and agents two blocks away and nowhere within striking distance? In hindsight, these are all necessary questions that must be answered when you are trying to determine if poor judgement or a faulty protocol led to an agent's death. There wasn't any lessening of grief or loss from the knowledge that all law enforcement personnel at every level are aware of the danger-factor in their choice of careers. Injury and death are a daily risk to agents and officers. It is always devastating to see a fellow officer fall; it further invokes rage and frustration when the killer is still not apprehended and nameless.

Doug was able to talk with Carl for only a few minutes after he landed back in Philly. "How are you, man?" was his first question of course. Even as he asked the question, he thought it was a dumb question to ask a person with two gunshot wounds who just missed death by inches or less, but it was a necessary one and it truthfully reflected his genuine concern for his friend who he had placed in harm's way. Carl just nodded. Doug had so many more questions and they were painful ones. He began but Carl cut him off.

"I'm so sorry about your friend." He mumbled in a low measured voice through his COVID mask. "He didn't have a snowball's chance in hell. It was a fucking ambush." Carl's voiced wavered, the medications he was given for pain were clearly affecting him.

"I know, Carl. There was nothing he or you could do." Doug adjusted his own mask as he moved closer to hear Carl. "Was there more than one person out there?"

"Just one man. He came from behind some trees." Carl winced with pain as he raised his bandaged head to see Doug more clearly. "I wasn't near your man. I stopped to call work. He had just put Marina in the car." Taking a breath and seeming to visualize his next words, he could be barely heard, "I looked up and I was shot instantly. I didn't see anyone else."

It was clear to Doug that Carl needed to rest. Doug wanted to know more but decided he would review the statements that Carl and Marina gave to headquarters yesterday morning. However, he did have one thing he wanted Carl to confirm. "I'm told the shooter fell into the river after you shot him. Did you hit him with your shots?"

"Yep. I'm certain I hit the bastard twice. Then he turned towards me with his weapon raised but he lost his balance and fell hard over the railing and into the river. I thanked God he did because I didn't have much energy left to stop him after the first two shots." Carl lifted his head and said quietly, "It was Jack's gun. Jack gets half the credit."

"You did great work." He patted him lightly on his good shoulder. "Get some rest." He turned and left the room. It was time to check in on Marina.

Driving back to his office, Doug thought it was very likely Sergei was dead, submerged somewhere in the river between the waterfall and the 30th St Penn Station Bridge, or entangled in the underbrush or trapped in the number of myriad items lying in the river bottom, watching with open dead eyes the thousands of gallons of water flowing above him. But he could be alive. The search for Sergei's body began immediately. All available river vehicles from nearby fire stations, underwater police divers, and assorted boats had been scouring the river, its banks, and inlets along the river since the shooting; a detail of officers and boats were in place at the base of the 30th Street Penn Station bridge operating as an observer and catch station for any large man-size object in the water. The Schuylkill River flowed past the city's busiest downtown traffic hub with multiple bridges crisscrossing the river from above the Philadelphia Zoo on the northern end of Kelly Drive down river to the Grays Ferry bridge in South Philadelphia; it wasn't uncommon to see people fishing off the bridges and banks. It was also the site of one of the goriest center-city seasonal pastimes: watching the recovery of the unfortunate persons who were lost every year in the river. The annual spring thaw regularly yielded a number of bodies dislodged from the tangled brush along its riverbanks or pushed bodies up from its depths that were locked in place until the powerful rush of heavy waters created by mountain snow thaws and spring rains freed them and carried them to Philly on a gruesome ride on the river's muddy surface. The bridge at Philadelphia's 30th Street station was one of the last calm places the bodies would surface and be unceremoniously dragged by hand into police and fire boats, or hooked by a boat crane, each body taken to the city morgue, eventually reducing the number of names on the missing persons list. All of this effort only intensified the media attention and crowds began lining both sides of the river from the Boathouse Row area to the shuttered coal power plant downriver on the east side of the city. Even if his body is recovered, Sergei's name would never appear on the missing person or recovered bodies list.

No name of a suspect was given to anyone. The police reported a dangerous unknown fugitive was being sought by the FBI. No one beside the FBI agents on the case and FBI personnel at the highest level were authorized to know it was a Russian assassin, and no one was to mention Sergei Gazunov's name. The motive presented to the media was an attempted abduction of a federal witness. No other details were given.

Chapter 32: The Prize

Following a brief interview at the gazebo immediately after the shooting, Marina was taken to the FBI office in center city; Carl was placed in an ambulance and treated by EMT personnel while on his way to a nearby hospital. All of the normal police protocols were performed: witness statements were taken from both of them and compared; local police and agents from the FBI scoured the grounds around the museum and Waterworks area; interviews were begun with secondary witnesses and persons of interest. The rush of activity throughout the day filled the large concrete Federal Building with a buzz that electrified the city. The crush of print journalists, radio and television reporters, and independent journalists threatened to block off the Federal Building from the rest of the city. The Philadelphia Police Department was placed on full duty to handle the traffic problems that arose.

Marina spent the day in the FBI offices inside the Federal Building. She spoke to her parents on her phone minutes after arriving in FBI headquarters. She assured them she was fine: jittery, tired, but OK. She agreed to stay the night with her parents as soon as she was released from questioning. Her Mom insisted she spend the night, maybe a few days, under her care. Marc was her second phone call, telling him in a brief conversation as much as she could about her ordeal.

She was advised she would remain under FBI protection; a detail of agents would be assigned to protect her for a day or so until it was clear to all she was out of danger. Without confiding to Marina, Doug knew the more likely scenario was that she would be in protective custody for several weeks at the least. She was told she was to have no singular communication with any media about the incident other than her personal feelings about her safety and any similar words regarding the two men who were shot while trying to protect her.

Marina's questioning was interrupted once after other agents who were sent to her apartment to retrieve her stained boarding pass envelope for blood DNA testing at the FBI lab, discovered the disorganized mess Sergei's ransacking rampage left in her apartment. They needed Marina to come over to determine if anything may have been taken. She arrived within minutes going from room to room with an agent, identifying what might be missing or damaged. She was told photos and fingerprints would be taken throughout the rest of the day - she could return the next morning after they were finished searching for any clue that might lead them to Jack's killer.

The next morning, Marc picked her up at her mom's house and drove her to her apartment followed by an unmarked black sedan and two handsome men in dark suits, dark shoes, and dark sunglasses who resembled agents who belonged in a sequel to Men in Black III. The FBI agents and local police teams did their assigned work but none of the assignments included cleaning up Marina's apartment. She and Marc began straightening up the rooms: putting objects back into cabinets; placing clothing back into drawers; stuffing her contents back into her makeup kit. Marina couldn't help thinking how desperate Sergei must have been to take the time to search every inch of her apartment. She lifted up her lone piece of travel luggage and surveyed the pile of clothing he left strewn outside her closet. She had been too upset, too worried about Sophia to even unpack from her trip. Among the mixture of clothing and shoes, she noticed a pair of dress shoes, lavish and fashionable high heels, she'd never seen before: they were definitely not her shoes. Inspecting them closely, she saw they were her size and found a price tag still attached to a strap on the right shoe.

"Holy crap!" she exclaimed to Marc. "Look at this price tag."

Wondering whose shoes they were, she realized only Sophia could've had access to her luggage; then she recalled Sophia arranged to have her luggage delivered to the airport terminal the evening before Marina's departure. She must've planned to do this last thing all along. Sophia bought them for her. Not hesitating to put them on, she stood against the closet door, bent over and slipped on the first shoe.

Overcome with emotion, she cried out. "My God." Then she whispered softly, nearly in tears. "My God. Sophia." While standing unsteady on one shoe, dangling her unclad foot in the air.

Marc heard her and walked into her bedroom from the kitchen. "Are you OK?" He asked her.

Marina balanced herself on one foot, then slipped on the second shoe. This time her foot struck an object in the toe of the shoe, something hard; she pulled her foot out of the shoe and thrust her right hand deep into the toe of the shoe. The object didn't move. She peered into the shoe and saw a clump of white masking tape crumbled in layers over something buried behind the tape.

Marc asked her "What's the matter? Are they too small?"

"No, I think they're going to fit but this left shoe has something taped in the toe of the shoe."

"Taped? Let me see." Taking the shoe from Marina, he held it above his head, then seeing the clump of white tape inside the shoe, he tugged at the tape and wrestled it loose. As soon as the tape was dislodged, a small dark object fell out of the shoe onto the floor.

Both of them stood staring at a two inch long rectangular metal object lying on the floor.

"It looks like a USB flash drive!" Marc exclaimed in surprise. He bent over and picked it up off the floor. "It's got an insignia on it."

The black USB flash drive was indistinguishable from any ordinary flash drive except for its iconic markings, a red soviet-era hammer and sickle logo engraved on each side of the two inch long drive.

"What the hell is this?" The sound of shocked amazement in Marc's voice startled Marina who stood as if she was under a magic spell. She knew instantly what had just been discovered. She was staring at the prize Sergei was sent to retrieve. It existed after all, it was in her possession all along. But what is it? And what should she do with it?

"Do you think this is what everyone is looking for?" Asked Marc.

"I don't know. It could be."

"Yeh, but it could be photos and stuff from your vacation week, something she wanted to surprise you with, right?"

"Maybe."

"Let's run it on your laptop." Marc suggested.

"I don't know. It might be better if we don't open it up."

"And do what with it?"

"Give it to the FBI."

"But then we'll never know what's in it."

"I don't care what's in it" Marina replied with a measure of fear in her voice." It makes me nervous. It's mine to decide what to do with it. I just want it away from me. It almost got me killed, and who knows someone else might still be looking for it."

"Right now, we don't know what it is. Like I said, it could be party photos." Marc stopped talking. Then his face lit up. "Well, we can find out real quick. It won't hurt to look at it." He stepped over to the laptop sitting on the night table next to the bed. It was already plugged into the wall outlet.

Marina stood transfixed. Silent. She watched as Marc inserted the flash drive into the laptop. After some minor whirling noises, a hammer and sickle image appeared on the laptop's screen; some additional whirling started again, then a click, and an image appeared with text in Russian. The whirling restarted, the screen blackened, for a few seconds nothing happened, nothing at all, then a single-word message appeared in large red block letters, blinking steadily on the dark screen:

ZAPRESHCHENO

Mesmerized, they looked blankly at the imposing, menacing blinking message, not knowing what to say, but both of them thinking the same thing – this is the real deal. Thirty seconds later, the screen went blank and the computer stopped its operation.

"It's encrypted." Marc said. He added an obvious understatement. "I'll bet there is more important stuff on this drive than your party photos."

Marina was shaken. "What do we do now?" she asked. "I'm afraid to be in the same room with it. Let's call the FBI. Doug will know what to do with it."

"Wait. I have an idea. If Sophia gave it to you she had a reason, and since some people are willing to kill you and her for it, it must be important to somebody. If we give it to the FBI, they'll have to give it to the DOJ who will give it to the White House who plays too nicely with the Russians."

"What do you mean?"

Politics wasn't something Marc shared with Marina. His interest in Marina was restricted to her, to whatever she wanted to talk about or whatever made her smile, anything that would keep him in her company: politics did none of that for Marina. So he kept his politics to himself when they were together but he was aware of the current president's refusal over the past four years to challenge Russia on any of its transgressions against the US political and military institutions.

"Who has anyone been able to trust these past four years? I mean really trust." He asked Marina. "The press. That's who: CNN, the New York Times, the Washington Post, the major credible news agencies. Let's give it to one of them. They'll know what to do with it." Holding the flash drive in his hand, he waved it back and forth like a banner, turned to her, and held it out towards her. "It's yours. Sophia gave it you. The chances are if she didn't disappear, she would tell you to share it with someone who can help her. I don't think the guy in the White House is going to help her."

"How do we contact whoever we decide to give it to?" was her next question.

"We can call the New York Times hotline, or I can call a friend of mine at the Inquirer who can give us a contact at the Times, or he can tell us what to do."

After a few phone calls, Marc spoke with a local journalist who called him back with a specific number for the New York Times hotline, at the same time, he offered to assist Marc with instructions on using the Times' own Secure Drop internet security program for tipsters. Within an hour, a more formal contact was made with the Times via Zoom where basic information was exchanged to help the Times determine if the news tip is news worthy. Remarkably, in less than six hours after discovering the flash drive, Marina personally handed it over to a Times' representative in a conference room in the Philadelphia Inquirer executive offices. In return she was given a receipt and several photos of the iconic flash drive. She was relieved to be freed from it. What happened next was up to someone else.

On her way home from the meeting, Doug called her with the FBI's test results on the blood-stained boarding pass envelope. It's makeup.

Chapter 33: Treason

The use of encryption to hide a message or information from everyone but its originator or from its intended recipient has been practiced from the beginning of written communication, possibly even earlier when single words or images were used as a code to relay a command to attack, to retreat, to stay, to declare love or loyalty, to disclose the whereabouts of something of value. The encryption on the flash drive Sophia gave to Marina was not difficult to remove nor was the information on it as noble as a plot to overthrow a cruel tyrant or to save an innocent life; not as exciting as disclosing where a fortune in treasure can be found in some long forgotten castle; nor as profitable as relaying a code for a locked Swiss bank account safeguarding millions in financial certificates. No. The encryption on this message was to safeguard one man's existence in a corrupt nation where friends routinely turned against one another. The small device held information that would serve as an insurance policy if he was threatened by friend or foe as happened often to those in his inner circle. He could use this collection of documents, photos, videos, and audio messages to blackmail them, individually or as a group. He would threaten to publish their private secrets and betrayals, thereby surviving the ugly fate so many others endured. The flash drive included the many plots and plans he and his co-conspirators agreed to and executed in the past twenty years for the sole benefit of the powerful men in Russia's new Federation. Under Vladimir Putin's authoritarian reign, Russian mobsters and voracious, greedy oligarchs illegally appropriated control of Russia's energy resources, soon acquiring complete control over the country's industries and financial institutions. Unfortunately, the FSB officer failed to keep one step ahead of his targets and he missed his opportunity to use his collection to blackmail them. Instead, his rumored trove of information proved too dangerous to ignore and earned him a premature and painful death but his cache of information was not found among his possessions.

Within hours of receiving the flash drive, the New York Times convened an emergency meeting with a team of executives, lawyers, journalists, and private intelligence professionals to confirm the authenticity of the flash drive and review its bombshell contents. There are always legal pitfalls to consider when publishing information that can be considered detrimental to the national security of the United States. There is the added responsibility to publish only the truth, the primary importance is to not be goaded or rushed prematurely into giving credence to a lie or a fraudulent event. Upon first viewing the data on the drive there was no doubt it was a colossal gold-mine of criminal behavior, state-sponsored espionage and murder, and a national betrayal beyond any treasonous acts recorded in the annals of American political history. The Times knew what it must do with it – give the flash drive with its windfall of subversive information to the highest law enforcement authority in the United States: give it to the Attorney General of the United States. But it was a dilemma! No one trusted the current Attorney General, not even the White House nor the AG's own Republican loyalists. The Attorney General's loyalty to the current president was plainly visible to everyone: his was a blind loyalty to the president's faults, but more worrisome, the Attorney General was blind to the welfare of the nation itself. Strangely he was singularly unaware his loyalty was not reciprocated by the president. As a consequence of this uncertainty, a number of side conversations and phone calls were exchanged between the New York Times and the Department of Justice. Though less formal at first, the deliberations became more formal and legally intense as a clear path evolved through the many discussions. A discrete number of senior members in the government were empaneled because the sensitive data was intentionally littered with concrete evidence – audio, videos, and photos of Washington D.C. politicians: persons who will be subject to inevitable extensive investigation and subsequent criminal charges.

A week passed between the moment Marina gave the flash drive to the Times and they delivered the drive to the office of the Central Intelligence Agency, a government institution independent of the DOJ and the FBI. The delivery was made only after the Times copied contents of the drive onto a secure database and safeguarded the data, the final agreement, and copious notes of its deliberations into a locked safe. The agreement included a document drawn up by the CIA, signed by the Times, the CIA, and several independent private citizens, approving the immediate release of some of the less explosive elements on the drive involving major players in the White House and in the Russian government. Within hours of the agreement, the New York Times published simultaneously in print and online its decision to handover the original flash drive smuggled out of Russia and acknowledged its agreement to withhold publication of some of the device's details with the understanding that publishing such details would jeopardize U.S. national security and hamper the legal defense and prosecution of some individuals' actions depicted on the device. A list of the more salacious details on the flash drive was published in the body of the story. The Times article also noted that the White House and several high profile congressional leaders were given a small window of advance warning before the news went public.

****

"Jesus Christ!" was Jefferson Crandall's mixed cry, likely seeking both divine intervention and acknowledging abject despair, when he heard the Breaking News broadcast on the television in his office. "Jesus Christ!" he repeated. His first instinct was to run down the hall to his boss' office which he had left only a few minutes earlier. But he was suddenly immobile. Instead, he called his boss, and though there was no answer, he knew he was in the office. Crandall didn't bother to leave a voice message: the boss had his own television, he would know why he was calling him. Now he'd just wait for all hell to break loose.

Marina was in the shower when her phone rang for the first time. By the time she dried off and brushed her hair, she had four more calls: her mom, Marc, Agent Frister, and Carl; the initial call was also from Agent Frister. She called Frister first because she thought he was probably a better source of information for what was getting her all of this attention.

"Hello. It's Marina. You called me twice?" She said in a questioning manner.

"Yes! Good morning, Marina. Thanks for calling me back." Marina did tell Doug a week earlier about the drive and how she met with the Times and handed it over to them and why she gave it to the Times and not to him. "I understand." is the only thing Doug said. Since then, he had been waiting for something like this to break. "It's in the papers." He said. "It's online, on television; it's everywhere. I wanted to tell you to expect some attention even though your name was not in any of the articles. Journalists have a way to uncover secrets."

She smiled at that comment, then he continued. "Even if the drive isn't traced to you, the coincidence will be connected to you so I wanted to give you a heads-up."

"OK. Thank you." Wanting to know more as fast as she could, she asked. "How much did the Times find out and share?"

"A lot. It's big. Gigantic. Bigger than the Mueller Report, bigger than the president's impeachment in February. It's bad." Pausing, he added more. "Remember, if you feel nervous, or have any questions, just call me. Hey, the FBI detail is out there if you need them for anything, even if it's just to wave back at you."

She smiled at that image. "Thank you, again. I'm OK. Bye."

"OK. Bye." Doug ended his conversation wondering where this would all end.

Marina had planned to share a training session with Marc this morning, then they'd have lunch together. She was glad she would be busy today. It would get her out of the apartment, onto the street and keep her mind on something other than the past week. She had stayed inside her apartment for most of the week, away from reporters, the public. She told Fred she needed the week off. He was wonderful; he told her to call him when she was ready to work. That was helpful; she did need the money. She wanted to move on from the recent events but she still hadn't heard from Sophia and no one in authority had given her any new information on Sophia's whereabouts. She wondered if Sophia would know her device is making news. Marina thought for a moment, maybe the FBI or the CIA can find her and bring her to America. She could hope.

Doug was correct. Before most people in Philly had their morning coffee, the world read about some of the information on Sophia's device at the same moment in twelve different time zones all across the globe. If you were asleep on the west coast or in Europe and Asia, someone woke you; if you were awake elsewhere in the world, you saw it on your cell phone or gawked, mouth open, at the nearest television screen. The story was carried in every newspaper and on every cable and international television network in the world. It wasn't an announcement of war but it was a stunning revelation.

The New York Times' morning headline was impressive, in large type and in the boldest font possible in newsprint, the headline read: *Putin and Trump: Art of the Deal*, with a subheading beneath it, *Quid Pro Quo: USA for Cash and More.* The entire front page and pages 2 through 6 were dedicated to the who, what, when, where, and why of the scandal including a listing of the contents in the device outlined in bulleted fashion in a lightly shaded vertical box in the middle of Page 3; hastily- penned articles on a few of the items were scattered on the remaining pages. The Times editor placed a heavy emphasis on advising the paper's readers that caution was being exercised in what was being made public based on restrictions enforced by the Department of Justice to protect the United States national security and the privacy of individuals and countries who would soon be embroiled in chaos by the information exposed in the device. The news coverage was crowded with declarations of alleged evidence and alleged crimes and alleged indiscretions.

The Final Victim

The Times made no mention of how they obtained the information or from whom, only that it was compiled by a senior member of the Russian government who the CIA had reported resigned his position less than a month earlier and hasn't been seen in public since doing so.

Marina's prime interest was directed to the vertical box on page 3. It was one of the last things Doug said to her before he ended his conversation with her. "You can see a quick summary of what is in the flash drive on page 3 of the Times."

And there it was! The heading within the vertical box had few details but the list invited one's imagination to roam wildly on the cooperation between Putin and the current White House administration.

Partial List of Conspiracies & Crimes Captured on Russian Flash Drive

- Transcriptions of private meetings between the current Russian and U.S. presidents: discussions of mutual-interest plans and goals for 2017 through 2020.
- Transcripts of undocumented private phone calls between both leaders on matters of U.S. security and policies.
- Audio recordings of Putin and FSB agents planning the poisoning of adversaries outside Russian sovereignty: Alexander Navalny, Alexander Litvinenko, Sergei Skripal, etc.
- Explicit videos and audio transcripts of goings-on at the Ritz Hotel in Moscow in 2013, and the disappearances of multiple participants and witnesses.
- Videos and photos of meetings, dinners, parties w/GOP legislators/Russians, 2015-2018.
- Quid pro quo agreements with GOP legislators for investments in U.S. and Russia.
- Lists of campaign donations from Russian oligarchs to U.S. GOP politicians.
- A copy of a formal agreement creating a New World Federation signed by the leaders of U.S., Russia, Turkey, and Saudi Arabia: a

goal to establish a cabal to dominate the world economy and military strength and weaken Europe, China, and Japan.

- A record of transactions detailing NRA's acceptance of $40 Million from Russia via Alexander Torshin for GOP presidential candidate in the 2016 campaign.
- Confirmation of Russian interference into, and acceptance of, U.S. Intel in 2016 election.
- Private agreement re: impunity for cyber-attacks on USA military, industrial and economic institutions.
- Details on Operation Omega, Russian/White House participation in a plot to restructure America as a straw democracy in the New Federation with the U.S. president positioned in a role similar to Putin's primacy in Russia.

The out-going White House administration was overwhelmed with requests for responses to the disclosures; the steady stream of new facts and the resurfacing of old rumors were now hardening into highly damaging truths. As usual, the administration issued a litany of complete denials accompanied by an expected loud chorus of their tiresome, childish chants of 'Fake News.'

Chapter 34: Final Victim

The following week, a daily parade of dark sedans and SUVs circled between the White House and the Capitol, between the Capitol and the Department of Justice, from the DOJ to the Federal Bureau of Investigation, back to the Capitol, onto the White House, and round and round again and again. This dizzying dance of chaos engulfed the nation's leaders and exhausted the public who remained glued to their choice of news outlets for their preferred dish of truth or fiction. On the truthful side of the news, the White House's primary occupant was under siege as each new day brought more revelations confirming the veracity of the device's bombshell allegations. On the fictional side of the news, the president denied everything. He denied it was his signature on damning documents; he said it wasn't his voice on the audio tapes involving private dealings where he is heard selling off America's political and economic security to the Russian president and oligarchs for his own personal gain and to advance his own schemes of sharing power with America's enemy; he even denied it was his face and form romping throughout a luxurious suite in a Moscow hotel in nothing more than his birthday suit.

It was a familiar scene that had played out for the previous four years on world-wide news broadcasts: a cycle of endless chaos initiated by the president who was always supported by his loyal and fearful Republican enablers who looked away from the lies they witnessed in those past four years and said nothing. Worse than saying nothing, they applauded their King's naked narcissism. Now they were abandoning him because their own greed and cowardice was exposed.

Amidst this clamor, Agent Frister arranged a meeting with Marina and Carl in a conference room at the FBI office in center city. Marc was added after Marina requested he accompany her. Doug deliberately chose one of the smaller conference rooms in the FBI office because he wanted to have an intimate discussion with the persons whose actions led to the discovery of these plots against America. Doug, as he was now informally addressed by all three participants, wanted to provide a bridge between the facts and the fiction of what was appearing in the news. He selected a room with wood paneled walls and no windows for its privacy; a large meeting table dominated the center of the room and a smaller rectangular table was placed against the wall nearest to the door; four framed paintings depicting scenes of Philadelphia's most famous open spaces completed the man-cave decor. This room wasn't used to impress visitors; its purpose was to conduct business, short and sweet.

Everyone around the table was masked. Doug was the last to be seated. He sat at the far side of the conference table, several chairs removed from the head of the table where he could comfortably face the entry door, allowing him to see anyone who opened the door or entered the room. His three visitors sat directly across from him, each place was equipped with a bottle of water, a pen and a note pad both emblazoned with the FBI insignia, Doug hoped it would lend a relaxed sense of equal importance to all four attendees. He didn't want any formality of authority and control to permeate this discussion.

He welcomed them with a warm and sincere smile. "Thank you all for coming into the office today. I know you've been flooded with attention from news media and friends, I also know you've been targeted with less friendly remarks from some crazies out there." He stopped and looked at each person, then continued. "I wanted to provide you with a few more details of the contents of the drive not yet shared with the public and which will not be shared publicly until after the inauguration of a new president on January 20th." Pushing himself and his chair away from the conference table, he added, "None of what I'm going to tell you can be shared with anyone outside this room." He smiled and said, "The pen and notepad are not to be used to take any notes here today. They are just a small inexpensive tribute to you for your courage in the past weeks."

Doug proceeded directly into his update referencing the released audio and video tapes as only a few of the many such items in the collection that could be made public now. Others were either too gruesome to share outside official government entities or required further verification.

"The audios and videos you've seen in the news media speak for themselves: it is clear who is speaking, who is seen; the content and the origin of the data has been analyzed in our labs and they are all authentic. The content in them is damaging to individuals and countries but of themselves they do not threaten our national security. The more sensitive disclosures are the pacts and various agreements recorded and seen on video. The New World Federation pact allegedly signed by the present leaders of Russia, Saudi Arabia, Turkey, and sadly, the United States, eerily echo the Axis agreement in World War II between Germany, Japan, and Italy. Whereas, the Axis alliance was an open declaration of war, this pact is more dangerous and devious for its secret alliance against the rest of the world, and for the alleged participation of our highest elected official who is accused of actively seeking to align the United States of America with hateful tyrants for his personal power and greed."

Pausing in between sentences, Doug opened his bottle of water, took a sip, and then continued. "Presently, you will see little action taken by our government besides the mountains of words spoken against this treasonous behavior but after the inauguration on January 20th, there will be indictments issued and arrests conducted based on the facts being continuously uncovered in this investigation. The world order may be slow to change in countries long afflicted with dictatorships and an absence of democracy but one person in Russia will not survive the disclosures, not because his citizens will turn him out, they have tried before, but because he failed to further enrich his oligarchs. Soon there will be onerous sanctions on Russia and the oligarchs which will create havoc in the Kremlin, threatening billions in assets and cash, some of it disappearing forever."

"Additionally, the Attorney General and several of his Assistant AGs resigned; the Congress is planning to meet to freeze the current presidents' powers, possibly invoking the 25th Amendment to remove him from office for his remaining weeks in office. You've read about the indictments being drawn up for several prominent Republican Senators and House Republicans. That is true but it is all I can share with you, there are no names to confirm now. Additionally, several individuals closely connected to the president will be investigated for domestic and international crimes."

There were additional comments from Doug and several questions from the three attendees. The meeting was concluded in less than an hour. Doug asked Carl to wait in the conference room as he escorted Marina and Marc to the elevator. When he returned to the conference room, Carl was admiring his FBI pen and notepad.

"Carl, I want you to know how thankful all of us at the FBI and the CIA are for your actions, for being so courageous and dependable."

"Thanks. I did what I had to do. Both times."

"The FBI also wants to present you with a commendation in a public ceremony after the inauguration. However the bigger news is they want you to consider becoming a formal part of law enforcement in this city that you love so much. The city and our office will be cooperating in a new program to improve the liaison between local law enforcement and the FBI on unsolved shootings. You will be our first sponsored candidate; the city will also assist you in your goal to obtain a P.I. license."

"Man, that's cool with me, dude." He looked skyward then shouted, "Hell yeah!"

Doug signaled a fist bump and laughed. He ended the conversation with a piece of humorous advice. "Well just for now Carl, as they say on the street, don't quit your day job."

****

In Washington, D.C., a cell phone rang several times before its owner limped across the room on the second floor of the cream-colored building at 2525 Massachusetts Avenue, Northwest in the quiet, tree-lined neighborhood referred to as Embassy Row.

"Privet. Da, Sergei." Answered the man who was still favoring his leg as it slowly recovered from the damn bullet that sent him careening head over heels into the river.

"Privet." replied the voice on the other end of the phone connection. "I have an important call to forward to you. Please end this call and wait for a return call from a secure phone." Immediately the call was ended. Sergei did likewise, and remained standing, holding his cell phone. In less than a minute, his phone rang. He answered it on the first ring. He wasn't certain who was calling but if it was who he thought it was, he didn't want The Man waiting on him.

"Privet." Sergei said brightly into the phone.

"Hello, my friend." It was exactly who Sergei expected it to be. "How are you feeling this day, Sergei?"

"I am feeling very well, sir. Thank you for asking. The medical care and the hospitality here have been excellent."

"That is good, and it is as it should be for your efforts."

"It is kind of you to say so but I did not succeed. I'm not worthy of any kindness from you "

For an instant, Sergei's mind's eye replayed a flashback of him plunging into the cold, murky river. In retrospect, Sergei thought the fall likely saved his life though at the moment he went over the falls and entered the water, he was thinking otherwise. Something, maybe the shock of hitting the water or maybe his instinct for survival awakened him, numbing his wounds as he fought to rise to the surface and began looking for a way out of the river. He was able to reach the river bank just below the retaining wall below the Waterworks. He laid there for a few minutes, fighting the pain, he scrambled up to the parking lot and was helped into the car that took him to safety and to much-needed medical care. He didn't know how long he was unconscious afterwards, only that he when he woke up, he was in this room at the Turkish embassy and he had been here ever since. He had limited conversations with his team and this was his first conversation with The Man since he failed to complete his mission.

"It is done, Sergei. It is done. Yes, this blow threatens both our retirements. It is creating many troubles and disappointments for me and new enemies who are getting stronger but we must somehow make our fate change directions. Don't you agree?"

"Yes, sir, I agree."

"Good. It is time to go to work."

The Man continued, "I have one last assignment for you. I am fearful the foolish man we compromised will inflict even more damage on Russia and on my friends. He has no strength, no character, and no loyalties to anyone. It was always so, knowing it was risky to join with such a fool was a thing I understood but it proved much easier and valuable once his own parade of fools were equally willing to sell out their country. Now he must be silenced, both as a punishment and as a safeguard to prevent him from firing bullets into my head and into the heads of the powerful men around me because he will turn on us. These men understand their black code; they want their pound of flesh."

As always, Sergei listened intently whenever The Man spoke to him. The details of his assignment were simple but dangerous – poison is always quiet but it is a lethal weapon and one that is equally dangerous to the assailant. Sergei had applied a variety of poisons in different ways in the past ten years but this strain was different. Though it was slow to act requiring as many as 12 hours from contact, it was fatal with the slightest amount of contamination. He did have one question he must ask.

"How do you expect to have me get access to him?"

"We can get you access to him." assured The Man. "Any friend of ours is a friend of his. It will be easy. He will see you. He is stupid. He loves everything Russian: the women, the drugs, our money, our power, and he will love you. He will welcome you as a wounded veteran of our Afghan war who still carries the pain in his leg from a wound received so long ago." The Man laughed at the ruse he had contrived on his own, then added in his formal voice. "He will also do as I say because he is Komprimat. He is ours for life." Then speaking with a voice of quiet self-satisfaction, he delivered his final words on the death sentence. "The day of delivery will be after the new president's inauguration."

"After the inauguration?" Sergei asked, puzzlement flooding his head.

"I am not a fool." The Man said calmly. "I will not have a dead USA president on my hands or in Russia's history books. No. You will receive the contaminant with instructions and the date for your visit to Florida." There was a brief silence followed by The Man's final words. "The package will come in a week or so, a call will soon follow. Farewell my friend. Do not fail."

The call ended abruptly. Sergei knew what was expected; he understood he was being given a chance to redeem himself. This third attempt at his final assignment cannot fail: his life and Sophia's life rested on his success. Now he will wait for his package and his business class plane ticket to arrive. He would leave his weapon behind in this little recovery room that served him well for the many weeks. He wouldn't need it. He only regretted his target was not still in D.C. If he was, he could simply take a short Uber ride from here at the Turkish Embassy to the White House; at this moment he was less than five minutes away.

****

Marina still recalls where she was and what she was doing late that evening when her phone buzzed louder, then even louder, demanding she draw herself away from Marc's over-zealous but welcome romantic maneuverings. Sex was finally a part of their attraction to one another. They could both relax now: some normalcy was beginning to replace the chaos that happened months earlier. It wasn't just their lives that improved; a new hope was raised for many in America only weeks before when a new president, a real president, was sworn in on the Capitol steps. Yes, there were many questions to be answered and much work to be done to heal America from the coronavirus, and from the past four years of ugly divisions in our union of states. Also, though there was still no word from Sophia, there was hope tomorrow would be different.

The buzzing increased in volume and repetitions. She picked up her phone, clicked the icon for Messages.

It was a short message, only three words. *"It was simple. Prostoy."* The text message was sent just before its messenger closed the flip phone with its pre-paid minutes and tossed it into a river in the Everglades. He got back in the rented car and began his long journey home, 5,000 miles away. Sergei smiled. He delivered his final victim. He was pleased with himself; he will be on a flight home before the poison completes its work.

Epilogue

A news bulletin was broadcast that same day before dawn announcing the former president was pronounced dead at his Mar-A-Lago estate in the early morning hours only weeks after the 46th President of the United States was inaugurated on the steps of the U.S. Capitol in Washington, D.C. The former president's cause of death was announced as a sudden heart attack possibly advanced due to complications brought on by a recent bout of the Covid 19 coronavirus.

Putin has been noticeably absent from his normal duties and gatherings in Moscow. Overall, Russia's economy is a disaster. Sanctions from the USA, Europe, the Far East and South America have decimated the oligarchs' stolen wealth. The Russian people are getting restless.

Two leading Republican senators from two southern states and eleven Republican congressional legislators were indicted on a wide number of criminal charges linked to crimes identified on the smuggled flash drive and related to acts of insurrection at the U.S. Capitol on January 6th.

Doug Frister returned to his field duties in Philadelphia. He was selected to lead a new class of diverse city and federal officers who will augment investigations into unsolved murders in the city of Philadelphia. If successful, the program will be exported to cities across the nation.

Carl Joseph Lewis enrolled as the first candidate in Doug's law enforcement program. He intends to get his PI license and maintains an informal affiliation with city and federal law enforcement. He hasn't quit his part-time job in West Philly, yet.

Marc's list of clients continues to grow. He continues to work harder at, and is having success on, being more than Marina's friend.

Marina still works at Le Café and assists Marc with fitness training clients. She enrolled as a full-time student in a local university and will resume class on a virus-free campus September 2021.

Two bodies were dragged from the Delaware River in late December. The bodies were not a match for the body profile of Sergei Gazunov. An un-lined dark brown jacket was found on the river bank below the Water-works. The clothing brand tag is from an overseas department store.

Sergei Gazunov arrived safely back in Moscow. He was decorated by The Man and received a large cash bonus for completing his last assignment. He retired to his home outside Moscow. Six months later he was killed in a fiery boat accident. He seldom ever went boating.

Sophia was smuggled out of Russia by Russian security personnel loyal to her father and at the expense of the CIA only three days before his fatal accident. She was spirited into the United States and is in protective cus-tody. She hopes someday to live in Philadelphia, the Cradle of Liberty.

The Covid-19 pandemic (novel coronavirus) began in January 2020 con-tinuing its deadly advance throughout the world. As of February 6, 2021, there were more than 466,000 reported deaths in the United States of America; the country with the next closest number of deaths is Brazil, 213,000. Worldwide the number of deaths through January 19 is 2.15 Mil-lion.

Acknowledgement

Beginning my journey for this third book brought to my mind the struggles and the fun that accompanied me on my earlier works and the need for the same support and encouragement for this book. At the center of all three journeys has been my best friend and the love of my life, Dorothy Elizabeth Donnelly McLaughlin. I thank her for her love and for the acceptance and understanding she generously gifted to me so I could complete these books. These are her accomplishments as much as they are mine. Our greatest accomplishments, however, are our love for one another and for our children and our grandchildren.

May they all be as happy in love and life as we have been.

Cloud9 Publishing Books by

Robert N. McLaughlin

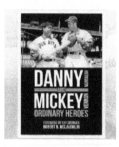

Danny and Mickey, Ordinary Heroes

The true story of boyhood friends, baseball, the Great Depression, WWII, and the World Series

Go to dannyandmickey.com

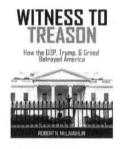

Witness to Treason. How the GOP, Trump, and Greed Betrayed America.

A fact-filled presentation of the people and events that combined to threaten American democracy before and after the 2016 presidential election.

Both are available on Amazon.com in print or as e-books, or can be purchased directly from the author, rnmbulldog45@gmail.com. Retail bookshop owners can order this author's books on http.www.ingramcontent.com/retailers/ordering

Bob McLaughlin was born and raised in Chester, PA. He is a graduate of St. James High School and Widener University and he is a life-long resident of Delaware County. He and his wife Dorothy live in Ridley Park. He has three children and ten grandchildren.

Bob retired in 2012 from a career as a Purchasing and Construction Manager for several international engineering companies and he was one of a three-person American management team hired to support the establishment and growth of the new Aker-Kvaerner Shipyard inside the former Philadelphia Shipyard in South Philadelphia. The shipyard continues its mission to build commercial ships in America for the past 23 years.

Naturally he is an avid Philadelphia sports fan who supports all of Philly's local teams. He only rooted one time for a team outside the city. That was the 1960 Pittsburgh Pirates, the subject of his first book, *Danny and Mickey, Ordinary Heroes,* available on Amazon and other retail book websites along with his other two books. *Spoiler alert here:* (The Pirates defeated the New York Yankees in 7 games.)

THE FINAL VICTIM

A Novel

Robert N. McLaughlin

Cloud9 Publishing

Philadelphia, PA

The Final Victim